HELLCORP

JONATHAN WHITELAW

Urbane
PUBLICATIONS

urbanepublications.com

First published in Great Britain in 2018
by Urbane Publications Ltd
Suite 3, Brown Europe House, 33/34 Gleaming Wood Drive,
Chatham, Kent ME5 8RZ
Copyright © Jonathan Whitelaw, 2018

A CIP catalogue record for this book is available
from the British Library.

ISBN 978-1-911583-72-1
MOBI 978-1-911583-73-8

Design and Typeset by Michelle Morgan

Cover by OR8 Design

Printed and bound by 4edge Limited, UK

URBANE

urbanepublications.com

To my darling (soon-to-be wife) Anne-Marie -
for living with me, The Devil and Him Upstairs.

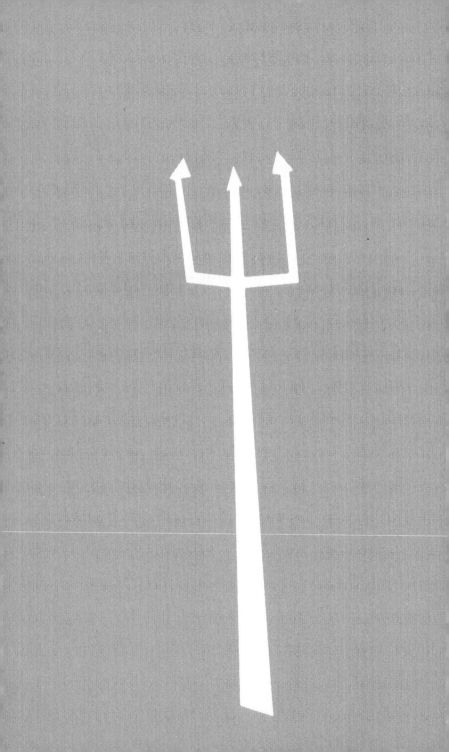

"Go to Heaven for the climate. Hell for the company."

Mark Twain

PROLOGUE

The chimes of the great clock rang out across St. Peter's square. The place was empty and quiet, save for the clangs of the ancient metal bell. A trio of pigeons fluttered in the colonnades that lined the square, scaring a dozing guard. Midnight had arrived in The Vatican City.

High above the plaza, the Pope sauntered into his private chambers. He locked the door, making sure he tucked the key back into the pocket of his vestments. It had been a long, endlessly infuriating day. They were all getting to be like that.

He let out a long, resigned sigh. His stomach didn't feel right, like there was a balloon inflated inside. He rubbed at the sagging meat and winced.

Stalking across the room, he felt something shift. He paused, leaned on one foot and felt his buttocks clench.

A loud, stretched out sound rang through the office. When he was finished, he relaxed, finally relieved.

"Mamma mia," He batted away the air from in front of his face, the smell a little overpowering.

At the far side of the office was a window that looked out onto the square. He hurried over and let in some air. A cold wind breezed in through the open panes, sending papers flying from his desk.

The hairs on the back of the Pope's neck stood on end. He turned to watch the files scatter. Something wasn't right. He could feel it. You didn't spend your life in the church and not know when there was foul play at work.

Outside, the bells kept going, now on their seventh chime. It was late and he knew he should go to bed. He rubbed his old face and blinked. Maybe just one little drink before bed. What harm could that do? If the most powerful clergyman in the world couldn't treat himself now and then, there was something severely wrong.

Inspired by his new thought, he trotted over to the huge, mahogany desk that dominated the opposite wall. Sliding out a drawer, he produced a bottle of single malt whisky, a cut crystal glass and a packet of cigarettes.

He pulled the cork from the bottle free with his teeth and poured a large measure. He sniffed the liquor before downing it in one swallow.

The rich, smoky taste made him bare his teeth. He licked his lips before pouring another. There were certain luxuries that came with being pontiff. A choice of rare whiskies was just one of them. Hand rolled cigarettes were another and he drew one out from the box. He lit the end, inhaled and basked in the rich taste.

Only in these few quiet moments did he afford himself some pleasure. Never in public. The good Catholics of the world wouldn't approve of their saviour drinking and smoking as he did. But he was only human after all. Being Pope was just his job, it wasn't who he was.

"Oh, I wish you would stop with your tin-pot philosophy," came a deep voice from nowhere.

The Pope froze, his arms and legs stiff. He looked about his empty office, clutching tightly onto his whisky glass.

"Che ha detto che?" he said, voice barely breaking a whisper.

There was no response. His heart was racing, faster than it had in years. His head was swimming a little from the Scotch and his mouth had gone dry. Suddenly all the mystery and mysticism he had been preaching for years was flooding back into his mind.

Being The Pope and talking about God, miracles and the universe was one thing. Experiencing it first hand was something completely different.

"Really, you Catholics, you love a bit of drama," came the voice again. "It can get a bit tedious at times, don't you think?"

The Pope was frightened. He pushed himself up quickly from behind his desk, slamming his knee into the hard mahogany. His crystal glass dropped from his hand, shattering as it hit the hard, wooden floor. It was an antique, irreplaceable. He bit his tongue and hobbled towards the door, cursing under his breath.

But before he could reach the handle, a figure appeared before him. A swirling, dark shadow stretched out from the creature's presence, a blackness that seemed to go on forever emanating from its centre.

The old man's eyes widened and his face fell slack in horror. He stumbled backwards, clutching at his chest. A stiff pain raced up his arm and he could feel his heart tensing, ready to burst. Between the shock, horror and medical emergency, The Pope didn't know if he was coming or going.

"Oh come on," said the figure, "I'm only here for a chat."

It reached forward and took The Pope by the hand. Stopping him from falling, it reached into his chest. In a second, the thumping stopped; the pressure relieved and The Pope began to breathe again.

He was sweating, his vestments clinging to his portly body. He looked down at where the figure had entered his chest. A shadow hung over him, darker than anything the old man had ever seen. He never knew blackness could be so black.

Then, as if the figure had read his mind, the shadow began to lift. In its place was what looked like a sleeve of wool, with pinstripes. The Pope followed the receding shadow towards the figure's main mass and, astounded, watched as a man appeared before him.

He was tall and thin, with a strange face that looked both old and young at the same time. His hair was dark and curly, slicked back behind his ears. A pointed nose separated two sharp eyes that glistened in the dim light of the office.

"Tu chi sei?" gasped the old man.

"Don't be thick," said the figure.

He took a step back, pulling his hand from The Pope's chest. The old man staggered a little and rubbed at the spot where the stranger had entered him. He felt ill but not as bad as he had been only seconds before.

A cold sweat broke out on The Pope's top lip. He wiped it and looked down at his finger. A sliver of blood was streaked over his skin. He touched his nose and saw more crimson. He looked at the figure expectantly.

"Oh yes, sorry," said the stranger. "A little collateral damage I'm afraid. Or should I say cholesterol damage," he nodded at The Pope's hefty gut.

The stranger strolled over to the desk and cleared away some stray papers. He sat down on the edge and straightened his tartan tie and cuffs. Spying the whisky, he lifted it up, smelled the top and nodded in approval.

"Not bad, not bad at all. Of course it'll kill you in the end," he said. "You humans, you're so frail and weak. Especially when you get old. But hey, who am I to argue with you know who." He pointed at a large, ornate crucifix which hung from the wall.

The Pope tried to speak but he was gasping for breath. The whole experience was something he was struggling to understand. Physically, psychologically, it was too much for an eighty-year-old. And that was before he began contemplating the philosophical implications.

"Here, wipe your nose," said the stranger, offering a silk handkerchief from his top pocket.

The Pope nervously took the gesture and blew his nose. He cleared away the blood and handed the handkerchief back.

"Blimey, I don't want it back," sneered the stranger. "Not after it's been up your hooter."

"Si, mi dispiace signore," said The Pope, cowering a little.

He stared at the handkerchief. The blood and snot began to move on the cotton. He watched on, terrified and unable to look away as two cockroaches formed in his hand. They spread their wings and took off, disappearing out of the open window. The Pope let out a frightened wail.

The stranger looked at him, chewing something over in his mind. He pursed his lips and leaned forward a little.

"You still don't know who I am, do you?" he asked, smiling a little.

The Pope said nothing. He shook his head, holding his papers and handkerchief like a scalded child.

"Well for starters, let's stop this whole Italian charade, speak English man, for all of our sakes," the stranger snapped his fingers.

"Shit!" shouted The Pope.

He clutched his throat and then covered his mouth. Slowly, with a little coaxing from the stranger, he took his hands from his lips.

"Go on, try it."

"Try what?" asked The Pope.

"Anything, I've made an arrangement with your vocal chords.

For the sake of this conversation, you'll only be speaking English. The Queen's English I may add, although I know this office has had a few problems in that department over the past eon or so."

"I don't understand," said The Pope. "Who are you? What are you doing here? Is this His work?"

"Whose?" asked The Stranger.

"You know," said The Pope. "Him," he nodded towards the crucifix.

The stranger smiled at the idol on the wall. He shook his head.

"No, not this time. Well, not directly anyway," he said. "But then again, it always sort of comes back to Him in a way. Creator of existence and all that game. Still, He didn't do a bad job."

"You… you're not Him then?" said The Pope.

"Nope, afraid not padre." The stranger hopped down off the desk and wandered over to the window.

"So, if you're not Him…" The Pope trailed off, his voice quivering with fear.

The stranger swivelled on his heels and extended his hands. He gave a little bow.

"The Devil, at your service papa," he said.

"No," breathed The Pope. "No, this can't be… this can't be happening."

He stumbled backwards towards the door, his faced etched with fright. All the colour had drained from him and he was as white as his vestments. He grabbed the handle and tried to pull it open but it wouldn't budge. Then he started banging on the wood, shouting and screaming for help.

"Oh give over would you," said The Devil. "We're both grown ups here, let's try and act like it shall we?"

He snapped his fingers again and the door began to glow. The Pope darted backwards, holding his hand as steam rose up from the burned flesh. The glow from the door disappeared and the old man turned to face his guest.

"What do you want from me?" he asked. "This is holy ground, you can't be here, you just can't. Be gone!" he shouted.

"That's not very welcoming," said The Devil nonchalantly. "Whatever happened to love they neighbour? Or is that yet another one of those rules you lot choose to ignore until you want to. Honestly, humans, you'll never catch on."

The Pope swallowed a dry gulp of air. He stalked around the room, never taking his eyes from The Devil. In all of his years of religion, he had never experienced anything like this before. Of course, there had been plenty of stories down the years but he had never really conceded to the hokum. Legends and fairytales were all well and good; he had an empire to run.

Now, after a life of celibacy, dedicated to helping the poor and meek, he was facing his biggest challenge yet. That was, he conceded, if he wasn't in the throws of a psychotic episode. He regretted having that drink now.

"Now I know what you're thinking," said The Devil. "Of course I know what you're thinking, I wouldn't be very good at my job if I didn't, would I?" he laughed a little. "How do you know I am who I say I am?"

The Pope nodded quietly, his eyes still wide. He bumped into a bookshelf in the corner of his office, stopping him dead.

"Well, apart from stopping your heart attack, breaking into what's possibly the most well protected room in existence and setting that door on fire, I don't really know what further proof you need," said The Devil, tucking his hands into his pockets. "Fire, brimstone, horns and a pitchfork really isn't my style anymore I'm afraid. But I could magic something up for you if you like."

"No!" The Pope blurted. "God, no, please, I believe you, I believe you."

The Devil grinned, a broad smile reaching out across his cheeks. He winked at his host.

"Good, I'm glad we've got that sorted then," he said. "Now, on to business."

"Business?" asked The Pope. "What possible business could I have with you?"

"I say business, it's not really business, not like the one you've got going on here anyway," he looked about the room. "Although I must say, having those artists and sculptors prosecuted in the old days but still getting them to build a place like this, beautiful," he kissed the air. "Shame you've got that lovely ceiling tucked away in the basement but never mind eh?"

The Pope didn't say anything, he didn't have the chance. The Devil scratched his cheek and ran a hand through his hair.

"What I've got to say is a bit awkward," he said. "I'm not quite sure I know how to put it."

"Well," said The Pope. "Why don't you start at the beginning? I'm a good listener you know."

The Devil smiled a wry grin at him. He wagged a finger towards the old man.

"Very good, I like it," he laughed. "Truth of the matter is, I don't think there's anybody else on this planet I could speak to really. I mean, who even believes in us anymore."

"I don't know about that," said The Pope. "I think you might be on your own there. Plenty of people believe in me."

"You!" The Devil choked. "Please, don't make me laugh. You're just as bad as the rest of them."

"The office then," the old man remained adamant. "And there there's always Him, of course."

"Him!" The Devil sputtered. "Don't make me laugh sports fan. If he knew what I had planned he'd have a fit!"

"You know I tell him everything though," said The Pope.

"Actually, I'm surprised you still believe in Him."

"How dare you," said The Pope, his eyes bulging.

"How dare I?"

"Yes, how dare you! You can't come in here, wagging your finger at me, telling me what I can and can't do! This is my house! It's His house! Be gone from here!"

He threw his arm out towards the door pointing. The Devil chewed on his lip and cocked an eyebrow.

"Are you finished?" he asked.

The Pope didn't answer. He was breathing heavily, a mixture of shock, terror and anger. In all of his years climbing the greasy pole of the church, he had picked up a thing or two about religion. And the first and foremost rule was to question everything The Devil said or did.

"I thought we could, you know, shoot the shit," said The Devil.

"Shoot the shit?" asked the old man, perplexed.

"Never mind," said The Devil. "It's what the kids say these days. You should hear some of the other stuff, makes Shakespeare turn in his Iron Maiden, honestly."

He parted his legs a little and squared his shoulders. Steepling his fingers, The Devil prepared to make his pitch.

"Okay, are you ready for this?" he asked.

The Pope did not reply. Not to be undeterred, The Devil pressed on.

"I'm going to make Hell a legitimate business."

The old man remained silent. For a moment, he thought over the words and then, still dumbfounded, thought how best to put across his confusion.

"How do you mean *legitimate*?"

"I mean *legitimate* legitimate," said The Devil. "I'm going to make it a business, a one-stop shop for anybody and everybody who wants to get on in life. Arts, culture, business, anything and everything. It'll be a school, a place for education, somewhere the mortal soul can go to learn all the tricks of the trade and be a success in this life. Going to call it Hellcorp. What do you think?"

"But that's absurd," said The Pope. "How would you even make such a thing? We can't go to Hell or Heaven, we're Humans?"

"Details, details," The Devil waved a hand. "We can iron out the finalities as we go. I just want to know what you think?"

"Details? What *I* think? You're insane," said the old man.

"You're swaying, I can tell."

"I am, most certainly *not* swaying. Of course I'm against it and I'll do everything in my power to stop you."

"Your power?" The Devil snorted.

"Yes. I'm The Pope."

The Devil pinched the bridge of his nose. He closed his eyes and tried to regain his composure.

"Yes, you are," he said slowly.

"Why?" asked The Pope. "Why are you doing this?"

"Why?" asked The Devil.

He turned back towards the window and stared out at the square below. A security guard was standing still in the middle of the plaza. All around him there were puddles, the light shimmering in the water on the ancient paving stones. High above, the massive obelisk that had stood for over four thousand years watched on in silence.

"That's a very good question," said The Devil, turning back into the room. "Pride I suppose, and to mix things up a bit. But mostly pride.

"Pride is a sin," fired the old man.

"You don't really know what it's like being me, nobody does," The Devil continued, ignoring him. "I'm alright with that, somebody has to be the bad guy. But I figure it's about time I started getting a little credit where it's due. I mean, I loved Dante's work, really top stuff, his vision of Hell was spot on. Then it came to me, three heads, are you serious? That's a tough pill to swallow, even for somebody with as big an ego as mine."

"So that's it then," said The Pope. "You're just doing this to make yourself feel better?"

"There are other reasons, sure, but we'll discuss them another time," he started for the door, breezing past The Pope who still held tightly onto the handkerchief.

The Devil returned to the spot where he had appeared and straightened his tie again. The Pope, sensing his guest was about to leave, scuttled forward.

"Wait, you can't go," he said. "I've got so many questions."

"Oh I'm sure you do," said The Devil. "But it's getting late, got a lot of work to do. Just thought I'd pop in and give you the heads up."

"But… but… but you can't just go," said the old man. "I mean, not after what you've told me. What am I supposed to do now?"

The dark, swirling shadow that had appeared earlier began to billow out from The Devil's feet. Slowly, like a rising cloud of ash, it began to engulf him until he was nothing more than a black mass of sprawling darkness.

"Improvise," came his voice through the cloud. "You lot have always been good at that. Oh and I must say thank you, before I go. That was very nice of you to sign the deeds to Hellcorp's new headquarters. And with Papal money too, you're not as bad as they say downstairs you know."

"Wait! What?" the Pope shouted.

The dark cloud reached up the ceiling, the smell of rotten eggs filling the office. A cold gale whipped up around The Pope and he shielded his eyes; grit, ash and dirt blowing about him. There was a bright, white flash and suddenly the room was still.

The Pope blinked and looked about his office, bewildered. He felt ill, quite sick. The pain in his chest was gone but his stomach was still doing back flips. He staggered over to his desk and leaned on the edge. Dropping his head, his eyes fell to the sheet of paper on top of a pile. Immediately, his blood ran cold and he gasped in fright.

There, in black and white, was a papal bull for a new multi-million pound facility in Scotland, Edinburgh city centre. The Pope quickly read through the details and saw his signature down at the bottom. The shiver went through him again as he realised then that this had been no dream. He had spoken with The Devil. And The Devil had won.

Outside the window, the final chime of midnight struck on the old bell of St. Peter's Basilica. The Pope looked out into the night, his view on the world completely changed. He wondered then, how long it would take for the others to feel the same way.

"Mamma mia," he whispered.

ONE

The Devil's office was a hellhole. As would be expected for the personification of evil, chaos and anarchy reigned supreme. Rather than the walls of flame, boiling hot lava and damnation torture, this hellhole was cluttered with paperwork and files.

Watching over the punishment and judicial system of the afterlife wasn't an easy task. Documentation had to be examined, double then triple checked to make sure the whole system remained ticking over. Since the dawn of time, The Devil's office was the go to point for any bureaucracy relating to Hell and the underworld.

Understandably, The Devil needed help when it came to maintaining the status quo. Indeed, the *Whatever You Want* album was kept on standby at all times. He didn't like the office staff getting too complacent.

That was why he employed the best organisers throughout history to keep the wheels of the machine turning. Although at times he questioned the term 'best' might have been a better description of his most loyal lieutenants.

Much like the cartoons and comics that humans loved to pour over, The Devil was surrounded by incompetent henchmen. He often wondered where humanity had come up with the idea. In his more arrogant moments, he put it down to a dropped whisper in the ear of some artist. More often than not, he calculated it was an error in the overall system. A rogue line of code that He had left in somewhere.

Regardless of its occurrence, The Devil had to deal with the outcomes every hour of every day. If he wasn't chewing out an office newbie, preferably a secretary or clerk in the mortal world, he was downing gallons of liquid painkillers to deal with his headache. Life as The Devil wasn't all it was cracked up to be.

That was why he was going legitimate. No more sneaking around, skulking in the shadows, plotting until doomsday. There was too long of an eternity to wait for that to roll around. Instead, he was taking the bull by the horns, the papal bull, and getting upwardly mobile. He could do that, he could become proactive.

He sat in his office, in the bottom tier of Hell, and took a moment. The flickering light above his desk was a pain but then again, everything was. That was the point.

"Alice," he said leaning forward and pressing the intercom.

"Yes," came a crackly voice.

"Could you come in here, I've got a memo I'd like you to take down."

"Right now?" was the response.

"Yes, please, if that's not too much trouble?"

The intercom clicked and there was a pause. The door slid open and in walked Alice, all eighteen stone of her. When it came to women, The Devil was a connoisseur. Although he couldn't take credit for their creation, he had spent thousands of years worshipping at their feet. And Alice, his personal secretary, was just one of many who fulfilled their jobs impeccably.

"Yes?" she said, a pen being tapped against a notepad.

"No good morning?" asked The Devil.

"Good morning," she said sarcastically.

"Is it even morning?" The Devil looked at the clock on the wall. "Oh yes, so it is, pardon me Alice."

She rolled her eyes impatiently. As far as secretaries went, Alice was top drawer. The problem was, she knew it. That meant she was in control. And if there had been a woman throughout history who shouldn't know her place in the universe, it was her.

The Devil had no real excuse though. He couldn't very well get rid of her. He was a glutton for punishment. Large rear ends too.

"That's quite alright," she smiled sycophantically, mouth small between two puffy, red cheeks. "What can I do for you?"

"What indeed," said The Devil quietly.

He stared blankly ahead, wrestling with his thoughts. In the past few days, he had been wracked with doubt. Never before had he felt less confident about himself and his abilities. The opening of Hellcorp was proving to be a challenge beyond even his abilities.

With every incident or problem, another crack opened in his Satanic armour. Although he rarely wore it anymore, he still didn't want it broken.

"Have we had any word from the architects about the building?" he asked.

"Yes," said Alice, her smile gone. "They said that there wasn't enough room for the six hundred and sixty-six rooms you asked for."

"How many can they do?"

"Forty-two."

The Devil's jaw clamped shut. A pulsing headache raced across his forehead but he kept his cool. Losing his temper wasn't going to get him or his machinations anywhere.

"Okay," he breathed. "Fine, so be it. What about the upholsterers, the interior designers, are they on track?"

"All in order, they're decorating the place as we speak."

"Matt black?"

"As you ordered."

"Lovely. I want it to look like the Trump Tower in New York, inside and out. You know the Trump Tower, don't you Alice?"

"No, I can't say I do," said the secretary. "A little before my time I'm afraid."

"Ah, a pity, you'll have to go see it when we move. Quite the sight. Plumbing?"

Alice let out a long breath. Everything about her screamed inconvenience. It was like serving the lord of the underworld was nothing more than a distraction from her day.

He didn't doubt that she could run the whole place by herself. She knew where all the files were kept, the records, the keys to the front door. He wanted it that way, he almost *liked* not being in total control. It was the sadist in him.

She took a quick look through her notepad. Drawing a finger down the lines of scribbled notes and dates, she found the one she was searching for.

"Yes, plumbing is coming along, although the contractors seem to be fussy about payment," she said.

"Payment?" The Devil blurted. "Who do they think they're dealing with, some cowboy outfit?"

"On the contrary, I think we might have put the scares up them a little."

"Hmm," The Devil mused. "Maybe offering the contract in a mass, communal psycho-telepathic dream *was* a little too much."

"You think?" said Alice.

"I could have just phoned them I suppose."

"Yes, you could have. I did suggest it, in case you'd forgotten. They're in the Yellow Pages. And have quite a nifty little website too."

"Yes, yes, I know," he flapped. "Are there any fresh problems with the construction? It's beginning to get right on my tits all of this."

The secretary looked through her notes again. She shook her head, her huge body taking up the majority of the office's front section. The Devil liked Alice for numerous reasons, but her figure was the most appealing.

He liked big girls, with big bottoms. The bigger the bottom the better. He had thought about getting that tattooed across his own bottom but had gone off the idea. Especially when he saw how much pain his invention inflicted.

"Just one," she said.

"Go on," he said, with trepidation.

"The council," said Alice.

"What about them?" asked The Devil.

"It seems they have a problem with the emissions coming from the site. One councillor has teamed up with a local conservation group and had some tests completed. Apparently, according to their figures, we're causing, and I quote here, 'more than the acceptable or regulated amount of carbon dioxide allowed for a construction site of this size.'"

The office fell silent. If The Devil had a pet peeve, it was do-gooders. He had been plagued his entire career by them. From the Good Samaritan to the dreaded Boy Scouts, they all drove him to distraction. Even Pilate had put up a mild fight, despite the outcome going The Devil's way.

It was their endless optimism that bugged him the most. Everything had a good side, every cloud a silver lining. Despite most creatures in all of existence happy to plough on through life's labours silently, this collection of societal misfits took it upon themselves to plague everybody's day with their tireless efforts.

And there was no talking to them either, that really got him angry. No matter how hard he tried, there was simply no getting through to them. He often wondered if they were rogue programs too. Even He couldn't have come up with somebody that obnoxious.

Environmentalists were at the very top of The Devil's hate list. He wanted to shove a car exhaust down every single one of their throats. Only a hectic schedule stopped him from carrying out his fantasy.

"Give me strength," he said at length.

"Quite," Alice smirked. "What do you want me to tell them then?"

"Tell them I'll be happy to meet with them and give them a tour of the building. And of course," he said with courtesy, "I'll be happy to answer any questions, concerns and tiniest of tiny problems that they have in Hellcorp's headquarters, with a smile on my face and a tune on my lips."

Alice underlined the last part of her sentence. She clicked her pen efficiently and filed it away in her top pocket, the bottom poking out beside her erect nipple.

"Is that it?" she asked with another sigh.

"Oh Alice," The Devil gargled. "If you only knew my dear, what else I would have you do for me. If you only knew."

"Believe you and me, I do know," she moved a little closer to him. "And don't think you'll be getting it any time soon!"

She ran a finger along the edge of his lapel. The Devil very rarely got shivers but Alice sent an army of ripples through his human form. He knew he had chosen wisely with her, another little victory for his judgement.

"I think you had better get back to work Alice," he said through gritted teeth. "We can't be slacking off in the office, can we?"

She bit her bottom lip and took her hand away. Turning back towards the door, she waddled, her large behind shaking in time with her every step. The Devil couldn't keep his eyes off of her. He was entranced, enchanted, completely consumed by lust.

"You know where to find me," she said, glancing over her shoulder, dark hair rippling down her back. She slipped out the door and closed it with a click, leaving The Devil on his own.

"Mercy," he said, slamming his hand down on the desk.

He stared up at the ceiling and the flickering light. Shaking his head, he grinned.

"Mercy, mercy, mercy. See what you do to me!" he said loudly. "And they call *me* the Devil. You ought to be ashamed of yourself."

He took a deep breath and wiped his brow. The morning's activities were running away from him already, he had to regain his focus. A distracted mind was a useless one, at least when it came to his own. Distraction had been one of his earliest creations. And like everything else, its simplicity was key to its success.

The answering machine on his desk was blinking. Slowly taking his seat, The Devil reached out for the small device. His technology was cutting edge, but then, so was everything in his office. He had been happy with his researchers in that department.

For every broken internet connection, every disturbed teen looking up adult videos online, he got a warm glow. Hacked accounts and explicit text messages were among his favourites, especially when they arrived in unknowing inboxes. Broken touch screens, leaked secrets, even something as simple as a battery running out of power, it all made him feverishly happy.

Now he was about to share all of his tricks of the trade with the Humans. Hellcorp would open a few eyes, he was certain of that. Humans might have invented technology but The Devil made it an art form.

"Let's see," he said. "I wonder how many messages there are?" He was talking a loud, deliberately.

He glanced at the red display and rolled his eyes. Three sixes blinked back at him.

"Honestly mate, you really should try something more original."

He pressed the play button and sat back.

TWO

The roar of jet engines sounded out over the assembled crowd who stood cheering and screaming. Huge banners fluttered in the wind as hundreds stood on the soft yellow grass of Arthur's Seat. The huge hill that overlooked Edinburgh had been turned into a congregating place, the atmosphere of a music festival hovering over the assembled mass.

The day was warm and balmy. As the jets streaked through the clear blue sky, children laughed and clapped, their parents hoisting them up as high as they could to see the aeroplanes.

Younger members of the seething pit of humanity were much braver. Drinks in hands, fashionable wellington boots on their feet, they smiled and waved and danced to the music. Huge towers of speakers had been erected near the huge, glistening building that was about to be opened.

The mood was positive, the vibe strong. Those who had answered the mass invitation were glad to be there. Never before had a thousand people ascended the summit of the hill and they were all glad to be a part of history. And they were there to be entertained at the expense of their mysterious host.

Standing like a great, medieval castle of shimmering glass and concrete, Hellcorp's international headquarters was looking majestic. Built from the most expensive, hi-tech materials known to mankind, The Devil had spared no expense in its creation. He couldn't afford to, there was his reputation to think of in the first instance and the overheads to worry about later.

The festival atmosphere seemed infectious. All up and down the hillside, a relaxed, friendly mood was creeping through those who had ventured out. Drawn in by the promise of mystery, intrigue and free t-shirts, none of them ever really stood a chance.

It had all been a deliberate move by The Devil. He knew what Scots were like. The smell of fatty food and a nice day, they'd jump through a ring of fire if they thought they were getting something for free. Add to that the opening being in Edinburgh and the launch of Hellcorp was almost too good to be true.

Unfortunately, he was unable to attend. There was nothing he would have enjoyed better than to be walking amongst the festival goers. Being in Scotland too, there were bound to be plenty of round figured women for him to enjoy.

But some traditions just couldn't be undone, even by him. Setting foot on mortal ground, unblessed and unholy was one of them. His jaunt to the Vatican had been a strangely liberating experience. Breathing the humans' air had reminded him just how putrid the atmosphere was in Hell.

While the party raged on into the afternoon, The Devil watched on his fleet of monitors and television screens. A special observation lounge had been created in his headquarters for just the purpose. Tuned to every media outlet around the world, he had unequalled access to everything that was going on at Arthur's Seat. Including, most importantly, the opening ceremony.

"Alice," he shouted, pacing back and forth around the room.

"What is it?" His helpful and attractive secretary popped her head around the door.

"Is everything still on course?"

"Of course it is," she said sharply. "What do you take me for? An idiot? The speakers are about to go on stage now. The doors will be officially opened for registration at exactly three thirty-three."

"Lovely."

"Is that it?"

"Yes, thank you Alice," he waved her away.

She vanished behind the door and he turned back to the wall of screens. The building was looking fantastic, even he had to admit so. Then again, he hardly expected anything less from the types of architects he had employed. Some of the greatest constructional minds had been put to good use in its design. If he was going to legitimise Hell, he was going to do it right.

"Any minute now," he mumbled to himself.

The Devil wasn't used to feeling nervous. It was a concept he had never bought into. As he stood waiting for the ceremony to begin, he reckoned that this was the closest he had ever come to the blatantly human emotion.

A fanfare sounded from somewhere and his eyes were drawn to one corner of the wall of screens. A small army of trumpeters, dressed up like knaves from a medieval court, head to toe in black and red, emerged from the huge central doors of the Hellcorp building. As they marched in perfectly timing, the crowd's anticipation grew and a huge cheer went up.

"Oh shit," said The Devil, conjuring a cigarette from a piece of fingernail he had bitten off with his teeth. "Here we go then."

The procession formed two symmetrical lines, all the while blasting out a specially written piece of music for the occasion. Handel and Bach had been up all night writing it, The Devil wanted it to be perfect.

A huge stage had been erected at the front of the shimmering building; great banners and drapes hanging from buttresses and pillars. In its centre was a dais, with the company's stylised letter H on its front. The knaves marched in procession and split in the centre, filing along the front edges of the stage until they were facing out at the baying crowd.

"Now the dry ice," said The Devil.

As if some stage producer could hear him, which they could, a rolling mist began to cover the stage. Multicoloured lights beamed from the rafters of the huge structure, dancing off the well-polished glass at every angle. The trumpets continued their melody, boosted by walls of amps hidden in the side sections of the stage and manned by a team of loyal roadies. Sweaty middle-aged men who had worked with the best had been drafted in for the occasion. Led Zeppelin, Queen, Kiss, these old rockers had form.

With the dry ice now flowing through the feet of the knaves and onto the front row of the crowd, the atmosphere and tension was building. The Devil could feel it, he could almost taste the nervous excitement that the humans were feeling. It fuelled him, made him excited, his skin trembling.

"This is good," he mused to himself. "This could be very, very good."

The trumpeters came to an end and the gathered crowd let out a huge roar of approval. The Devil spied a beach ball being bounced around their smiling faces and waving hands. He took it as a seal of approval.

But before he could enjoy the moment, his attention was drawn back to the central dais. Now was the moment of truth, the money shot, the part where everything could take off or crumble to dust in front of him. It was time for the world to be introduced to Hellcorp.

The Devil straightened himself and took a deep breath. He fixed his tie and rolled up his sleeves, flexing his fingers and rolling his head. Every screen narrowed in and focussed on the dais as a tall, slender man with silver hair and frameless spectacles took up a position. He adjusted the mic, flicked through a stack of papers and looked out onto the crowd.

"Good afternoon ladies and gentlemen," he said. Or technically The Devil made him say.

Speaking in his private observation chamber in Hell, The Devil's words were projected through the man at the dais. A simple enough trick for the Lord of Evil, it was a handy way of getting around the old rules and regulations.

"My name is Creighton Tull, the CEO of Hellcorp."

Another huge applause went up from the crowd. The Devil smiled to himself. Give the Scots sunlight, booze and a bit of music and they were anybody's.

"Thank you all for coming out today, and I must say, it's a wonderful day to be here in Edinburgh," another cheer. "I cannot describe to you just how wonderful it is to see such a response from the open letter we issued. Having you all here in your thousands and the millions watching around the world at home, means a great deal to myself and the rest of the staff at Hellcorp. And I want to take this opportunity to thank you personally from both myself and the board of the corporation."

Tull clasped his hands together and shook them at the crowd. The Devil was proud of his work with him. He had been little more than a corporate stooge, sent to Hell for drunkenly murdering a prostitute. Yet here he was, less than twenty-four human hours later, standing on the cusp of the biggest and best corporation in Earth's history. The Devil made a special note to thank the boys in Hell Labs for their work. They had particularly outdone themselves this time with whatever they had pumped into Tull's body.

Regardless of the methods, it was working. Tull had mastered the crowd with his easy smile, natural charm and easy on the eye middle-aged good looks. Tanned skin, white teeth and a muscular physique, he was the housewives' favourite and schoolgirls' guilty little secret.

"I suppose you're all wondering what it is we do here. Well, I'm here to tell you. And for starters, I'm going to say it, I'm here to be honest with you" He turned a page of blank paper over on his podium. "We at Hellcorp are here to facilitate your dreams. We're a place where you, the public, can come and learn from some of the most accomplished minds and figures in their fields that the world has to offer. From business to athletics, science to philosophy, art and crafts, there's nothing Hellcorp doesn't facilitate to."

Tull adjusted his spectacles as the crowd watched on in noisy concentration. The huge screens at the side of the stage projected his face to those unlucky enough to be at the back of the throng, his voice blasting out through the speakers.

"Our door is always open, our tutors always ready to listen to those who wish to learn. When you pass through the doors of Hellcorp, you're entering a world that was previously thought impossible. This is a new dawn for humanity, one that we can all embark on together. Hand in hand, mind with mind, the future is ours to make what we will. And with Hellcorp, the only limitations are the ones that you set yourself."

The Devil took a moment to think. His speech writing was immaculate; he had been doing it for a very long time. Honed to perfection, he could talk one person into doing what he wanted and a million into following him. What was more, after millennia, he still enjoyed the showmanship of giving a good speech. Albeit, across the ethereal plain and through the mouth of a puppet.

"My friends, Hellcorp is the new kid on the block and we know that we have to convince you to use our services. After all, there are many, many fine organisations and outlets for you out there. But, as I mark the official opening of this, our spectacular global headquarters here in Edinburgh, I want to personally assure each and every one of you that this company will not stop until every single customer has achieved what they wanted from our programmes. That's my guarantee to you and the guarantee of Hellcorp."

The crowd cheered again but it was starting to wane. The Devil knew that time was short. Keeping humanity's attention for longer than five minutes was a challenge even he didn't dare try and break. He needed to wrap things up, keep up the mood, play to their spirit of selfish endeavour and hedonism.

"I can see that you're all in the middle of a fantastic party and I'm not so out of touch to know that you want an old duffer like me lingering around all the time" There were a few laughs. "So I'll close by saying thank you once again. Without your support and presence, Hellcorp wouldn't be in existence. It is with you and you alone that we can service you and help deliver everything you want in this life. Thank you for your time and please, welcome to the stage, a group a young men I know are going to go far. Ladies and gentlemen, Hyway!"

Tull stepped to one side as a motley crew of long haired rockers came shambling onto the stage. They picked up their guitars and one of them dashed to the front of the stage, grabbing the mic from the dais before a roadie pulled it away.

"Hello Edinburgh how you doin?" he screamed at the top of his voice. "You guys look great. We've got some songs for you, you ready!"

The crowd's roar was deafening. The only sound that was louder was the three chord riffs that now pummelled out of the speakers.

The young heavy metal band, plucked out of obscurity by The Devil, kicked off what would be a twelve hour sweat-fest to mark the opening of the company. And the crowd were lapping up every second.

Down in Hell, The Devil was pleased. He examined every screen in turn, watching the faces of the humans in attendance. He could hear the telephones ringing already outside the room as the legion of spies and statisticians all gathered up information from around the world. Viewing figures were important but more urgently, the subscriptions to Hellcorp's classes.

Phone operators sat on tender hooks at ten thousand receiving stations across the globe. All armed and ready to sign up the faithful and enrol them on courses that would cost both money and souls. The website had been designed to cope with high amounts of traffic, the highest ever recorded, should it need to. It was a well-oiled, well-practised machine. The Devil was providing a service and he wanted it to be top flight from start to finish.

"Alice," he shouted.

His faithful if slightly unappreciative secretary appeared in the doorway, taking up the doorway, looking a little dishevelled. She had a phone in her hand, another one ringing in a holster on her substantial waist.

"What is it?" she said, a little out of breath. "I'm up to my neck in it here!"

"Better boil some coffee darling," he said. "We're in for a long one."

THREE

The Big Red Phone sat on a plinth in the back of The Devil's private room. He didn't like to keep it on show. Something as bright and big as that always attracted attention. The less people who knew about it, the better

More importantly, the phone could only dial one number. And that number was the closest guarded secret in all of existence.

Why He had chosen a phone, The Devil had never understood. For a being of total omnipotence, surely having a device, a manifestation like a telephone, was a little underwhelming. Even before humanity had been able to catch up with the technology, The Devil had thought it was a little dated.

Not that any of that mattered. The Big Red Phone was The Big Red Phone. And when He wanted to chat, He would ring the number.

The Devil sat on a long, black leather sofa in the middle of the darkness. The move to legitimise his own business was a trying one, much more so than he had ever expected. By the time five o'clock had rolled around, either afternoon or morning, he had decided he had taken enough abuse.

He sat with the lights switched off. Somewhere, beyond the confines of his room, the low, constant, sub-sonic hum of his kingdom could be heard. If he closed his eyes and concentrated hard enough, he could just about ignore it. Ahead of him was The

Big Red Phone, a pillar of light bathing its Bakelite contours. That light was always on; he couldn't turn *that* one off. Pure, brilliant, endless, He liked to keep an eye on the phone at all times.

A tall bottle of gin sat on a table beside the couch. There was a glass beside it, ice tinkling gently as it slowly melted in the heat of the underworld. He would pour himself a drink, eventually. But for now, he wanted to sit in peace.

Just as the throbbing in his temples began to ease, the phone rang. The Devil's eyes shot open quickly, narrowing on The Big Red Phone immediately. The hard, buzzing bell that emanated from the infernal contraption was burned into his mind. He was certain the whole of Hell could hear it.

"Honestly," he said, pulling himself to his weary feet. "You get five minutes to yourself and the phone rings. I thought that only happened to Them."

He slowly picked up his empty glass and walked across the room, bones aching. Lifting the receiver, he held the ice cold flute to his forehead in a vain attempt to relieve his headache.

"Hello," he said, wearily.

"How are you?" came the His voice from the other end.

"You know how I am, why bother with the chit-chat?"

"I always like to ask. Sometimes I don't ask and people get the wrong impression. I would have thought you would know all about that."

"Yes, well, what can I say, I'm good at my work."

The Devil wasn't in the mood for pleasantries. He wasn't in the mood for anything. He wanted to lie down on the floor, hold his knees and sleep for a thousand years. Hibernation had a great habit of changing one's viewpoint of the world.

Then he remembered the last time he had tried something similar. The Humans had called it The Renaissance. When he came back from sunning himself in the south of France, he had his work cut out for him. Arguably, he had never really recovered.

"Are you busy?" He asked.

"Of course I'm busy," The Devil snapped, his temper frayed. "You know all of this, you know the answer to every question, even before it's been asked. What do you want, so I can scurry off back to the rock I've climbed out from under."

Silence ensued from the other end of the line. There was a slight, static buzz from the phone line, there always had been. The Devil had always thought to look into it but had never gotten around to the job.

The buzz was interrupted again by the sound of Him. He cleared His throat and spoke again.

"Why don't you come up and see me in the morning," He said gently. "Just for a chat."

"A chat?" said The Devil. "What do you mean *a chat?* I don't like the sound of that."

"I don't mean anything by it, you know that. I just want to have a private word with you, see how things are ticking over," He said. "There's nothing devious in it, that's your department. Or, as I've been hearing, *was* your department."

"Ah…" The Devil let out a long sigh. "I see it now. They've been chatting to you, haven't They."

"Whatever do you mean?"

"Oh come on you old bastard, you know exactly what I mean. My little trip to Italy the other day there, old Popey has been on the phone, letting you know what we discussed."

"I wish you wouldn't call him that. He does his best with the tools he has." He sounded almost sympathetic.

"Well why don't you give him some better tools then?"

"That's not how it works."

"That's your answer for everything."

The Devil wasn't in the frame of mind to let that one go. Credit where it was due, he might have had the image of being unfair but in reality, he liked to award praise if and when it was applicable. He, on the other hand, seemed to be a random number generator when it came to approval.

"He's a bloody Human, he can't be trusted, You know that and I know it too," he said.

"So you're saying I should ignore him then? He's way off the mark?" He asked.

"Well, no, not exactly," The Devil murmured. "There's some truth in what he says."

"That you've gone and made Hell a legitimate business?"

"Yes."

"And that you're going to help the humans commit sin."

"No, I never said that to him."

"That's what he said to me."

"Well it's not what I said to *him*," The Devil made sure he got his point across. Yes, he was a liar, yes, he was a cheat, but he didn't like being accused of those things when it just wasn't true. Being the personification of evil was an art form, a talent he had mastered over more years than anybody could remember. He deserved to be quoted accurately.

"Bloody Chinese whispers," he said at length. "Still, it just proves my point, They can't be trusted."

"Did you ever think to ask me about any of this?" He asked.

"Well, no, quite frankly. It's of your concern, yes, but you're not going to be landed with any of the paperwork. Of which, may I add, there's been plenty already."

"I'm sure there is," He said. "But a little courtesy would have been nice."

"I don't do nice, remember," The Devil fired back.

There was a sigh from the other end of the phone. He knew better than to toy with Him. While they were opposed in almost every way, they also needed each other. At least, that was what The Devil liked to think. Being a creature beyond the comprehension of anything in the universe could be lonely. They each needed somebody to talk to.

"Can I speak with you first thing in the morning please," He said, a little more sternly. The Devil knew when his luck was out. He wasn't stupid.

"Very well," he said in indignation. "The usual place."

"The usual place."

"Will there be anything else?" as he said it, The Devil regretted being so forward. Mercy wasn't His strong point, despite what had been written down in black and white.

"No, no, that'll be all. For now," He said. "I'll have the usual accoutrements delivered to you first thing, make sure you take note."

"Really?" moaned The Devil. "We still go through all of that rigmarole."

"I'm afraid so," He laughed. "Anyway, I'll let you get back to your paperwork. No rest for the wicked and all of that."

"Touché," The Devil cocked his eyebrow.

The line went dead. He stood still for a moment, staring at the receiver. Carefully, he replaced it down and he paced back over to the couch. He grabbed the bottle of gin and poured a large measure into his glass. The ice had melted, the water pooled at the bottom.

Choking the gin down in one quick gulp, he made a large belch. While humanity had it's many faults, their form was still about the most functional. He gave a quiet thanks to still retaining his ethereal powers though. Without them, he'd be lost.

"Shit," he said loudly. "Shit, cock, bollocks and all!"

His voice echoed off the dark walls and came back to him. What had been a royal pain in his Hellish backside of a day had just got worse. There was nothing he hated more than being called to the headmaster's office. Suddenly he wasn't quite so confident that Hellcorp was a good idea.

"That old bastard," he said, pouring another drink. "He always does it, he always bloody gets to me. That seed of doubt. That seed of bloody doubt. If only I knew how he did it. If only. Bastard!"

He looked up at the ceiling and extended his hands, the anger rising from the pit of his stomach. With a mighty roar, he unleashed his rage.

"You bastard!"

Somewhere across Hell, a mountain crumbled to pieces, sending out a huge ash cloud that engulfed a small town. The denizens of the underworld all slept a little uneasily that night, for fear their master was in one of his moods.

Meanwhile, on Earth, the phone lines were ringing non-stop. Hellcorp was doing a tidy bit of business, its courses filling up quicker than the operators could subscribe them.

FOUR

The Devil woke with a startle. For a moment, he thought he might have slept in. Being in His bad books was enough of a bad trip without adding tardiness to the rap sheet. He took comfort in knowing it wasn't the worst thing he would have ever done.

He yawned and scratched his potbelly. Ever since he had taken human form, since They had been created, every day had felt like more and more of a struggle. Tiredness and fatigue, those were humanity's biggest enemies. He was a little peeved he hadn't been the one to think of them.

A wry smile etched its way into his sharp features as he rubbed his eyes clear. One snap of his fingers and he was back to feeling one hundred percent. The perks of being an ethereal entity were plentiful, something he was greatly appreciative of.

For appearances sake, he dressed in his familiar pin stripe suit and tartan tie. Appearing in front of the Masses of the Damned required a certain level of pomp and discipline. Fear and loathing couldn't be conjured up in one's underpants.

He stormed in towards Hell's central offices nodding firmly at those who halted in his wake. He reached his own little den and smiled at Alice behind her desk.

"Oh Alice, my dear, how are we this morning?" he asked.

"Really?" she asked. "You're asking me that? Here I am, running your empire and you're asking me how I am. Unreal."

"If only I had a legion of Alices," he said, raising his voice. "The world and everything in it would be mine. To dream Alice, to dream."

"And don't you know it."

"Any messages?"

He leaned forward on the desk and took a sniff of the air around her. She ignored him, rifling through a stack of papers.

"Nothing urgent really, I make sure of that of course. The usual forms for you to sign, permission slips, appearance schedules, record label deals, all the normal things."

"Good. Any developments on Hellcorp?"

"A dozen or more local complaints but nothing outstanding."

"Wonderful," he started off towards the door.

"Actually, there is one thing," she called after him.

"Yes?" he cocked an eyebrow and slowly swivelled on his heels.

"This, it arrived for you this morning."

Alice ducked beneath her desk, affording The Devil a quick glimpse down her low cut top. He licked his teeth at the sight of her wobbly breasts but composed himself before she sat up straight.

She looked confused as she handed over a plain, white shoebox. The Devil looked at it curiously before examining the tag. His name was written in neat, cursive handwriting.

"Bastard," he said under his breath.

"What is it?" asked Alice

"Nothing," he held the box close to his chest. "Look, Alice, I'm going to be out for a while this morning, I won't be able to take any calls or deal with any business. Do you think you could steer the ship while I'm gone?"

"Isn't that what I do every day?" a devilishly wicked smile made her lips curl at the sides. "How long will you be away for this time?"

"It's hard to say," said The Devil, his eyebrows arched. "I'm not quite sure, hopefully not long."

"Your wish is my command sir," she bowed a little.

"Oh Alice," he said with a sigh. "Whatever would I do without you my darling?"

He gave her a sad smile and turned the handle of his office door. As he stepped through, a wave of bright, white light engulfed him, knocking him backwards onto his rear end.

When his mind was restored, he blinked his eyes open. The light dimmed a little, the whistling wind in his ears dying down and he was able to regain his breath. The Devil knew when he had been tricked, and that made him mad.

Upstairs was a much nicer place than Hell. Though it pained him to admit it, and he would never say it aloud, the notion drove him mad.

One of its big advantages was space. Acres of room for anybody and everybody who was lucky enough to get real estate there. Fresh air, pristinely cut lawns, the whole place looked like one huge golf course. It was no coincidence, He loved golf, to the point of obsession. Yet one more reason why The Devil had never gotten along with Him.

One quick look about him and he knew he had been summoned.

"I was on my way you know!" he shouted to nobody in particular. "Can't a guy make his own travel arrangements? Sheesh."

He stood up and dusted off his jacket and trousers. The shoebox had been thrown out of his hands and he gathered it up. Inside was a crisp, white rose with a long stem. He lifted it out and discarded the box, the container disappearing before it reached his feet.

"We're still using these then?" he said. "I thought your people would know me by now. I don't do flowers."

He sniffed the centre of the rose. It was sweet and a little sickly, like the smell of all ancient cathedrals. There weren't that many odours in the universe, some of them had to double up.

He tucked the rose behind his ear and looked about his surroundings. He began to whistle, keeping in time with the birds that cooed overhead.

"No greeting party this time?" he said. "I thought I'd at least get a guide."

"You talk too much, sometimes," came a voice from behind him.

The Devil swivelled, a little surprised. A tree had appeared from nowhere, leaves making a gentle hissing sound in the light breeze. They were gold and orange, red and brown, rich in autumnal colouring. Beneath the tall branches, a man sat on a bench, scattering seeds. He was broad shouldered but slouching, his crumpled suit, shirt and tie matching the colours of the leaves.

"Nice outfit," said The Devil, sitting down beside him. "Is that an Armani?" he scoffed.

The man smiled gently but said nothing. He was focussed on the small group of pigeons who had gathered near his feet. They were pecking at the seeds, making satisfied sounds as they filled their beaks.

"Do you know what the humans call those birds?" The Devil said, nodding towards the flock. "They call them flying rats. Charming lot aren't They."

"They have their moments," was the response.

"Yeah, well, I suppose," The Devil was fidgeting. He always felt a little uneasy in His presence. Talking to a being capable of creating whole multiverses within the blink of an eye could be a rather daunting task. Even to the personification of evil.

"Look, I'm sorry alright," he said at length, unable to bear the silence.

"What for?"

"You know what for, snapping on the phone last night. I'd had a long day."

"How do you think I feel?" He said, that gentle smile on his face.

His features were much like The Devil's own. Young and fresh but carrying the weight of a billion lifetimes. There was an experienced wisdom in his cool, grey eyes but also an innocence.

The Devil knew it was all deliberate. He was a master of disguise, the definitive lord of illusion. Nothing was ever left up to chance with Him. This form he had taken, it was designed to keep The Devil's attention. It mirrored him, appealed to his selfish nature. He was clever, brilliant even, a total professional. The Devil was jealous.

"Do you ever get lonely?" he asked.

"Lonely?" He returned the question. "What do you mean lonely?"

"You know exactly what I mean. Do you ever get lonely, up here, on your own?"

"I'm not on my own," He replied politely. "How can I be, I have all of Them to keep me company."

"I know, but I get a lot of Them too. And They're still human after all. Not like... you know. Us."

"Us?" He asked, looking at The Devil.

"Oh come on, don't be so bloody obtuse."

That drew a laugh. He tucked away the bag of seed into the inside pocket of his suit jacket and stood up.

"Come on," He said. "Let's go for a walk."

"A walk," The Devil grunted. "Bloody hell."

The pair began to stroll away from the tree and the bench. A path of soft grit appeared beneath their feet, cutting through the short, neatly primed grass that stretched off into the distance. High above them, in the clear blue sky, a flock of birds were flying off in perfect formation.

The brightness was hurting The Devil's eyes. He was used to darkness. Dank, shadowy gloom was more his style. Being in the daylight, it made his skin itch.

"So what are we going to do then?" He said, scratching the silvery beard that had grown around his chin.

"What are we going to do about what?" The Devil tried to play it smart, buy himself some time.

He wasn't having any of it. Rather than rise to the antagonism, He continued walking, his head bowed a little.

"I see," He said.

There was no menace to his voice but it was laden with disappointment. Ordinarily, The Devil could care less about letting somebody down. Then it hit him.

An almost burning sensation in what felt like the depths of his blackened soul began to bubble. He stopped in the path, letting Him walk on a little further. He rubbed at his chest, trying to source the sensation.

"What have you done?" he shouted after Him.

"Pardon me?" he asked, turning to face him, His beard now grown down to his waist.

"You've done something, something to me. I can feel it!" The Devil shouted. "What have you done old man! What have you done!"

He shook his head and shrugged. Tucking His hands into his pockets, he rocked back and forth on his heels, whistling.

The Devil kept rubbing at chest. He pulled open his shirt but there was nothing there. His pallid skin looked back at him, unperturbed.

"What *is* this!" he shouted again. "What are you doing to me?"

"I've done nothing," He said.

"You have done! You've done something. I feel like my chest is on fire! Bloody shit, cock and bollocks man!"

"I'm telling you, I haven't done a thing," He said again.

"You're lying!" The Devil spat.

"Come come old boy," He said, smiling. "We both know that's simply not true."

"Then what *is* this!" he pointed at his chest, rubbing, scratching, kneading with his knuckles.

"You have to believe me though, I didn't do it," He said calmly, starting back down the grit path. "I need you to tell me you believe me."

"What? Piss off!"

"If you don't believe me, there's nothing I can do."

"Now that *is* a lie."

He shrugged his shoulders. A calmness fell over him, his eyes almost closed completely. The Devil wasn't quite so peaceful.

"Do you believe me?" He asked.

"Yes, yes, yes, whatever you say, just make this stop!"

"Alright then, but you're not going to like the answer," He produced a white golf ball from his pocket, popped it on a tee and took a step back. Lining up the club, which had miraculously appeared in his hands, he steadied himself for a shot.

"That strange, burning sensation in your chest," He said, peering off over the rolling fairway, "is guilt."

"Guilt!" The Devil sputtered.

He took his swing. The club head connected with the ball perfectly and gave a satisfying clink. Zipping off into the clear sky, the shot was straight, high and true.

"Guilt," He said again, shouldering the club.

"How could I possibly feel guilt!" The Devil shouted. "That's impossible."

"Not impossible old boy, just a little improbable. Remember where you are."

"Guilt, the nerve," he said, still fidgeting with his chest. "Can you imagine. Well, I suppose you could imagine perfectly well, but you know what I mean. Guilt. I've never heard of anything so preposterous."

"I told you you wouldn't like it," He said, starting off over the fairway.

"You would say that though, wouldn't you! Bloody hell this is annoying."

"Oh man up about it," He smiled. "They deal with it all the time, down there."

"And whose fault was that!"

He didn't answer. Despite driving the ball a solid four hundred yards, the duo found themselves at its resting place immediately. Sat on top of the fine grass, He lined up His club once again and prepared to swing.

"This whole business, with Hellcorp and what have you, have you given it any thought?" He asked.

"Of course I have," answered The Devil. "What do you think I am, thick or something?"

"Don't tempt me," He said.

The Devil rubbed at his chest. Thankfully, the irritation was beginning to ease. He buttoned up his shirt and adjusted his tie.

"I thought I would mix things up a little you know. After thousands of years, make it a little more interesting, that sort of thing."

"Interesting?" He asked.

"That's right, interesting. You have to admit; it's all been a bit boring down there for ages."

He laughed to Himself and shook his head. Turning back to His golf, He pulled back the club and swung elegantly. The ball zipped up into the air, The Devil wincing as it vanished into the glare of the sun.

"A little wide right," He said. "Don't you think it's a bit, well, cheeky of you, to go interfering."

The Devil was cautious. He knew what He was capable of, all too well. If humanity had painted him as a trickster, He was surely the best in the business. Not that any of Them knew or cared much about that. Or, more importantly, had documented it in their history.

He swallowed his disgust and thought carefully. Taking Him on at anything, head on, on the golf course no less, was a very dangerous game.

"I don't really see it as interfering, not really," he offered. "I'm just giving them the choice, that's all. If they want to live a life of so called sin, dedicated to money, power and greed, then they're going to do it anyway. My way merely means they can do it to the best of their abilities."

He didn't look impressed. Lifting up His club, He stared down the shaft, measuring it. For a moment, The Devil panicked, expecting it to be wrapped around his head before he could even scream. While he liked to dish out pain, he couldn't stand the stuff being inflicted on himself. Devil's Irony, he called it.

"I'll give you that much," He said. "They have been driving into your building in droves."

"Flocks even," The Devil afforded himself a little smile.

"Quite."

"You have to see it from my point of view, those people *you* created, Them down there, they've been at it since you first gave them life. I'm merely here to facilitate the process."

"Yes, but not being part of the solution is being part of the problem," He levelled, rubbing his hefty beard.

"Oh give it a rest, would you?" said The Devil, throwing his hands up in the air. "You sound like those bloody self-help gurus They are always listening to. You know that's all a con right? They're money grabbers, thieves, telemarketers."

"I know," He said. "But sometimes you find a pearl amongst the pollution. That's how I see it anyway."

They started off again over the gentle slope of the fairway. The Devil was beginning to tire of his company. He always did, after a short while. The sunlight, the fresh air and the nagging questions. He was altogether tired of His company but he knew he couldn't simply flee. Not without great difficulty anyway.

"Besides," said The Devil. "Don't you think I deserve a bit of a rest?"

"A rest?" He asked, sounding genuinely perplexed.

"Yes, a rest. We've been at this for a very, very, *very* long time you and I. Isn't it just exhausting? I mean, really. I'm absolutely knackered."

He said nothing. The Devil had the bone between his teeth now and he wasn't going to stop.

"That said, you get it easier than I do, when we count up the chips. I mean, when was the last time you were depicted with a bloody goat's head and snarling horns eh? Do you know what that does to one's self esteem?"

He laughed a little. His ball appeared on the horizon, another four hundred yards away. This time the laws of perception weren't bent and the pair walked in silence. They reached the ball and He took aim for a third time.

"Did you see the opening ceremony?" said The Devil, trying to make conversation. "It was quite a show no?"

"I did," He said. "I was there."

"You were there?"

"Oh yes, I wouldn't have missed it for the world. The crowds, the drinking, the sheer anarchy, yes. Right in the middle of it I was."

"Blimey," The Devil scratched his head.

"What's the matter?" He asked.

"Nothing, no. It's just, well, had I known you were going to be there I would have… you know."

"Toned it down a little?"

"Ramped it up actually," The Devil laughed.

He shook His head. The Devil was only half joking. Knowing that He had taken the time to appear in person, in secret, at Hellcorp's opening was something of a mild honour. After all, He hadn't even shown up at Golgotha for the main event thousands of years ago.

The Devil had been there, amongst the onlookers. Certain moments deserved a front row seat. And back then he was still young and keen to impress. The party afterwards had been a night to remember. If only he could.

"You know I can't do anything to stop you," He said, interrupting his daydream.

"Pardon?"

"You've made your bed, you'll have to sleep in it now. I'm not going to interfere. If that's what They want then They can deal with the consequences. I've always said that."

"But you're not happy," said The Devil.

"Old boy, I'm never going to be happy with *anything* you do, am I?"

"I know, but that little attack back there, the guilt thing. That was terrible, really shocking. If I had to live with that all the time, man. No wonder so many of them are turning their backs on you."

He looked up from His golf ball and darted The Devil a hard look. There was a darkness there, an ominous foreboding that came straight from the Old Testament and pre-history.

Gone was the happy, casual golfer, lost in an ocean of foreboding anger. In his place was a powerful being from beyond the comprehension of the conscious mind.

"Sorry," said The Devil. "Bad habits, bad language and all of that."

"That's alright," He said, and the dread was gone. "But I can't let you off easily old chap, not by a long shot."

"Oh," said The Devil. "I thought as much."

He knew it wasn't going to be that simple. Nothing ever was with Him. There was always ambiguity, never a straight answer. If it seemed too good to be true, it almost always certainly was. The Devil had learned that fact the hard way, over millennia.

"What's the catch then?" he said, testing the water.

"It's not a catch old boy, I don't do catches."

"You know what I mean."

"I do but I assure you, there's no catch," He took another swing and struck the ball once again. This time, it shot straight up into the sky, faster than was natural. The Devil watched it streak through the air until it vanished beyond his sight.

"If this Hellcorp is what you want, and with it a relief from your duties," He said, looking directly at The Devil, "then you're going to have to prove yourself worthy."

"Worthy?" he asked. "How could I be any more worthy!"

"Worth, old boy, isn't the same as circumstance. If you really want this to work, then there's nothing I can do to stop you. Not really."

"But…" The Devil drew out the word.

"You'll have to prove to me that what you're doing is for the right reasons."

"And how do I do that?"

The words were out of his mouth before he had a chance to stop himself. A terrible sense of responsibility made his skin creep. He knew then that he had played straight into His hands.

"I'm sure I can think of something." He smiled a broad grin and nodded towards a small building in the horizon.

"Shit," said The Devil as they made their way across the fairway.

FIVE

He always had a knack for the dramatic. Burning bushes, epic floods, the projected end of the world. If The Devil was supposedly famed for his extravagance, he was a two-bit Z-Movie director compared to Him.

And what was worse, He liked to show it. As the pair approached the clubhouse that had appeared on the horizon, The Devil wrestled with his own thoughts.

He didn't like the sound of the challenge being laid at his feet. Sure, he was always up for proving how good he was at his job. That was all well and good when the challenge came from Them. Ultimately, he would always win, the odds were permanently stacked in his favour. When He was in the mood, that was a whole different ball game and one that The Devil was unsure he was willing to get into.

The fairway retreated and a large, open square appeared in front of them. The clubhouse loomed large on the opposite side of the forecourt. Tall, grand and made from dusty, white sandstone, it was everything anybody could expect from the Ultimate Golfer.

A few of the Upstairs residents were present too. They smiled politely, saying their hellos in a thousand languages. The Devil walked cautiously a few paces behind Him, still a little nervous. The rose in his lapel would only provide so much protection and he didn't want a full scale riot on his hands. Not yet.

"I'm parched," He said, smiling warmly at a young couple walking their dog. "Would you like a drink before we continue?"

"Got anything alcoholic up here?" asked The Devil boorishly.

"I'm not going to dignify that with a response," came the answer. "You know fine well that stuff is bad for you."

"Eh, hello?" The Devil made two horns with his fingers and flapped his tongue. "Master of Evil here, I know that. Blimey."

They continued into the clubhouse where the air was cooler. The Devil was glad to be out of the sunlight, his skin blotchy and red with hives. The thought of Alice rubbing lotion into his wounds made him perk up a little and he fought the urge to smile.

"Steady on there," He said.

"Sorry," The Devil blushed, remembering his company.

A long hallway stretched into the distance of the clubhouse. Inside there were people chatting, sitting at tables, reading newspapers, enjoying the delights of the afterlife. The whole place seemed easy going and light, the quiet hubbub of pleasant conversation filling the air-conditioned air.

The Devil was about ready to be sick. All of these people, enjoying each other's company. What was that all about? Had this been what they were like on Earth? Surely a peaceful afterlife for them would be to avoid all of that small talk nonsense and be left alone. Do-gooders, he thought, they just can't help themselves.

"What do you think of the place?" He asked, stopping at a large, mahogany reception desk.

"It's alright, yeah," said The Devil, spying the frescos on the ceiling. "Bit ostentatious though, don't you think?"

"It's nice to look at," He answered. "We have some wonderfully talented people here, it would be a shame if they didn't put those talents to good use."

"Hmm," The Devil grumbled.

Before he could mount an argument, a slender, balding man with a thick, bushy grey beard appeared behind the desk. He was wearing a yellow polo shirt, grey slacks and the type of trainers elderly people were seen in on Earth. The Devil bit his tongue, determined not to make a sarcastic comment about the height of the man's waistline.

"Ah, good morning sir," he said in an obviously forced voice. "How are you today?"

"I'm very well Pete, how are you?" He replied.

"I never complain sir, always happy to be here, doing the job," he flashed a sycophantic smile.

His eyes fell to The Devil. The smile dropped as his mind ticked over. When he spied the white rose, he broke out in a sweat.

"Sir…" he stammered.

"Oh come on," The Devil leaned on the desk. "I don't bite, blimey."

"That's alright, calm down," He said. "We're here for a meeting. Do you have the keys to the Seventh Room?"

Pete was lost for words. He tripped back a little and kicked over a dustbin, scattering the carpet with waste paper. He nervously fumbled with his hands, unsure what to do.

The Devil was enjoying the panic. He liked that he could still force that reaction, even on somebody as ancient. He missed all the drama and back-and-forth rivalry he and the Old Man used to have. That was part of his desire to make a change, to give something else a try. Feng shui was what the humans called it, and they had been doing alright for themselves for a good while now.

"Yes sir, of course," Pete snapped out of his panic and began scurrying about under the desk.

There was a clanking and more bumping before he popped his bald head back up over the counter. He produced a large, golden key and handed it to Him.

"There you are sir," he said. "Everything has been prepared just as you requested."

"Lovely, a sterling job as always," He said, taking his leave. "I'll speak to you soon and explain everything. But don't panic Pete, there's nothing to worry about."

The receptionist watched the two head down the hallway. As he was leaving, The Devil puckered his lips and blew a kiss at Pete. The old man looked outraged and terrified in equal measure.

"Still got it," he said cackling.

"I wish you would try and get on with Them more," He said, counting the doors that lined the hallway.

"What are you talking about, I get on with Them fine," The Devil explained. "It's just some of them, the ones that have their noses so far up your back side that get on my tits. Him back there especially, he was always at it, even when he was down there."

He didn't respond. He came to a halt in front of a huge, ornate pair of doors. Two golden knobs stuck out from the dark wood, the metal polished enough that The Devil could see his reflection in them. He looked at Him for a cue.

"Well?" he asked. "What's this then? Is this my challenge?"

"Yes," He said. He didn't move, instead standing at the doors, staring into the swirling grain of the wood.

"What's the matter?" asked The Devil.

"Nothing," He replied.

"Then let's get on with it."

"I just like to take a moment, that's all."

"Take a moment?" The Devil scoffed. "Take a moment for what?"

"You'll see," He said, shoulders slumped, eyebrows arched. His eyes had turned a little glassy and he was chewing on his lips.

"Bloody hell," The Devil moaned. "Can we get on, I'll be here until Ragnarok at this rate."

He took a big gulp of air and perked Himself up. Fishing out the key, he placed it in the lock and pulled on the handle.

"This is the part I always hate," he said, throwing open the doors.

Immediately, the two ethereal figures were swamped in a bright, white light. The Devil's breath was taken from him again, a huge force barrelling into him faster than he could have expected. Wind howled in his ears and his mouth was filled with thrusting air, sending his skin rippling over his cheeks in waves.

The strange power evaporated and the world came back into view. The clubhouse was gone, the plush upholstery and lavish décor replaced with something altogether more sterile. The Devil rubbed his eyes and found that he was in an operating theatre.

"What's all this then?" he said in a panic.

He didn't answer. Hands clasped, He stood watching on as a team of doctors, wrapped up in operating robes, volleyed and jostled for position over the table. Bright beaming lights hung from the ceiling, instruments bleeped and whirred around them. Bloody instruments sat on trays as nurses dashed about the periphery.

The mood was taut. Panic was beginning to set in, tempers fraying. Doctor shouted at doctor, nurse shouted at nurse. And all the while a body lay motionless on the slab.

"Why did you bring me here?" The Devil shouted. "What could possibly come from any of this?" He waved at the unfolding drama. "And won't they worry about us being here?"

"They can't see us," He sniffed, wiping away a tear from his cheek. "We're beyond their level of comprehension. And besides, they've got much more important things to worry about."

A shout went up from the table and The Devil snapped his head around. The computers, life support machines and other devices all began to blare loudly. Strobing red lights, warning signals, screens flashing messages made the whole place seem almost dreamlike in its terror.

The doctors screamed at each other like pigs around a trough. A nurse dropped a tray near the door, the clatter ringing out loudly over the din. More instruments were fetched, their glistening surfaces splashed with blood instantly.

Arms flailed wildly over the body on the table. The Devil watched on from a distance with Him, the heaving green mass huddled together like a giant wounded spider. This was a side of humanity he didn't see often. Raw, warts and all, it made him feel a little sick.

Then it was all over. The commotion stopped, the voices died down and masks were removed from the pale faces that surrounded the operating table. A single, high pitched drone came from an unknown machine marking the end of the race. The patient was dead, the doctors had finished in second place.

He stood sobbing in the corner. The Devil was numb. He wasn't quite sure how he should be reacting. Death was as much part of his job as it was His. They dealt with death every day of their existences. Humans were born to die; they were brought into life dying. That was the natural order of things.

Yet he felt strangely hollow. Witnessing the final moments of a life was no great thrill. He had never been there to see it, he had never had any reason to. Now he stood amongst the wreckage, the humans mourning the loss of another of their kind.

"He is gone," He said solemnly, wiping his eyes.

"Where to?" asked The Devil.

"He is yet to be judged, that comes later."

The Devil nodded sombrely. The paperwork process of death and human souls now seemed a million miles away. All he could see and feel was the operating theatre, the downtrodden medical staff removing their gloves and bloodied robes with frustration and anger.

When they were clear, The Devil caught sight of the deceased. He was old, in his seventies, pipes and tubes protruding from his face. His chest was wide open all the way down to his belly button, the blood shining under the hard lights. The Devil watched as colour slowly drained from his skin, the final elements of life leaving their mortal vessel.

"Hell's bollocks," he said quietly.

"I thought you should see it," He said, coming up beside him. "For the sake of your task. I thought you should see Anton's final moments."

"Anton?" said The Devil, his eyes fixed on the gore.

"Antonio Baggio, a shopkeeper, from Govan in Glasgow. Came over to Britain in the nineteen fifties, Their time, from a place called Sorrento in Italy and spent his life raising a family. A good man, honest man, hard working, always attended church. When he was younger, he played football for the parish. He has seven children, thirty-two grandchildren and a dozen great grandchildren you know, all very young. They're about to find out what happened," He sighed. "Dreadful business."

"You designed it this way," said The Devil. "If you think it's that dreadful, you wouldn't have allowed it to happen."

"No interfering," He said strongly. "That's the key part."

"Whatever." The Devil took a step back as the nurses began to clean up the body.

They covered Anton's corpse in a sheet, blood soaking through onto the white linen like tears of red. The doors of the room swung open and two porters appeared, ready to take the cadaver away.

The Devil suddenly felt cold. He looked at the backs of his hands, his skin covered in goose-pimples. He shivered and stamped his feet.

"What's this all about?" he asked, filled with renewed curiosity.

He followed the stretcher out of the room and into the corridor, The Devil close behind. Standing at the swinging double doors, He reached up and tapped a flickering light bulb. The twitching stopped and the bulb grew a little brighter, bringing a smile to His face.

"I want you to solve a puzzle for me," He said, turning his attention back to The Devil.

"A puzzle? What kind of puzzle."

"Anton there, was murdered."

"Oh come on," said The Devil. "Don't start with all of this Sherlock Holmes crap. I'm not your bloody lackey you know, there are plenty of cronies Upstairs who would jump at the chance to kiss your feet for the umpteenth time."

He smiled and crossed his arms. The Devil stared down the hallway, the porters carrying Anton's body into a lift with morbid efficiency.

"Murdered how?" asked The Devil, after a moment of contemplation.

"I don't know," He said.

"What do you mean you don't know? You know everything!" The Devil shouted.

"Despite everything that you think *you* know old chap, there are still things in this universe that are a mystery even to me."

"Bull. Shit," The Devil spat. "I refuse to believe any of that."

He shrugged His shoulders. Closing His eyes, He smiled again weakly.

"It's true, I can't explain it. Sometimes there will be moments that I just can't see."

"But you built the fucking thing!" The Devil screamed. "How can you not know what's going on here! That's like saying you made dinner and forgot what ingredients you used in the first place. Come on, don't insult my intelligence."

He walked off a little down the corridor. The Devil hated being spoken to like a child. It was one of His little traits that could be totally irritating. The simple, feckless way that He would dismiss His own abilities and powers as little more than trivial or, worse still, non-existent.

"So what anyway," said The Devil. "Literally thousands of these rats are murdered every day, what difference does this one make. Why does he get special treatment?"

There was silence between them. The whole corridor seemed to grow a little darker. The Devil panicked, thinking he might have finally pushed the Old Man too far. But the response was as gentle as ever.

"Quite simply, old fellow," He said, "he was murdered forty years ago."

The Devil let the words sink in. He knew that He had always enjoyed being cryptic, but this was a whole new level of obscurity. Shaking his head in disbelief, The Devil twirled his fingers around.

"Let me get this straight for a moment," he said. "You want me to solve a murder case, that happened forty years ago, even though we just saw the guy die."

"Yes," was the answer.

"Okay, once more, just for old time's sake. You want me to solve a crime, a murder no less, that you just said happened forty years ago, four decades. Yet the victim, old Anton down there with the gully of blood where his chest used to be, has only just died right now."

"That's exactly it," He smiled.

"Right, I see," said The Devil, clapping his hand against his forehead. "Yes, of course, that makes perfect sense, doesn't it? Why didn't I see it sooner. You want me to solve a murder that took almost half a century to happen. Brilliant, absolutely brilliant."

He walked over to The Devil and clapped him on the shoulder. He smiled, his teeth white through the fluffy hair of his brilliant beard.

"See, I knew you were the man for the job," He said, starting off down the hallway. "And if you get stuck, you know where to find me." He pointed at a small sign that read Chapel nailed to the wall.

"That's it then," said The Devil. "I do this for you, I get some time off?"

"That's the plan," He called back over his shoulder.

"And I'm not getting any other clues?"

"You'll figure it out." He conjured up a golf club and began twirling it around in his hand, whistling as he went.

"When do I start?" asked The Devil.

"You already have, old boy," He said, reaching the lift and opening the doors.

"What, right now?"

"Right now," He nodded. "And just one more thing."

He turned to face The Devil and flashed a mischievous grin. All at once, The Devil's insides clamped tightly together, his buttocks firming up like concrete.

"What?" he asked.

"You might want to get that seen to," He pointed with His club at The Devil's stomach.

He looked down and saw a cloud of blood ebbing out from his left rib cage. A sudden shock of pain erupted through his body and he collapsed to the ground. He tried to speak but his mouth was filled with more crimson.

"What?" he gargled. "What have you done?"

"Human bodies aren't used to all that anger you've got inside of you old boy," He smiled. "You had better get used to that while you're on the case."

The doors slid shut and He vanished. The Devil tried to stand up and chase after Him, ready to throttle Him with his bare and bloody hands. But he couldn't, he was paralysed with pain.

The last thing he remembered, before he keeled forward onto the floor, was thinking about how awful it would be to be human. As the thick, dark, blanket of unconsciousness wrapped itself tightly about his mind, he was glad he was only dreaming. At least, he hoped he was only dreaming.

SIX

All about him the world was bright. For a brief moment, he thought he was in another one of His portals. But there was no gusting wind, no imposing force knocking him backwards.

He was already on his back and he could feel something wriggling about near his abdomen. He tried to push himself up but his arms were tied down. Only then did he realise he was wearing an oxygen mask.

"What the bloody hell is going on here!" he shouted, his voice brittle.

A shadow fell across his face. Above him, a hazy silhouette focussed to reveal somebody looking down on him. Eyes widened above a surgical mask and the piece of the puzzle began to take shape in his mind.

He was being operated on. The blood, the pain, the passing out. It all came flooding back into his mind.

"Let me up!" he shouted, struggling.

"Please sir, keep calm, we'll give you something," said the face with the mask.

"I don't want anything, let me up," he said.

Two forceful hands pinned him down to the table. The wriggling started again and he squirmed.

"Sir, please, for your own safety, try to lie still."

"Nonsense, let me up, there's nothing wrong with me! Don't you know who I am?"

The Devil lifted his head a little so he could peer down the rest of his torso. A number of pasty-faced doctors and nurses were scrambling about over him. For a moment, he wondered if He hadn't swapped his place with Anton Baggio. No, He wouldn't do that, that was too cruel, even by His standards.

"What are you doing to me?" he shouted, shifting to get a better view.

He spied something moving in his stomach. The flesh peaked and then disappeared. Then it happened again, a few inches above the last time. There was something inside of him.

"Bloody shit, cock and bollocks!" he shouted. "What are you people doing! What have you go inside of me!"

"Please sir, hold still!" the face with the mask was firmer, more authoritative. "The rectal probe examination has to be completed before we can let you go!"

"Rectal examination!" The Devil screamed. "You mean to say you've got… a camera… up my…"

He trailed off, feeling his freshly made human body. As he checked all the vital signs, his mind drifted below the waistline and around the back. And, sure enough, there was a cold, metal pipe somewhere it didn't belong.

"Get that out of me!" he shouted at the top of his voice. "Get that out of me right now!"

The camera pushed itself against the inside of his stomach again and he struggled. Having a piece of machinery lodged in his rear end was not how The Devil had envisioned his time of Earth beginning.

"Sir, if you don't stop fidgeting, we won't be able to remove the probe!" shouted the face with the mask.

There was a surreal logic to the words. The Devil conceded that whoever this woman was, she was inevitably going to be right. If he was to survive his little trip to the surface, he was going to have to play ball.

"Alright," he said, lying back down. "Alright, fine. But I want that thing out of me right now. Do you understand?"

The woman wearing the mask didn't answer. He stared into the bright light, breathing the medicinal smelling air that was being pumped through his mask. There was a sense of motion all around him as shadows and figures scurried about the bed. Was this what human life was really like? How glad he was that he didn't have to suffer it.

Down below, something began to tug. He gripped onto the side of the bed to steady himself. It felt like his whole intestines were being sucked out through his backside. Gritting his teeth, he closed his eyes and thought of home. Dorothy had been right all along.

With one final, hard tug, the probe was yanked from his flopping human body. Much to the disgust of those gathered around him, and to The Devil's own personal embarrassment, he proceeded to soil the bed.

"Shit," he breathed, bathed in sweat. "I've gone native."

If he had been hoping a quiet moment to examine his new mortality, The Devil wasn't going to get it. Wheeled into the corner of a huge ward, the beds around him were full of chattering people. Old and young, ill and healthy, they continued to pour into the sprawling room and talk themselves dry.

He couldn't quite believe They could talk so much. And the innocuous nature of that chat was enough to drive him to distraction. His teeth had been ground down almost to dust as he sat in his health service nightgown, an intravenous drip attached to his hand.

There was a large bandage around his stomach and a dull ache coming from his side. He hadn't been quite sure what had happened in the corridor but he supposed it was down to the transition. An adjustment to a new climate always took a while and he hadn't been counting on being caught so short.

He examined his bed and spied a table beside it. A large bouquet of white roses had been placed on the top of the cabinet. A small card hung from one of the petals, with some strange scribbles on it. The Devil had never bothered to learn to read human languages. It was much too uncivil and crass.

"Aww what's the matter?" came a voice from the end of his bed.

"Excuse me?" he looked up and saw a young, fresh-faced doctor examining his notes.

"You're face, it's like a bulldog chewing a wasp," she smiled. "You looking for some company?"

"Believe me madam, the last thing I need is more company," he looked about the room. "This is more than enough for anybody."

"Yeah, we are rather busy tonight. Still, plenty worse ways to spend a Saturday, or so I'm told."

She scribbled something down on his notes and rounded the end of the bed. She tapped the bag of fluid that hung above him.

"You feeling alright?" she asked.

"I've been better," said The Devil, a tinny, metallic taste coating the back of his throat.

"I'm sure you have been, you were in quite a state when you were found."

"Not my finest hour, I'll grant you."

"No, I'll bet," she smiled warmly. She was tall and thin, her arms sinewy and toned. He supposed she was a runner, or some sort of gym fanatic. They all were these days.

"What's your name?" he asked.

"I'm Jill," she smiled. "What's yours?"

"I'm The Devil." He extended his hand.

Jill cocked her head and squinted her eyes. She took his hand and shook it, measuring him up.

"Are you serious?" she said.

"Of course I'm serious," he replied. "Why would I lie about a thing like that?"

"Well you did lose a lot of blood back there. I wonder if I should maybe fetch somebody from our psych unit to give you the once over."

"Psych?" he asked.

"Psychiatry," said Jill. "Just to make sure you're feeling okay and you're not a danger to yourself."

"Believe me Jill, I am a danger to myself, and everybody in this room," he smiled, scratching at the needle in the back of his hand. "But there isn't a physician alive who would be able to crack this nut."

Her initial surprise turned to suspicion. Slowly, she began to edge away from the bed. He could see that she was nervous, her friendly demeanour evaporating quickly.

"What's the matter?" he asked.

"Nothing, nothing at all," she said. "I'm just going to get some help, that's all. I'll be right back."

"Jill, wait, hold on." He threw back the bed sheet.

There was a gasp from an elderly lady sitting at the bed beside him. A few others sucked in more air than they were used to, one little boy having his eyes covered by his mother.

"What?" said The Devil. Then he looked down. "Bloody hell, where did that come from?"

Jill raced over to him and covered up his crotch with his gown. She pulled the curtain around the bed quickly.

"Jesus Christ," she said.

"No, he doesn't work weekdays," smiled The Devil.

"You can't do things like that, there are kids out there, old folk."

"I assure you madam, I didn't do it on purpose."

"No?"

"No," he said flatly. "I may be a lot of things but I'm not a flasher. It's this new body; I'm still getting to grips with all of its nuances. And anyway, it's nothing that old bird hasn't seen a hundred times before."

The doctor ignored him, fastening the ties of his gown about his shoulders. He could smell her short, dirty blonde hair, the aroma of deodorant and soap wafting up his nostrils.

"Alright," she said. "Let me just go get you something that'll calm you down."

She moved towards the curtains but The Devil grabbed her wrist. She looked at his hand and then to him.

With one quick, swift movement, he was twisted around, forced face first onto the bed, with his own arm angled up his back. He blinked as the pain set in.

"Holy bollocks!" he cried. "What are you doing! Have you lost your mind?"

"Don't touch me, do you understand!" she said sternly. "This is self defence."

"Self defence!" he sputtered. "If this is you defending yourself I'd hate to be even close to you in a bad mood."

"Just relax," she said, twisting his arm up again. "I'm going to get you a sedative and you'll be fine."

"Listen love, it's not me that needs a sedative!"

"Take it easy."

"Please, would you let me go, I'm not going to touch you, honest."

Jill kept a firm grip on his arm. She manoeuvred herself until she was close to the head of the bed. A large, red button sat beside patients' tables and lockers, designed to call nurses in the even of an emergency. She set her sights on it and thought how best to juggle her assailant.

"I'm going to call for help," she said firmly. "Now I don't want you kicking up a fuss, okay?"

"Please, would you just let me go, I need to leave, I need to get out of here."

"You're not going anywhere pal," she said, her accent thick Glaswegian.

"You don't understand, none of you do. I'm not here as a bloody patient, I'm here to catch a murderer."

The Devil could feel her tense. She flexed her grip on his forearm. He knew that the seed of interest was about to blossom. He had to capitalise on grabbing her attention.

"Jill, if you let me up, I promise you won't need to call security," he said coolly. "Look at me, I'm attached to this bloody drip, where could I possibly go?"

He counted the seconds in his head. Usually it took two or three for the decision to be made. Any earlier and she wasn't buying it, any later and she would need more convincing.

"How do I know you won't try to grab me again?" she said.

"Please," The Devil smiled into the sheet. "If you thought that, you wouldn't be asking, would you?"

The seconds ticked down. He was about to conjure up more convincing arguments when the pressure was relieved from his arm. He pushed himself off the bed and rubbed his wrist.

"That's quite a grip you've got there," he said. "I like a woman who can hold on to things."

She remained stern, half a step away from the button. Her brow was narrowed, dark eyebrows serious above a pair of emerald eyes.

"You need help," she said. "You need medical attention."

"Hello," he said. "Look where we are, we're in a hospital, remember. I've had enough medical attention."

"I don't mean bandages and stitches," she said. "I'm talking about therapy."

"Get over yourself," The Devil dismissed her, prodding his side where there was a large gauze panel taped to his skin. "If you really believed that you wouldn't have hesitated in shouting for help."

"No?"

"Of course not. You're human, what, about late twenties, single, by the looks of your skin and in a room full of people."

"The looks of my skin," she touched her face instinctively.

"Yes. It's clear and tight where it should be. Anybody your age who doesn't start to look like a used paper towel is obviously still hunting for a man. Or a woman, it's the twenty-first century after all. Actually, that reminds me," he pointed at her, "what year is this? When are we?"

"You really don't know?" she said.

"If I knew that, I wouldn't be asking, would I? Come on, what year?"

"It's 2017, March in fact."

"I see," he said. "That means it happened in the sixties."

"What are you talking about?" she asked.

"It would take too long to explain," he said. "Come on, chop chop, take this thing out so I can get on with His business," he raised his hand with the IV line sticking out of it.

"Wait, hold on, time out here. Who's business, what do you mean? And what's this about a murder?"

The Devil gritted his teeth. He could feel the tendons twitching in his cheek. He hated repeating himself. He hated it even more when what he was trying to explain wasn't being understood.

"He, as in the Ultimate He, the man Upstairs," he said with a sigh.

"Who," she lifted her eyes towards the ceiling. "You mean…"

"Yes, Him, now hurry up would you, I've already wasted too much time."

"But I thought you said you were The Devil?" she asked, her eyes closing to slits.

"I *am* The Devil."

"Then why are you working for Him?"

"Why do you think?" he fired back.

Jill contemplated this for a moment. When her head began to spin with the theological implications and a world of fantasy mixed with the reality she knew and loved, she gave up.

"I'm calling psych," she said, sucking her tongue and reaching for the button.

"No wait!" The Devil shouted.

She stopped just short of the button. He had her at a crossroads, ready to choose a path. If she pressed the buzzer, he would be delayed even further. He needed her help and that galled him to no end.

"Do you see those flowers there," he nodded towards the vase sitting on the table beside his bed.

"Yes," she said.

"Check the card and tell me who it's from."

Jill stepped away from the button and examined the flowers. She took up the greetings card and read it to herself. The ruddy redness in her cheeks began to fade a little, her eyes widening at the same time.

"Well," said The Devil expectantly.

The doctor didn't answer. She kept staring at the card and then back up at him. Red rings formed around her eyes and she began to cry. Suddenly, The Devil had a hysterical woman on his hands.

"Oh don't do that," he said. "No, no, no, don't start all of that crying nonsense. Please, I don't have time for any of this bullshit. Pull yourself together."

"How did you know?" she said, holding her mouth.

"Know what?" he asked.

"This, this, how did you know that about me?" she flashed the card.

"I can't read love, not my style. Why, what does it say?"

Jill shook her head. She was all tears and snot and unable to speak. The Devil's patience was wearing even thinner than usual. Humans were terribly emotional creatures, that was why he didn't bother with them. His one brush with guilt on the golf course had been more than enough to remind him.

"I need to get out of here," he said, moving over to the curtain and peering out through a gap. Outside, the ward was still busy. Families and friends still visiting their loved ones. They were gabbing away like hens in a battery, clucking over each other in a competition that would crown the loudest.

"Are you really who you say you are?" Jill said, appearing behind him.

"Sheesh," The Devil said with a fright. "What? Yes, of course I am, why would I say otherwise? For fun?"

She stared at him, face streaked with tears and drool. She wiped her nose on the back of her arm, still holding onto the card from the flowers.

"This," she said, waving the card in front of him. "Only a handful of people could ever know this, what this says on here. And they're all dead."

"I've got news for you madam, it's still the same. Like I said, I can't read."

"Then that means whoever sent you this knows. And if you are who you say you are, then this could only have come from... well... you know."

The Devil shook his head. She pointed upwards.

"Ah," he said. "I see. I get it. One word from me and you're about ready to rip my arm from its socket. But one greeting card from Him and suddenly it's all tears and bogies. That's gratitude for you," he snorted.

He turned back to the ward. Jill was confused and emotional, frightened and comforted all at once. She wasn't sure what exactly was going on but the card in her hand gave her great faith. She touched The Devil on the shoulder lightly.

"What can I do to help you then?" she said quietly.

"I need to get out of here," he replied. "And then, I need to have a look at your records. There's a body bag sitting in the mortuary with one Antonio Baggio inside of it."

"So?" asked Jill, listening intently.

"So, I need to find out who killed him. And you are going to help me."

"If that is what has been asked of me. Then it will be done," she stood to attention.

The Devil cursed under his breath. The only thing worse than a zealot was a converted one.

SEVEN

The lift stopped with a hard, metallic bump. The Devil did his best to steady himself, a cold gust of air blowing up his gown. He made a mental note to look into having them installed in Hell. Walking about, with no underwear on, in a hard, almost plastic robe was strangely irritating.

"Here we are," said Jill, the door sliding open. "The mortuary."

A small reception area opened up ahead of them. Behind a desk sat an old porter, his glasses slid down his nose, mouth hanging slack. He was asleep, a thin trail of drool staining the collar of his shirt.

"Are all of your staff as efficient and keen as this one?" asked The Devil.

"No, this one's a real go-getter, career minded, aiming for the top," Jill volleyed.

"Touché," he smiled.

"Ahem," she cleared her throat loudly.

The man behind the desk woke with a startle. He fumbled his glasses and rolled his thick tongue about his mouth, the sleep clearing from his eyes.

"Yes?" he said snippily.

"I'm here to see a body," said Jill. "Doctor Gideon."

"Gideon?" spluttered The Devil.

Jill threw him an expectant look. He composed himself, wiping away a little spit from his mouth.

"Excuse me," he said. "Must have been something I ate."

Satisfied she had put him in his place, she turned back to the porter.

"Yes, Doctor Gideon, I'm here to examine a cadaver."

"I don't have anything on record doc," said the man, tapping some buttons on the keyboard of his computer. "You sure it's been filed properly, the request I mean?"

"No, I haven't filled out the paperwork," said Jill. "But I was wondering if you could let me off, just this one time."

The porter chewed his lips. Jill appeared to be appealing to his sympathy, something The Devil had no time for. He stepped forward and slammed his fist down hard on the desk.

"Look chappie, listen here," he barked. "Let us into the body or we'll report you were sleeping on the job!"

The porter and Jill blinked, both taken back by his actions. He stared at both of them, unsure what he had done wrong.

"What?"

"If you pardon my patient here," said Jill, nudging him out of the way. "He was close friend, relative even of Mr Baggio. He wants to see the body, before it is sent to the undertakers."

"Yes," said The Devil. "Yes, that's exactly it."

"I don't know," mused the porter, scratching the white bristles on his chin. "It's not really allowed, you know that doc."

"I know, I know," she clasped her hands together in prayer. "But it would mean a great deal to me. And… you were sleeping on the job."

That was enough to convince the porter. He pushed his glasses up his nose and headed for the door. Unlocking them, he stood to one side.

"Baggio you said."

"That's right," answered Jill.

"Vault twenty, you have five minutes doc and then I'm flinging you out on your ear," said the porter. "And your friend here," he shot The Devil a strange look.

"You're a star," she said, hustling The Devil into the room beyond the doors.

"A real professional."

"Come on."

The doors closed behind them. A wall of small hatches stood ahead of them, each with a faded number beside a handle. There was a strange, eerie silence about the place. The mood of a mausoleum hung heavy in the air.

"What are we looking for?" said Jill, locating the twentieth door and pulling it open.

"We?" said The Devil.

"Yes," she said as she slid out the tray and with it, Anton's body.

"I work alone love," he said, pulling back the sheet to reveal the corpse.

Anton's rigid face stared up at them. His skin was greying around the edges and his lips were blue. His white hair stuck out in great clumps, beads of frozen water glinting amongst its folds.

"Here are his notes," said Jill, taking a folder from the side of the tray and handing them to The Devil.

"I can't read," he said. "Tell me what he died of."

Jill sucked on her tongue and began pouring through the sheets of paper. Her eyes scanned over the details, assimilating information with the speed that only professional physicians could.

"Well," said The Devil, taking in every detail of the body. He had never seen a cadaver up close and was enjoying the education.

The staples on Anton's chest particularly interested him. He counted them in turn, admiring how simple yet gruesome the whole process looked. Care and attention seemed to be abandoned by the Humans once life was gone. Staring down at the body on the tray in front of him, it was hard to believe that They were capable of any compassion.

"It says here he died of a bowel obstruction," said Jill, interrupting his thoughts.

"A bowel obstruction?" he said. "No, that can't be right."

"That's what it says here," she tapped the file. "He died from a bowel obstruction due to ventral hernias secondary to remote exploratory laparotomy after a stab wound to the lower chest."

"A stab wound," he said, raising his voice. "He was stabbed?"

"That's what it says here, on the death certificate."

"When?" he asked.

"When what?"

"When was he stabbed?"

Jill sighed loudly and looked at the files again. She shook her head.

"That's strange," she said.

"What is?"

"It says here he was brought in for the obstruction, not that he was stabbed."

"Which means what?" asked The Devil.

"It could mean a whole lot of things," said Jill. "To my mind though, if he was brought in for this, he was stabbed. But that would mean there would be police kicking about and we certainly wouldn't be allowed near the body just now. It would be under guard."

"So what are you saying?" asked The Devil, his mind ticking over.

"It means that he was either stabbed and didn't tell anybody. And by that I mean he was stabbed and no doctor was able to see a wound. Or…"

"Or what?"

"Or, it happened before today."

"How about forty years ago?" The Devil ventured.

Jill's face contorted into a grimace. She shook her head, unconvinced.

"That would be just, odd," she said.

"I agree," The Devil mused. "But I wouldn't put it past Him to make this the oddest bloody murder in the history of your sorry race."

The doors behind them swung open behind them and the porter stood swinging his keys. He pointed up at the clock on the wall.

"That's time doc," he said.

"Yes, of course," said Jill, replacing the file. "Thank you for all of your help, I've seen all that I had to."

"And what about him?" asked the porter, nodding at The Devil.

"Him has a name you know," he said.

"Yes, he's been able to say goodbye, haven't you?" Jill stood on his toe, causing him to yelp.

She pushed Anton's body back into the fridge and locked the door. Pushing The Devil towards the doors, they eased past the porter quickly and stepped into the lift.

"Thank you again," she said, pressing the button.

The doors closed, leaving the porter behind, scratching his head. Jill slapped The Devil's shoulder, staring at him intensely.

"You stood on my foot you bitch!" he protested.

"You need to learn how to interact with human beings!"

"I don't need to learn anything Doctor Gideon!" he said. "Which reminds me, were you ever going to tell me your last name?"

"Why, what does it matter?"

"It matters quite a bit!" said The Devil, hopping on one foot and examining his other. "Especially when you come from my realm and that name has implications."

"What do you mean, implications?"

The Devil let out an infuriated breath. He rubbed his foot and, still unsatisfied, sneered.

"There's one thing you should know about this little, insignificant existence and world you inhabit," he said. "There is never, ever, *ever* coincidence. Everything is planned; everything is put together in a way that means that the outcome is already pre-determined. You helping me, you knowing what killed Anton Baggio, you being a Gideon, it's all part of His plan."

"So if it's all part of a plan, then why is he got you looking for a murderer?"

The Devil shrugged his shoulders.

"Who knows," he said. "Who knows?"

The lift came to a halt and the doors opened. The busy front lobby of the hospital was ahead and beyond, the front door.

"I have to go," said The Devil, stepping out of the lift.

"Wait, you can't just go," she said, following him. "Where will you go?"

"That's none of your concern Gideon, you just scuttle about with your own business and thank Him Upstairs that you've done your bit."

"Done my bit!" she shouted. "But… the card… it said."

She stopped herself before she said anything further. The Devil was suspicious, she was hiding something. He didn't have time to ask, he didn't much care anyway.

"What if I could help you, more I mean," she said. "I could help you find out what happened. At the very least I can give you some clothes."

She looked at his gown. While The Devil was still adjusting to the rigours of human life, he knew he couldn't run around the streets wearing next to nothing. Above all else, it was hugely unfashionable.

"We must go at once then," he said, reaching the front entrance.

"Wait, no, I'm on shift!"

"Shift?" said The Devil. "I'm quite sure I don't know what that means. Come on."

He took her hand and she clenched her fist. Half expecting to be clumped around the head, The Devil winced.

"My car," she said. "It's in the car park, a blue Mini, on the bottom floor. I'll be there in ten minutes."

She pulled her hand away and dashed off back towards the lift. The Devil felt a cold gust of wind blow up his gown again, another shocked gasp coming from a woman standing smoking in a dressing gown.

"Oh," she said. "Hello."

The Devil covered himself up and raced off towards the car park across the street.

"You wish love."

EIGHT

Jill hurried down the stairs, hopping two, sometimes three at a time. She could hear her breath in her ears, rasping away. The keys to her car were in her hands scraping against the metal banister of the stairs.

She didn't know what she was doing. She was hopping out of what had been a hectic shift already, all for the promise of a lunatic. Not just any lunatic, one who was claiming to be The Devil. When she said it again in her head, she was tempted to stop and return to the ward. Or better yet, call the police.

But something kept driving her on. She couldn't explain it, perhaps she didn't want to explain it. As soon as she had met him, whoever he was, she had been drawn into his world. Was he really deranged? Was he actually The Devil? She couldn't tell.

She was a woman of science, a doctor no less. Logic, statistics, cold, hard facts were her world. So why was she suddenly racing off on what was a wild goose chase? None of it made any sense. Not one detail.

When she thought about it though, she knew exactly why she was going. Divine intervention or not, she believed this man. Something about the way he carried himself, the way he spoke, he was more than a simple delusion case. The conviction of his ideas, his self-assured swagger, the way he insulted almost everyone he came into contact with. If Jill was going to paint a picture of The Devil in human form, he ticked every single box.

Who was she kidding? Nobody, not least herself. She had been drawn to him for one reason and one reason alone. She found him attractive.

Jill wasn't stupid. She was also desperately lonely. Being in the company of a man, any man, every man, was enough to make her knees weak. That was why she was running down stairs, ducking out of work and possibly putting her career and life in danger.

"Unbelievable," she said, skipping down the last of the steps.

She bolted into the car park, catching her breath, and spied her trusty car sitting near the entrance. He was nowhere to be seen though.

"Hello?" she shouted. "Are you there?"

There was no answer. The place was quiet, dead. A few other cars were dotted about but their owners were long gone. The public were kept away from this section of the car park, only staff were allowed here.

Jill had never really noticed how desolate and creepy the place was. She had passed through there almost every day for two years, thinking nothing of the bland concrete and dark decor. Now, though, it all seemed a little more sinister.

A chill went through her and she rolled down the sleeves of her scrubs. She treaded carefully towards the car, looking about, flinching at the faintest sound. She reached the door and unlocked it.

"Are you here?" she said again, this time barely louder than a whisper.

There was no answer. Somewhere in the distance, the hiss of traffic was filtering over the shrubbery and foliage of the hospital's grounds. Jill had started to sweat, the salty taste edging into her lips. Something was wrong; she could feel it, burrowing into her core.

"Don't fucking move!" came a hard male voice from behind her.

A hand reached around her throat and pulled her backwards. She felt something hard pushing into the base of her back.

"Oh god!" she coughed. "Please, don't hurt me, oh god, don't hurt me!" She was panicking, her heart throbbing so hard she could feel it pulse through her legs.

"Shut the fuck up!" shouted the voice from behind. "Give me your purse bitch or I'll fucking shoot you!"

"I... I... don't have my purse," she said, gasping for air.

"What?" the hand tightened around her throat.

"I don't have it, I'm a doctor, I don't carry it with me." Her vision was blurred with tears and she couldn't think.

"Don't fucking lie to me!"

The man shoved her forward into the car, the hard metal winding her. She could hear him breathing in her ear, the smell of alcohol strong and sickly. Her worst nightmares were unfolding in front of her eyes, she was being mugged, or worse.

"I'm not going to ask you again!" said the man, pushing himself against her. "Give me your fucking purse or I'll fucking kill you."

"I can't," she sobbed. "I don't have any money. I don't have my purse with me. Please, please you have to believe me. Please, just let me go."

"You just don't fucking get it, do you bitch. You're a fucking liar!"

He pulled her back up and spun her around. Forcing her back against the car, she caught sight of him for the first time. His face was covered by a balaclava and he towered over her, his shoulders broad and chest thick. There was no way she could tackle him, she would never stand a chance.

"This is the last fucking time!" he shouted, grabbing her by the throat. "Gimme the fucking cash and I'll let you go."

Her eyes fell to the small pistol in his other hand. A cold, hard dread washed over her as she realised he wasn't going to give up.

"I'm sorry," she stammered. "I'm sorry, I can't… I can't."

The thug made a roar and jammed the barrel of the pistol into her temple. He forced it into her skin hard as she continued to shake. Adrenaline was coursing its way through her veins but she was paralysed with fear, limbs locked like blocks of concrete. She was as mobile and useful as a statue. She closed her eyes tightly and prayed.

"When I count to three, I'm going to blow your fucking head off!" he screamed at her. "One. Two. Th-"

"Three."

Jill's eyes snapped open immediately. There, behind the thug with the gun, stood The Devil. He was smiling, calm and collected.

"Who the fuck are you?" said the thug, twisting to get sight of the man who had suddenly appeared from nowhere.

"I'm your worst fucking nightmare mate," said The Devil. "And your luck just ran out."

The thug didn't answer. He spun around quickly, bringing about his pistol. He smashed The Devil in the face with it, sending him staggering to the side, a fountain of blood spurting from his mouth.

"Oh god!" Jill shouted.

"Holy fuck!" said The Devil, swaying on his feet near the front of the car. "That really fucking hurt!"

He touched his lip and stared at the blood. Spitting, he wiped his mouth on his bare arm and charged forward for another attack.

The thug saw him coming and side stepped him before he could connect with an awkward fist. He grabbed The Devil by the arm and swung him into the car with a thud. Two solid punches to the gut and The Devil slid down onto his knees, wheezing.

"Hold on," he said. "Hold on, this is supposed to be a rescue."

He made a loud retching sound before throwing up all over the ground. It was putrid, Jill smelling it through her snot. The thug leapt back a little, avoiding the puddle.

"Oi!" he shouted. "These shoes are brand new!"

Jill blinked, totally flummoxed. She was convinced then that she was in the middle of a psychotic hallucination.

"Sorry about that," said The Devil, still doubled over. "You see it wasn't quite meant to happen this way."

"No?" said the thug, lowering his gun.

"No. You see, I was meant to come in here, rescue this fair lady here and look like the hero. But, as you can see, it's gone arse over elbow hasn't it."

"I'll say," said the thug.

Jill watched the two men arguing. She realised that she still had the car keys in her hands. Thinking quickly, she leapt forward and jabbed the metal point of the key into the man's neck.

"Fuck!" he shouted, dropping his gun.

The pistol hit the ground hard and went off. The shot rang out throughout the car park, the bullet pinging off an expensive looking SUV on the far side. The glass of a window shattered and the alarm began to blare.

"You bitch!" said the thug, slapping Jill hard. She toppled over as he leapt around the car and took off towards the exit.

"You better run!" The Devil shouted. "You better run!"

Jill picked herself up off the floor and rubbed her cheek. She was still shaking, her eyes wet from tears. The thug had disappeared and she was left with her useless, but no less brave for the effort, have-a-go hero.

"Christ almighty," she said, stooping down to help The Devil.

"I wish you would stop mentioning him," he said. "It gets right on my tits."

"Sorry," she said. "You're bleeding again."

"Of course I'm bleeding. That bastard smashed me in the face with his gun."

"No, I mean, there," she pointed at his side.

A large red patch of blood had formed in his gown. She pressed it hard and he winced.

"We need to get that seen to," she said.

"No, not now, we need to go," said The Devil, opening the door of the car.

"But you'll bleed out, you'll die." As she said it, she realised what she was talking about. "How does that work anyway? Can you even die?"

"It's a human body," said The Devil, easing himself into the passenger seat. "I suppose so, although what happens after that is anybody's guess. I can't very well punish myself can I?"

"No," she mused.

"Now hurry up and get in, I don't know how to drive one of these bloody things. They're too complicated."

Jill rounded the car and scrambled into the driver's seat. She started the engine and eased it backwards, passing the car who's alarm was blaring loudly.

"You know, for the Lord of Hell, you don't know how to do very much," she said, leaving the car park and joining the traffic.

"It's because I *am* the Lord of Hell that I don't know how to do these things," he explained, lifting up his gown to examine the damage. "When would I ever have to learn how to do things? There are people for that. *Lots* of people."

The whole of his gauze had been turned to a red mush. He

peeled it back and saw the large gash in his side had been burst open, probably from the punches. He cursed loudly.

"This needs re-sewn," he said. "It's all opened up again."

"I have a kit at home, I'll be able to do it there."

"Are you sure?" he asked.

"Yes," she said, looking down at the wound. "I'll be able to -"

"Look out!" The Devil screamed.

Jill instinctively slammed on the breaks. Her seatbelt tightened about her collarbone as the car screeched to a halt. When they came to a rest, they were only a few yards from a huge, double-decker bus that was blocking the road.

People were rushing to the front, shouting and screaming in panic. Jill followed the traffic, slowly rounding the big vehicle. She looked at the scene unfolding in front of them and felt the air leave her body quicker than it was going in.

A body lay in the middle of the road. Arms spread wide, legs at unnatural angles - it was a large, square-set man. He had been hit by the bus, the onlookers rushing to his aide. One of them had bent down beside him and was removing something from his head. Jill realised then that it was a balaclava.

"Holy fucking Christ," she said, turning to The Devil. "It's the man, the man who tried to rob me."

The Devil grimaced and looked over her shoulder. He sat back down and shrugged his shoulders.

"Guess you've got some friends Upstairs," he said. "Either that or we're in a lot more trouble than I first thought."

"Friends Upstairs," she said quietly to herself.

She thrust the car into gear and sped down the road. Her mind had been made up.

NINE

"Come in, don't mind the mess," said Jill. She stepped through the door and started gathering up dirty towels and pairs of pants that were strewn along the hallway. The Devil followed her at a distance.

"My dear," he said, wafting away the smell of damp from his face. "I was at the fall of Sodom and Gomorrah, the start of the flood, Woodstock in 69, 79, 89 and 94, although I did miss the 1999 version, spot of tummy trouble. Believe me, Gideon, whatever forsaken mess your flat is in I'll be able to handle it..."

He trailed off as he entered the living room. In the centre of the room was a large, cast iron bathtub. Cardboard boxes were piled high within its chipped sides, books spilling out over the top like the froth of a pint of beer. The Devil caught himself staring and closed his mouth.

"I told you," said Jill. "Don't mind the mess."

"What..." he pointed at the bath.

"Oh that, yeah, don't mind that," said Jill, skipping over to the bath. She threw the pile of dirty washing over the stack of boxes and books, trying to hide it. "Yeah, I'm going through a bit of a transition at the moment."

"A transition?" The Devil scoffed. "It looks like a bomb of sadness and depression went off in here and wiped out the whole place."

Jill sucked her lips and threw down the last of her towels. She took The Devil by the arm and forced him back into the hallway. She didn't stop until they were in the kitchen, throwing him towards the windows.

"Steady on, would you," said The Devil, rubbing his arm. "You know, you said I had a bad attitude. Maybe if you tidied up a bit here and there and didn't shove people around, you wouldn't be living with a bathtub in your living room. Did you ever think about that?"

She didn't answer. She grabbed the kettle and filled it with water. When it had started to boil, she fetched two mugs and threw a teabag in both of them.

"I take it you drink tea," she said.

"I've been known to," said The Devil.

A sharp pain was racing through his jaw. The swelling was beginning to take shape, the whole lower left side of his face gradually getting bigger. His body hadn't been made mortal for twelve hours and already it was in worse shape than it had been in twelve centuries. He cursed his luck and he cursed Him.

"We'll have a cup of tea and then see to that," she pointed at the blood patch in his gown.

"Shouldn't you do that first," he said. "I mean, I'm no doctor or anything, but this seems to be bleeding an awful lot."

"How do you feel?" she asked.

"You mean apart from eternally pissed off, surrounded by all the worst aspects of creation and continually dumbfounded by humanity's stupidity?"

"Apart from that," she said.

"I'm actually in quite a bit of pain. Not that I talk about it of course."

She stepped forward and took his face in her hands. She moved his head from side to side, tracing the swelling around the base of his jaw.

"I don't think it's broken," she said. "Which is a minor miracle."

"Ahem," he coughed.

"Sorry. That wound though, in your side, it's going to need more stitches and I don't have any anaesthetic."

"What else is new," he groaned.

The kettle clicked, steam spewing from its spout. The Devil seemed a little surprised by this. He stepped over, cautiously, to the device and peered at himself in the chrome finish.

"You alright there?" she asked.

"No, I'm not," he said, pulled the skin down from beneath his eyes.

He checked both cheeks, prodded at the swelling and bared his teeth. Finally, he let out a defeated sigh.

"Really, you would think He would give me something a bit more helpful to play with," he said.

"What do you mean?" she asked, pouring the tea, she stirred in some milk and handed him a mug.

"This," he pointed at his face. "It won't do at all. Look at it, it's all lopsided. I'm used to being handsome you know. Not like this, not like a shaved ape."

"Beauty is only skin deep," she said.

"Ha!" he snorted, taking his cup. "I assume this is still the same."

He slurped quietly, raising his little finger as he did so. It took all of Jill's effort not to laugh, her grunting causing him to level a look of suspicion at him.

"Are you alright there?" he asked suspiciously.

"Yes, fine," she smiled.

"You know, if I wasn't so blinded by agony, I'd say you were laughing at me."

"Me, laughing? Not at all."

"Well wipe that stupid bloody smirk off your face and sew me up."

He stormed off into the living room, leaving her behind. She shook her head and left her tea. He was a demanding patient but not the worst she had ever had.

"I'm waiting!" he shouted.

"Alright, fine!" she yelled back. "Honest to god."

"I thought I said I didn't like you mentioning Him?"

"Yeah, something like that," she fired back, pulling her doctor's bag out of a cupboard near the door.

She lugged the heavy leather bag into the living room and stopped. Composing herself, she tried her very hardest not to look at The Devil's naked, bruised and bloody body now sprawled out on her sofa.

"Making yourself at home are we?" she said, opening the bag and digging out a packet of sterilised cloths, a needle holder and suture.

"Have you washed your hands?" he said.

"What do you think I am, a dimwit?"

"Don't tempt me Gideon, don't even think about tempting me."

She examined the bloody wound again and began to dab it with the sterilised pad. The Devil winced every time she neared the cut, the flesh still raw and bright red.

"Would you please be careful!" he hissed.

"Think about something else," she said. "It helps ease the pain."

"Rubbish," he barked. "How could that possibly ease any pain?"

"It's what I tell all my patients who burst their stitches while fighting masked gunmen," she laughed.

"Nonsense."

"If you're not going to think of something else, talk to me then."

"Talk to *you*?" he asked. "And why would I want to do something as bloody stupid as that?"

She dabbed a little harder and he yelped. He stared at his side and then back at her.

"That was deliberate!"

"No, that was you concentrating too much on the pain," she lied. "Now sit back down and let me sew this back up."

Reluctantly, The Devil settled back onto the couch. The wound was almost clear and Jill could see where the flesh had split apart. Unlike any wound she had ever seen before, the cut was almost perfectly straight. It appeared like a split in a cushion that had been filled with too much stuffing.

"Extraordinary," she said quietly.

"What?"

"Nothing. Go on then, you're meant to be talking to me."

She took the needle holder, clamping closed the needle inside. Digging the needle into The Devils flesh, she passed it through his skin and out the other side of the wound. He quivered with pain, his hands digging into the cushion of the sofa.

"There we go," she said. "First one done."

"The first one!" he yelled. "Hell and damnation woman. Do you know how much agony this is!"

"Yes, I do as a matter of fact, I am a doctor you know."

"Then do it quicker!"

"Are you ready to talk to me yet?"

The Devil groaned. He was in pain, he was frustrated and there was a strange lethargy hanging over him. He supposed it was what the humans called tiredness but he knew that wasn't possible. He could go whole centuries without sleep.

"Fine," he said, gritting his teeth again as she dug in for another stitch. "What am I supposed to talk about?"

"You could tell me anything," she said, concentrating.

"Now we know that's not true," he said. "Are you forgetting who I am?"

"Listen mate," she said loudly. "As far as I'm concerned, you're just a nutter who I'm still reasoning as to why I've invited you into my flat. Anything you tell me right now is only going to help me believe you."

He sneered. He hated being upstaged, most of all by a human. There was no dignity in that, not after the way they behaved.

"Well, what do people talk about? That is, when you savages are digging needles into them."

"It depends."

"Depends on what?"

"Depends on who they are. Some people like to talk about their jobs, their families, where they come from. You know, small talk."

"Small talk," he growled. "Don't start me on small talk."

"Why not?"

"Because it's right down there with children's theatre, bad cooking and moral obligation when it comes to the worst things ever invented by Him Upstairs."

"How so?" she asked.

"There are too many reasons to go into Gideon. Believe me, if I started, we'd be here until the end of time and I wouldn't have touched on half of it. But the one thing, above all else, that I really, really despise about small talk is the title."

"The title?" she laughed. "What do you mean?"

"The title, 'small talk,' it's so utterly inane," he said. "I mean, what good could possible come from something that calls itself 'small talk.' What does it even mean anyway. Is it reserved to small people, does the topic have to be mass, weight and height restricted? You lot thrive on it, especially the British. And for what, to pass a few measly moments in your days, weeks, lives even? No, believe me doctor, if I had my way, small talkers would fry in their own private furnaces."

"There we go," Jill rocked back on her knees.

"There we go what?" he asked, surprised.

"You're done, all sewn up."

"You're kidding."

He looked down at the wound. Seven little stitches held his pale skin together in a strip of red. The wound was angry and inflamed but it was back together. All that remained was to clean up the excess blood.

"I didn't feel a thing," he said.

"See, I told you." She got to her feet, wrapping up her instruments and bloody cloths. "It's amazing what a little small talk can do, when used in the right dosage."

"I'm still not convinced," he pouted, folding his arms across his chest. "And anyway, it was my first time, I'm sure it won't happen again."

"Oh, if I had a pound for every time I heard that," she said wistfully.

"Pardon me?"

"Nothing, never mind. Come on, let's get you some tea and food, you've lost a lot of blood."

"I assure you madam, I don't need any food, I'm quite alright."

As he got to his feet, he began to wobble. He swayed in a small circle before almost toppling over. Only Jill's quick reaction stopped him from clattering into the bathtub.

"Is that a fact?" she said. "You're depleted, you need energy. I'll make us something and you can get some rest."

"Nonsense!" said The Devil, opening and closing his mouth. "I'm not eating the muck you'll cook up."

"Oh, sorry," she said, steadying him.

"I only eat the finest cuisine, or at least, the finest cuisine you lot can attempt to produce."

"So what do you suggest?"

The Devil looked at her. His broad, toothy grin extended across his strange old and young face. She tightened her lips, unsure just what to make of it or him in general.

"Get your glad rags on Gideon," he said. "We're painting the town red."

TEN

Glasgow was at its busiest worst. Saturday night and the mob were out in force. Huge swathes of people marched along the streets singing, shouting, looking for trouble. Ironically, Devil's Irony, there wouldn't be any trouble without them.

The taxi pulled up outside the huge City Chambers building in George Square. At the insistence of the punters, Jock the driver had taken a long, roundabout route throughout the city. The woman in the back seemed a little miffed at this but her man, her husband he reckoned, had been borderline rude about it happening.

For Jock, the world wasn't the same place it used to be. He had driven cabs for the better part of thirty years. In that time, he'd been cursed, applauded and offered everything from a million Greek Drachma to a blowjob every Saturday night for the rest of his life.

No, the life of a taxi driver wasn't anything like the way people pictured it. But the people were changing and for Jock, that signalled danger.

The pair he had now were among the new breed coming through. Surly, angry, drawing each other looks. It was no way to be with each other. Life was too short to be spent fighting, especially when it came to loved ones and the people you shared the adventure with.

He and his wife Agnes had been together for fifty years. Five decades, married for forty-seven of those. When they had first met, he was a spotty teenager and she wasn't much better. Now, years on with two kids, five grandchildren and a paid off mortgage, he was finding time to enjoy his work again. Going home at night after a shift wasn't the arduous chore it used to be. That was what life was all about.

Not for these two though. Every time he looked in the rear view mirror, the man was scowling. When he did open his mouth, it was derogatory, inflammatory, meant to cause offense. She seemed nice, if a little snooty. Jock could hear the private school education in her voice. He knew a half-baked toff when he saw one and she ticked all the boxes.

Still, she had nice legs. Her dress was slit to her hip and he caught sight of more than a little flesh when she wasn't looking. That made him smile, it was the small victories.

"This do you folks?" he asked, turning off the meter.

"Yes, thank you," she said, digging out her handbag.

"Ten-eighty," said Jock automatically.

"Ten-eighty what?" said the man.

Jock swivelled in his chair. The bloke, trussed up in an ill-fitting suit and tie, had a face like a red raw backside. His eyebrows narrowed above his pointed nose, rising near his temples, making him look like a sort of eagle.

"Ten pound and eighty pence," Jock spelled out to him.

"For what?" asked the man.

"You kidding me on?"

He didn't respond. A jolt of fear went through Jock's spine and his grip on the steering wheel tightened. There was something odd about this bloke. Something didn't quite sit right with him. He looked calm but Jock could tell he was secretly angry. But it was a different kind of anger. Something wholly dangerous, malicious even.

Slowly, he let a hand drop from the wheel and down to the side of his seat. He kept a wrench down there, just for emergencies. And he wasn't taking any chances with this one.

"Here you go," said the woman, breaking the tension between the two.

She handed a crumpled twenty-pound note through the Perspex screen. Jock looked at the money, then to her and back to the man. His gaze hadn't shifted, he didn't even look like he had blinked. Jock let go of the wrench and snatched the money.

He moved to get his change tin but the door flew open and the pair got out. The man said nothing but kept looking at Jock as he crossed the street, heading into the square. When he was far enough away, the cab driver let out a throaty sigh of relief.

"Bloody hell," he said. "Bloody hell."

He was sweating. He rubbed his moustache, wiping his brow on the arm of his jumper. He checked the heating of his taxi but it was turned off completely. He rolled down the window and gulped in some air.

"Hello."

Jock almost jumped clean out of his skin. His head bashed off the top of his cabin and he let out a roar of anger, fright and frustration. When the pain died down, he peered out of the window and saw two students staring at him.

"Could we get a lift to the west end please?" one of them asked politely. Jock shook his head.

"No chance mate," said the taxi driver. "I'm aff duty."

He rolled up the window, turned out his light and pulled off. He didn't even stop for the red light at the edge of the square. Jock was going home to Agnes, locking the door and getting in to bed. And nothing on this earth was going to stop him.

ELEVEN

The Devil fidgeted with his tie. The damn thing wouldn't sit straight and it was choking him. He hated it already. He hated the stupid shirt she had given him and the shoes that were two sizes too small. But most of all he hated the flapping suit that was now hanging from every bone in his body.

"Where did this bloody thing come from?" he asked, rolling the sleeves up his arm for the twentieth time since leaving the flat.

"You don't want to know," said Jill.

"If I didn't want to know I wouldn't have asked, would I?"

"You still don't want to know."

"Fine," he said. "Be like that. But remind me not to put a good word in for you when all of this is finished."

Jill ignored him. She was learning to do that quickly.

"Is this one of these Human things where I'm supposed to badger you until you cave in?" he asked. "Because if it is, you're going to have to tell me. I'm new to all of this and quite frankly, after the day, no, *millennia*, I've had I'm really not in the mood to be playing along with your bloody games."

"No," said Jill. "It's one of those, you really don't want to know, things."

"Am I to assume then, that the previous owner of this dreadful suit is dead then?"

"You don't give up do you?"

"If he's dead, maybe I know him," smirked The Devil. "His taste in fashion is crime enough to warrant a trip Downstairs. In fact I'd say, judging by the poor cut of this suit, this garish tie and frankly everything else, an eternity of damnation and punishment is the very *least* he deserves."

They crossed the road onto Buchanan Street. The pale blue street lights made the whole street look and feel like it was submerged in water. The ancient sandstone buildings that had stood since the city's glory days in the nineteenth century towered over them. The glory days of tobacco and trade sailing into Glasgow were now a distant memory. For the people that called it home, they didn't know half of the history and they didn't care about the other.

For those who had ventured out on a Saturday night, the historical nuances of their city were so far from their radar, it didn't even warrant thought. This bothered The Devil more than he had expected it would. While his reputation was that of a cruel and callous puppet master, he was actually more fair than that. Credit was awarded where and when it was due. And he detested anything being taken for granted. That included city heritage and where people came from.

He kept his frustrations to a minimum as he walked with Jill down the centre of Buchanan Street. The immaculate suits on shop front models silently mocked him as he shuffled past. He ignored them.

"Where are we going anyway?" asked Jill.

"I was rather hoping you would be able to tell me," he said, watching a shambling group of drunk teenagers shout, scream and stagger their way past them.

"You mean you got me all dressed up and didn't even know where we were going?" she asked. "Some date you are."

"This is most certainly not a date Gideon!" he proclaimed.

"Alright, blimey, keep your hair on," she said. "I was only messing with you."

"Well don't," he sulked.

"Fine," she huffed. "Where are we going then?

"I told you, I don't know. You live here, pick somewhere."

"It depends on what you want to eat though. Forgive me but I've never chosen a restaurant for the lord of darkness before. I'm a virgin."

The Devil raised an eyebrow. He was going to make a joke but decided against it.

"Fine, where can I get oysters?"

"Oysters," Jill mused. "I think I know a place."

"They have to be fresh oysters, none of this frozen nonsense. I can tell you know."

"I think this place is fresh." She took his arm and started walking further down Buchanan Street. "Although don't quote me on it."

"I wouldn't dream of doing that, believe me."

They walked quickly down the street for another twenty yards before Jill angled them down a side street. A large, neon sign blinked on and off, casting a warm, oozing glow down the dingy alley.

"Nice place," he said. "Reminds me of home."

"Are you being sarcastic?" she asked.

"Oh no, not at all. I just love dining out in a place that smells of cat piss and, oh, has a broken sewage pipe for decor," he nodded at a flow of putrid water running into a drain.

"Come on."

She bundled him into the entrance and they stepped down the narrow staircase. At the bottom, the dimly lit restaurant appeared like a boat emerging from the mist. Dark and shadowy, the vaguest outlines of people could be seen sitting at booths and tables that clung to the walls.

Pictures of faces The Devil didn't recognise decorated the walls, faded over time. He, begrudgingly, acknowledged that Jill had made a good choice.

"Ah, good evening my friends," said a tall, thin maitre d'. He was old and gaunt, his neck scraggy and flopping over his tight collar and tie. "Welcome to the *Red Herring*, Glasgow's premier fish restaurant."

"Lovely," said The Devil. "I must say there, you have a nice establishment."

"Thank you sir," smiled the maitre d', his pencil thin moustache stretching and a set of crooked yellow teeth appearing between his lips. "Are you here for dining or will you be enjoying a drink at our bar?"

"Dinner please, just the two of us."

"Of course, please, follow me."

He led the pair through the tables, gliding effortlessly over the dark carpet with ease. Satisfied with a table, he stopped and offered a chair to Jill.

"Thank you," she said.

"No, thank you madam. You'll find the wine list on the table along with a separate menu detailing our specials this evening."

"Good," said The Devil. "Bring us one of each of them, from start to finish."

"I beg your pardon?" It was the first time the maitre d' had looked anything but stoic and polite.

"I said. Bring us one of everything on the menu. And your most expensive wine."

"But sir."

"No buts," said The Devil, taking his seat. "And oysters. My colleague here tells me you serve oysters, is that correct?"

"Yes sir, it is," answered the maitre d', trying to recapture some of his composure.

"Then bring me a platter for starters. Then in intervals of thirty minutes. I don't want my plate empty." He threw out his napkin and replaced it over his lap.

The maitre d' couldn't believe what he was hearing. That was of no concern to The Devil or Jill though. In an instant, he remembered where he was and who he was, snapping into his most comfortable and serving self.

"And for the lady?" he asked, bowing.

"She'll have some of mine," The Devil drummed his fingers on the table. "And as quickly as possible, there's a good fellow."

Clicking his heels together, the maitre d' quickly marched towards the bar and beyond it, the kitchens. Jill stared hard across the dimly lit table at The Devil.

"What are you looking at?" he said bluntly. "I'm starving. These bodies of yours, they don't half expend energy quickly. Hells teeth, I'm falling apart here. Look."

He held up a trembling hand. Jill pushed it out of the way, her face twisted with anger.

"Never, ever order for me again, have you got that?"

"Oh give over." He waved her away.

"I'm serious," she slammed her hand down on the table and made the cutlery jump.

The Devil blinked, surprised at the force. She was still staring at him, her eyes firmly locked on his. Was this human anger in all of its glory? He couldn't be sure. She was already pretty unstable, even for a human female of her age. He was glad he kept that thought to himself.

"Alright, alright, fine," he said. "I apologise."

Her anger seemed to subside a little, although there was still some rage bubbling away beneath her calm surface. He thought it best to sit in silence until the food arrived.

And when it did, he was glad he had an appetite. A small platoon of waiters and waitresses, all dressed in matching white shirts and red bowties, delivered the platters of oysters in succession. They had barely landed on the table when The Devil began filling his grumbling stomach.

"Oh my," he said, choking down one oyster after another. "Now this is living."

He snorted and coughed, slurped and savoured, devouring each of the shellfish in turn like a machine. Jill watched on, a little in horror, as the sight unfolded. A shell was scooped up, lifted high, his head thrown back and the contents swallowed. The same process was repeated until there was only an empty platter.

"Fuck me that was good," he said, leaning back in his chair. "Why don't you lot do this all the time?"

"Because some of us have learned self control," said Jill, still holding her first and only oyster.

"Bah, who needs that," he said. "You've got an eternity for all of that rubbish. You should enjoy this while you can."

"So what you're saying is, all the negatives, excesses and downright greed that humanity has to offer is a good thing?"

"I never said it was a good thing," The Devil belched. "I said you should enjoy it. Believe me, what's waiting for you in the after life, Up or Down, it's not going to beat any of this."

"I disagree," she said, replacing the oyster and crossing her arms. "How could any of this be better than what's in Heaven? It's paradise, in case you didn't know."

"For some people, maybe," said The Devil, scooping up the abandoned shellfish. "But I know you, you'd hate it."

"You know me do you?" she laughed. "You've been in my company for a few hours and suddenly you're my best friend."

"Listen love, I'm your *only* friend."

"Now that is nonsense," she quickly dismissed. "I've got hundred of friends. I'm never short of a bit of company."

"Is that so?" he pressed.

"Yes, it is," she replied adamantly.

"Then answer me this, Doctor Gideon, what are you doing with a bathtub in your living room and a man's suit, shirt, tie and shoes in your cupboard?"

Jill motioned to answer but stopped herself quickly. She tried to think, tried to conjure up a clever, witty response but nothing was forthcoming.

"Oh stuff you," she said eventually.

"I knew it," he scoffed as two huge steaks were set down in front of them. "It's a man, a boyfriend, a lover even? Go on, tell me, I love a bit of gossip."

There was a mischief to his face. She didn't want to tell him anything, she still wasn't sure of who or what he was. But there was something undeniably charming about him. Charm, she had found, was in very short supply in her life.

"His name was Goeff," she said.

"Of course it was," he shoved a large chunk of steak into his mouth and chewed noisily.

"And he broke my heart, quite frankly."

"Oh boo-hoo, pass me a napkin while I dry my eyes."

"Do you want to hear this or not?" she hissed.

"Not really but you're on your high horse so go right ahead."

She thought about being quiet. He didn't deserve to be in the same room as her with that type of attitude. Yet she couldn't help herself. There was a magnetism to him, a strange, almost ethereal conviction and honesty. Ironic, she thought, given who he said he was.

"He was cheating on me," she said, swallowing a lump in her throat. "We'd been together for ten years and he had been sleeping with somebody from his office."

"I bet she was younger than you," The Devil pointed with his knife. "I'll even wager that you had met her at office parties, had spoken to her, maybe even shared a joke. I'll go out on a limb here and say that this Geoff character was the one who introduced you to each other."

Jill was speechless. How did he know these things? Was her depression and loneliness broadcasting so loudly even a complete stranger could pick it up? She wouldn't have been surprised. Just another way that Geoff had won.

"And the bathtub?" he asked.

"What about it?"

"Well, I'm no expert on the human condition but the last time I checked, you lot weren't prone to keeping bathtubs in your living rooms."

"It's a monument," she said, gritting her teeth.

"To what?"

"To the fact that that bastard left me without saying goodbye, taking all of his stuff with him. Including, may I add, the bathroom suite."

"Good grief," The Devil muffled a laugh. "You mean to say he took the taps, the toilet, all of that and left you a bath?"

"That's right."

"In the middle of the living room?"

"No, I put it there," she said. "I've been meaning to take a sledge hammer to the thing, you know, just to let it all out but I haven't had the time."

"You won't do it," he said.

"Yes I will," she remained firm.

"No you won't. If you were going to do it, you would have done it by now. You don't hate him enough."

She could feel her muscles tensing. Whether she liked it or not, or even cared to admit it, this man, this strange, lopsided man in one of Geoff's old suits, had called her bluff. She wasn't used to being trumped. She normally made sure it never happened.

"You're not right all of the time you know," she said, taking up her own cutlery. "A lot of it looks like blind luck to me."

"Darling, when you've been around for as long as I have, nothing is blind luck," he cut a huge chunk of meat and stuffed it into his mouth. "You don't get to where I am by lucking out. That would just be silly now, wouldn't it?"

She flipped him her middle finger and shoved her tongue into her chin. He feigned offense as the wine arrived and a nervous looking waitress poured out two glasses.

"Lovely, another bottle please," he instructed and she scurried off.

"You're going overboard aren't you?" Jill questioned.

"I have a reputation to uphold," he said, sniffing the claret.

"That may be, but in case you haven't noticed, nobody knows who you are."

The Devil stopped mid-sip. He sloshed the wine around in his mouth and looked about the room. The place was nearly empty, only an elderly couple wedged into the far corner and two drunk businessmen at the bar. There were more staff in the place than customers.

He swallowed and rasped. The wine was slightly bitter and left an uncomfortable taste in his mouth. Although he couldn't be sure it hadn't been caused by Jill's frankness.

"Bullshit," he said under his breath.

"It's not bullshit," she said adamantly. "Think about it. To the rest of the world you're just another bloke. The only reason I believe who you are is because no other man, sane or insane, would behave like a lunatic as much as you do. I mean, there's rude and reckless and then there's you."

"Are you quite finished?" he asked.

"No, I'm not. You need to get it into your head mister that while you're here, for whatever cosmic purpose that may be, you have to play by our rules. You might not like it, in fact I'd say you'll hate it, but that's how it goes."

She was out of breath. The makings of tears were beginning to form in her eyes but she held them back. She was more angry than upset. The Devil couldn't really blame her.

"Well I'm glad we've sorted that out," he said, raising his glass. "Now, if you're over giving me a lecture about mortality and the human condition, why don't we drink to it and enjoy this fine meal the restaurant has laid on for us."

Jill was still seething. The Devil tilted his goblet towards her and raised his eyebrows, trying to be diplomatic. After another short moment of quiet, angry contemplation, she finally conceded. She raised her own glass and clinked it into his.

"Cheers," he said, a waiter delivering a fresh platter of oysters. "Now let's see if we can't get stuck in, shall we?"

TWELVE

The same nervous waiter who had served them at dinner stood with his hands shaking. He cupped the frail light of his Zippo lighter around the end of The Devil's cigar. Concentrating with all of his might, he managed to spark the huge Cohiba into life.

The Devil took long, deliberate draws on the cigar and swirled the smoke around in his mouth. Satisfied that the taste had filtered into every blood vessel and cell, he blew it all out in a murky grey cloud.

"Delightful," he said, licking his teeth. "You know, you really should be lighting these with matches young man."

"Yes sir, sorry sir, it's just, well, I'm not allowed to carry matches, restaurant rules," the waiter fumbled with his words.

"Then I shall have a word with management before I leave here," The Devil chewed down on the end of the cigar. "Now, if you would kindly light my good lady friend's cigar, we'll have no further need of your services."

"His good lady friend, doesn't want her cigar lit," said Jill, holding up her hands.

The waiter dithered, caught between his sense of duty and a direct command from a customer. The Devil watched him and let him squirm a little longer before nodding.

"She's a doctor," he said with a languid sigh. "You can't take them anywhere."

Jill threw him a contemptuous look. She thumbed the cigar in her hands, prodding the lengthy shaft with her fingers.

"Do you know how many chemicals are in these things?" she asked, holding up the Cohiba.

"Undoubtedly thousands," said The Devil. "That's why it tastes so good."

"Do you have any idea what those chemicals do to your lungs? You might as well stick your mouth around an exhaust pipe and breathe in."

"Steady on love," said The Devil with a smile. "All this talk of putting your mouth around things is getting me all hot and bothered."

Jill cocked an eyebrow. She denied herself even the slightest bit of pleasure from his statement. Not that she would have said no to what he was implying. But she wouldn't let him know that.

She took the cigar in both her hands, tightened her grip and snapped it in half. The Devil began coughing and spluttering, smoke pouring through his teeth and out of his mouth.

"What's wrong with you woman!" he gasped, catching his breath. "Do you have any idea how expensive those things are!"

"I don't care," she said. "I'm a doctor, you can't take me anywhere, remember?"

He recomposed himself as she threw away the broken ends of the cigar. She began to rub her bare arms, a chilly wind gusting down the alleyway outside the restaurant.

The smoking section was just outside the front door. Two large canopies extended out from the venue's front and there were tables and chairs for sitting and dinning. A bouncer stood by the front door, face like untreated marble. Beside him was the puny waiter, fumbling with his tray and bowtie.

"I'd forgotten just how much I enjoyed these," smiled The Devil, looking at his cigar. "There's something wholly satisfying about the way you people are bent on self destruction. But not content by simply throwing yourselves off of bridges or blowing yourselves up. You prolong the agony and take great enjoyment out of it in the process."

"Not all of us," said Jill.

"No," he agreed. "Not all of you. But enough to warrant it's continuation. You see, that's where you all fall down. You're essentially sheep, all programmed to follow one leader and do what he or she says."

"Again, not all of us," she said, feeling the chill.

"The majority. Don't get me wrong, it has it's uses. I wouldn't be in a job if you lot weren't so impressionable. And more importantly, neither would He." He pointed upwards.

"What's He like?" asked Jill curiously. "In real life I mean."

"Real life," The Devil laughed. "If you only knew what reality really was Gideon. It would turn your shit white."

"I'm asking a question," she said sternly. "Seriously, what's He like? Is He like the paintings, you know, the Sistine Chapel and all of that?"

The Devil rubbed his cheek. His jaw was healing remarkably quickly. It was a pleasant surprise and one he wasn't going to dwell on.

"The thing is," he said, taking another long draw. "Any concept you lot might have about him is entirely created by you. He didn't have any influence over your art or your perceptions of science, time, reality et cetera. And, I should point out, neither did I."

"So what are you saying?" she asked. "That we came up with it all by ourselves?"

"Essentially, yes."

"How is that even possible?" she asked, stepping a little closer to him. "I mean, surely he's had a guiding hand in it all. He created us for god sake."

"And that's where the story ends," said The Devil. "You see, he had this strict policy of not getting involved. Not interfering. Yes, he created you, yes he made everything you can see and even the stuff that you can't. But that's it. Everything else, your concept of time, of your place in the multiverse, even your ability to think, that was all you."

He shrugged his shoulders as she digested the secrets of existence. Usually when he did that, it took a Human several decades to even begin to comprehend what it meant. Philosophers had written great poems about it, artists turned to their work to try and fathom out what he was saying. Even Einstein had gone out and theorised almost everything as his brilliant mind struggled to keep up with something it wasn't naturally meant to.

Much to his surprise, however, Jill Gideon seemed to click instantly. She shrugged her own shoulders and clapped her hands against her arms.

"Fair doos," she said.

"Fair *doos*?" The Devil repeated, more than a little astonished. "Is that all you've got to say? Fair doos? I've just revealed what is perhaps the biggest secret in all of reality and you're taking it like that?"

"And how would you have me take it?" she said.

"I don't know," he said. "Something, anything. Not a simple fair doos. Blimey."

He took a few more draws on his cigar and began to laugh. He conceded that he didn't know very much about Humans and their ways of thinking. But he thought he knew more than he did.

Maybe that had always been his downfall.

"Unbelievable," he said quietly to himself.

"Anyway, enough of all of that," said Jill. "What are we going to do about your murdered Mr Baggio?"

"Ah, I was wondering how long it would take you to ask," he beamed. "Took your bloody time too I may add."

"What's the plan?" she ignored him.

The Devil rolled a little piece of ash around on his tongue before spitting it into the gutter. He rubbed his lips, face twisted into a bitter frown.

"Yuck," he said. "Bloody tobacco leaf."

"The murdered man!" she said firmly.

"Yes, Anton Baggio. You said he was stabbed, yes?"

"Yes."

"Well it's simple then. All we have to do is find out who stabbed him and I'll be free."

"Oh yeah, really simple that," Jill scoffed. "If it was that simple, you would have done it by now instead of swanning around, living it up at swanky restaurants."

She had a point but The Devil was never going to concede. Instead, he tapped the end of his nose.

"Watch and learn Gideon, I'm about to teach you the first rule of planning," he said smugly. "Always have a get out."

He spun quickly on his heels and waved over at the bouncer. The stoic security guard ignored him, instead choosing to look straight ahead.

"I say, fatty, would you mind holding this for me," The Devil said, pronouncing his accent.

The bouncer didn't budge. He needed more encouragement and The Devil knew just what he was doing.

"I said fatty, yes, you fatty, what's your name?" He reached the bouncer and, standing at least an inch and half shorter than him, he stared up into his big meaty face.

"My goodness you're ugly," he said with a laugh. "I mean I've seen ugly in my time but you really do take the biscuit. Or should that be carrot, after all, there's no human on the planet could be *that* ugly. You must be a horse or something. Am I right?"

He nodded at the waiter who was standing nervously beside his colleague. Twitching and rocking between his feet, the young man looked about ready to burst with nerves.

"Sir, don't you think you should return to your lady friend?" he mustered the courage to say.

"What? Her? No, she's fine. I'm more interested in this big, bulging bag of shit. Bloody hell, I had no idea they stacked dung heaps so high. Where are you from?"

Despite The Devil's efforts, the bouncer remained calm. He stared blankly ahead, huge hands crossed over his black suit jacket.

"I'm talking to you boy!" The Devil turned on the aggression. "Don't you know who I am? Look at me while I'm talking to you."

The bouncer, much to his credit and The Devil's chagrin, remained firm. It was time to kick things up a level.

"I bet you're Polish," said The Devil. "Or Irish, or maybe from some back water shithole that used to be on the other side of the Iron Curtain. Am I right?"

"Sir, please, don't. Pavel has done nothing to-"

"Pavel!" The Devil laughed. "Did you say Pavel? You mean to say this towering mass of rotting, self serving, over bearing worm food is called Pavel? What kind of stupid name is that anyway? Pavel. I wouldn't even call my dog Pavel and I hate the fucking thing. Are you listening to me?"

He gave the huge bouncer a little slap across the face. If there had been a camel present, the smack would have been the straw that broke its back. Like a huge, bubbling volcano about to blow its top, Pavel the bouncer erupted in a fit of rage.

"Oh shit!" cried the waiter, ducking behind the door of the *Red Herring*.

"Oh shit is right!" said The Devil backing off.

He tried to run but the bouncer grabbed him by the lapels. Pulling tightly, the huge man mountain brought his thick brow down into The Devil's. The world went white and then dark and the metallic ooze of blood filled his mouth.

He staggered backwards, clattering into tables and chairs, knocking over glasses and candles. Eventually, his balance threw in the towel and he flopped heels over head into a pile on the ground.

Pavel wasn't finished with him though. The huge bouncer untangled the arms and legs and lifted The Devil back onto his feet.

"Hold on!" he said through bloody teeth. "I don't think I quite caught the last thing you said. You want to what to me in the showers?"

A mighty fist barrelled through the air and collided straight into The Devil's nose. There was a loud crack that echoed off the damp, slime covered walls of the alleyway and sent two pigeons into the night sky. More importantly, The Devil careened backwards, smashing into Jill.

The two companions collapsed to the floor in another pile. There was blood everywhere, Jill's shoes lost somewhere in the maelstrom. She pushed The Devil off of her and tried to sit up.

"You're a bloody idiot!" she screamed. "Why would you do that?"

"Do what?" asked The Devil groggily.

"Pick a fight with a Polish doorman who was twice your height, three times your weight and as down with his anger management issues as you are!"

Before he could answer, Pavel shoved two tables out of the way and came charging towards them. He lifted them up, each in one hand, and threw them down into the alleyway. He shouted something in his own language but The Devil didn't understand. He didn't need to, it was no doubt an insult to his mother.

"Joke's on you!" he shouted back, lips swelling up like balloons. "I don't have a mother!"

"Come on!" Jill shouted. "Let's get out of here."

The words were no sooner out of her mouth when the whole alleyway was lit up. Bright blue and red flashes danced off of the dirty puddles and dingy décor as a police car pulled up at the end.

"Oh fuck," said Jill, helping The Devil stagger forward. "Now you've done it."

"On the contrary my dear Gideon," he smiled, nose crooked and leaking crimson down his front, "a job well done."

Four police officers met them half way down the side street and took them into custody. They were escorted into the back of the waiting squad car and read some statutory rights.

The Devil didn't care; he was in too much pain. Above all that though, he was feeling rather proud of himself. The smile on his face lingered long after he had passed out.

THIRTEEN

The crowds were getting restless. They had been shouting, screaming, clamouring all night. Alice didn't blame them, she shared many of their worries.

She wasn't being paid to be part of the mob though. She wasn't being paid anything. Her soul had been sent Downstairs for the rest of time. Helping out The Devil with his filing was a small price to pay for being spared eternal torment.

"Excuse me please," she said. "Get out of my way!"

Pushing people left and right of her, this wasn't her usual trip to work. She could do without it too. Order, discipline, those were her friends and allies. This was as far from that as possible.

"Would you get out of my way!"

She began shoving bodies out of the way. Her patience had been worn away, she was now angry. And when Alice got angry, there would be Hell to pay.

She reached the office door. Forcing it open and then closed again, the silence of the familiar surroundings afforded her a brief moment of rest. Then the phones started ringing. They had been ringing non-stop for almost a week. They had rung so much she had stopped answering them. The chorus of metallic bells and buzzers were driving her mad.

The Devil was gone. He was prone to popping out of the office from time to time. She took great delight in reminding him he was slacking off. But it had never been for this long. Never had she been left in charge for so long.

There was only one thing for it. She would have to use The Devil's office. It was against all the etiquette she had mastered over a few centuries but drastic times called for extreme measure. The Devil going missing was as drastic as it got.

She hurried past her desk, ignoring her phone and fax machine and into the office at the back of the room. She hesitated at the door. She had never opened it up without first being instructed. She wondered if there would be any booby traps, some sinister workings that the Lord of Hell had placed as security.

Then she remembered she was already dead. What was the worst that could happen.

She turned the door handle and pushed it open. Nothing happened. Feeling brave, she stepped inside and waited. Again, nothing happened. She closed the door. Still, nothing happened.

The ringing phones disappeared, the shouting quietened down, everything went silent. The office that she knew so well had a different feel to it though, almost like it was sad. The missing presence of The Devil appeared to be affecting the ambience slightly. For the nerve centre of Hell, it was surprisingly gloomy.

A chill ran down her spine. She shivered and rubbed her arms. It was an odd sensation, not least of all because she hadn't felt it in close to two centuries. The dead very rarely got chills, especially if they lived in Hell. Something wasn't right.

"Hello?" she asked, not quite sure why. "Is there somebody here?"

Silence answered her. She felt uncomfortable, like she shouldn't have been there. Yet, something was drawing her further and further into the room. She moved forward, carefully choosing her steps, taking in every little detail of the office. It was exactly the same as it had been since the last time she was there. It was exactly the same as the first time she had been there.

Her mind travelled back to that first, fateful day in Hell. She didn't know what to think. Guilt played a large part of it but it wasn't enough to repent. She had murdered her husband and boiled his limbs. It was no more than the bastard had deserved.

But she knew she had to be punished. You couldn't go about killing people everywhere you went, just because you thought they needed it. So, after the initial shock, she had accepted her eternal fate Downstairs.

The Devil had been kind to her. He had seen something in her that nobody ever had. Maybe it was his charm that had won her over. Maybe it was the way he looked at her more than ample rear-end. She had never been sure which came first. Either way, she had settled into her new role as his personal secretary with ease. After all, what was another set of chores to be done, even if it was in the blazing inferno of Hell?

Now though, she didn't feel so comfortable or so cocky. There was an eerie presence about the office. She looked about the walls, half expecting to see eyes peering out at her. Living in Hell meant taking certain supernatural occurrences as a given. But this was something altogether different.

"Where is he?" came a question.

Alice stopped. She turned to face the door but there was nobody there. She looked back towards The Devil's desk, it was still empty. She was alone in the room. The voice she heard was inside her head.

"Who is this?" she asked. "Do you know who I am? You can't go invading my head like this. I'll tell him, he'll be angry. You don't know who you're messing with."

"Where is he?"

"Didn't you hear what I said? I've got influence, get out of my head right this instant or there will trouble, I guarantee it."

Her words were empty, she knew this. She was gambling on whoever was talking to her to not be so well informed.

Being The Devil's secretary afforded a certain lifestyle in Hell. It was a glamorous if menial position. However, as Alice had made it her own, she knew she could yield a certain decorum of power over other not-so-civil servants. She was counting on this helping her out now.

Whoever was inside her head was powerful, powerful enough to be operating in The Devil's private office. She knew she had to be careful.

"Where is he?" it asked again.

"Look, would you please get out of my head?" she asked, changing her tact. "I'm sure if you just appear in front of me in a relatively suitable form we can work this out, together, and there won't be any need for trouble."

There was a still moment. Alice was sweating, another first in a few centuries. While she may have taken a human form in Hell, there were certain biological functions that hadn't followed her Downstairs. She tried to remain calm, to seem unfazed by what was going on. It was difficult.

"Where is he?" asked the voice again.

She laughed a little. This was getting ridiculous. Was this some sort of test? Was it a little joke The Devil was playing on her? Maybe this was the booby trap that had been set up in the event of somebody entering his office without permission. If so, the question wouldn't have an answer and she would be stuck with it in her head until the end of time.

"Trust The Devil to play semantics with a rhetorical question," she said aloud, hoping it would break the spell.

"Where is he?" asked the voice.

"I don't know," she said, a little frustrated. "I don't know where he is, alright? Why do you think I'm in here, in his office, to have a nosey around? Whoever or whatever you are, you know who I am; it's not my style. I'm in here to hide from all of them out there? They're asking the same question as you, they want to know, I want to know where he's gotten to. This place is falling apart without him. We need him back!"

She was panting, out of breath. Her hands were shaking with a mixture of anger and fear. It had been the first time she had admitted, out loud, that she was worried. The Devil's disappearance was most unexpected and definitely out of character. That meant there was something seriously wrong. And if there was something wrong with him, with his stature in the multiverse, then it didn't bode well for any of the rest of them.

"I will find him," said the voice.

Alice was a little surprised. In the short moments she had been haunted, she had grown accustomed to the voice. But more worryingly, the message had been changed. That meant it wasn't a trick, it wasn't a booby trap. Whatever was inside her head was a living, thinking being. And it was on the hunt.

"No wait, hold on, are you there?" she asked in a panic. "Hold on, wait a minute, you've got to tell me where you're looking. Maybe I can help you, maybe we can help each other? How does that sound? Take me with you, wherever you are going, please, I can help, I know him, we can help each other."

There was no response. She dashed about the office, hoping to hear the voice again. Only silence, still, pure silence.

"Hello? Are you there? Hello?" She sounded like a lost child. "Hello? Hello! Where are you! Take me with you! Answer me! Damn it answer me right now!"

Hell had its own, dark secrets. Certain parts of it were out of bounds, sealed off from even Alice. The Devil rarely talked about them, what could be found there. She had always thought he was a little ashamed of them, what they could become.

As his loyal servant, she had always remained coy and silent on the matter. If The Devil didn't want to talk about something, then that was entirely up to him. She wasn't about to go dabbling in affairs that were nothing to do with her.

Another cold shiver went up her spine and then back down again. Suddenly, all she could think about were those dark secrets. What were they? Why were they so terrible that he couldn't confide in her? And most importantly, had she just spoken with one of them directly?

Her panic and worry were now a hundred times worse. What had she done?

"Oh no," she said aloud, hoping that her own voice would provide some comfort. "This can't be good, this can't be good at all."

There was no comfort to be found. She dashed to the door and pulled it open. The phones had stopped, as had the shouting and screaming from the crowd outside. The silence prevailed.

"This can't be good," she said again. "This can't be good at all."

FOURTEEN

"You want your head examined son," said the policeman. "Fighting with a Pole, you're lucky you weren't killed by that big bastard."

"Is that your medical opinion nurse or are you trying to chat me up?"

The police officer wiped away stale blood from around The Devil's nose with a cloth. He pinched it between his two fingers and pulled up with a sharp tug.

The Devil let out a wail as his face burned. The policeman let him go and he sank back down into his chair.

"Oh, sorry pal," said the cop. "Didn't realise my own strength."

"No, I'm sure you didn't," breathed The Devil, still wincing.

The policeman peeled off his rubber gloves and closed his medical kit. He tucked it under his arm and made for the door of the interview room.

"You better watch that lip of yours, son," he said. "This DI is right bastard."

"Noted," said The Devil. "Although he can't be any worse than you."

"You'll see," laughed the officer. "Hell mend you."

He closed the door behind him, leaving The Devil on his own. Tentatively, he prodded his wounded nose. Pain bit with every touch and he began to rue his decision to go fighting again.

Sitting in the silence of the interview room, he suddenly had time to think. Since his arrival on Earth, he had barely been given two moments to himself. It had been one hectic problem after another. From his tumultuous arrival on the golf course to bleeding out in the corridor of a hospital, everything had been a speedy whirlwind.

Relatively speaking, The Devil wasn't used to things moving quite so quickly. Time might have been a human invention, but that didn't mean he wasn't affected. Ethereal creatures like him were subject to progress and they had to keep up. The alternative was being left behind.

With that firmly on his mind, he stared up at the hard light shining down on him. He closed his eyes and tried to centre himself.

"Humans," he said aloud. "They'll never take off."

The door swung open and in charged one of the angriest looking men The Devil had ever seen. Flushed face, wild eyes, his suit was as cheap as his.

The man stormed up to the table and leaned over, grabbing The Devil by the lapels. He snarled, the smell of bad cologne and coffee creating an odour pungent enough to bring a tear to The Devil's eyes.

"What do you think you're playing at you little shite!" barked the man.

"Please to meet you too," The Devil said calmly.

"Don't give me that! I've been dragged back into work on a Saturday night because some half-baked toff thinks he can go about slapping Polish waiters."

"Actually," The Devil held up a finger, "we don't know he was Polish and he most certainly wasn't a waiter. You'll have to get your facts right if you want to prosecute."

The angry man let go of The Devil's lapels, thrusting him back into his chair. He stood back up and straightened his greying comb-over, the last hints of ginger retreating towards the back of his head. His face was etched into a permanent scowl, the acne scars thickening his cheeks, making him look like a handbag.

"Oh great," he said to the officer standing by the door, the same one who had treated the Devil, "we've got another comedian on our hands."

"Am I to assume you're the inspector I've heard so much about?" said The Devil. "The one described as a 'right bastard' by his colleagues?"

The inspector's face dropped from a scowl to a grimace. He threw a glance at the officer by the door who didn't react. He let out a throaty laugh and fished a packet of pills out of his pocket.

"Is that so?" he mused. "That might be the case but you can call me Garfield."

"First or last?" The Devil fired back across the table.

Inspector Garfield cracked open two tablets and swallowed them dry. He snorted loudly, pacing around the room.

"Any more of that cheek son and I'm going to throw you in the cells with the biggest bunch of queers we've got."

"Please," said The Devil. "You're threats of homoerotic violence are totally futile. I practically invented it."

For the first time since he entered the room, Garfield let his guard down. He was confused, perplexed, unsure what the perp in front of him was saying. He quickly remembered where he was and strapped on his armour again.

"Right, let's get down to business then shall we?" He leaned on the back of the chair across from The Devil. "What's your name?"

"I've got lots of names, mostly ones that you lot have given me."

"If you've got lots of names then you can give me at least one.

Come on," Garfield growled.

"The Devil will do fine."

"Okay. That's a start. Address?"

"I don't have an address."

"What do you mean, you don't have an address?"

"Being who one is, I don't have a postcode or permanent residency on this astral plane inspector. Really, try to keep up would you."

Garfield ground his teeth loudly. He pulled the chair out quickly and sat down in a flurry of drama. The Devil wasn't sure if he was supposed to be impressed or intimidated. As it happened, he felt neither.

"Is this how you want to play it?" Garfield asked.

"Play what inspector?"

"You're in some serious trouble boy-oh and it could get a whole lot worse for you unless you start playing ball."

"Boy-oh? Playing ball? Honestly inspector, if we're going to talk in buzz words and slogans, at least give me a chance to catch up on the parlance. I've only just arrived and, by your own medical examination report, have suffered severe head trauma."

"It won't be as severe as it is when I'm finished with you!" Garfield screamed.

A fleck of spit flew from his mouth and landed on The Devil's chest. He looked at it with disdain and then to Garfield.

"I don't care much for that type of threat inspector. You don't know who you're dealing with."

"Oh, I see," Garfield pushed out his chest and began to crack his knuckles. "I don't know who I'm dealing with is it? Son, when you've walked the streets of Glesga' for as long as I have, you learn a few things. First is-"

"Yes, yes, yes I've heard it all before," The Devil yawned. "Honestly, you lot, you think you invented the wheel sometimes.

And you never, ever like to let anybody forget it."

Garfield was baffled by his new charge. In all of his long serving decades in the police force, he thought he had seen and arrested it all. Especially chinless wonders like the one sitting in front of him. Yuppie types were among the easiest nicks he would ever have. Yet this one seemed strangely aware, acutely intelligent.

"Let's start again then, shall we?" he said, calming himself down.

He was going to need to try a different tact with this one. That was what good policing was all about. Adaptability to the situation and person. At least, that's what the head doctors had told him at the annual conference.

"What's your name and address?" he asked, a little softer.

"We're wasting time," said The Devil. "And I don't have much of that to waste inspector. I need your help."

"Name and address first."

"I told you! I don't have an address and my name is The Devil."

This was getting nowhere. Both parties were as frustrated with the other yet neither could back down. If it had been in Hell, The Devil would have been quite proud of such an endless loop. Hell Labs worked around the clock to create logarithms like this one. He had managed it successfully in five minutes.

Garfield, on the other hand, didn't have such responsibilities. He was more worried about his wife's steak pie getting cold on the dinner table back home. And, more importantly, his wife getting cold at the same rate.

"Out there, I've got a database of every wino, glue sniffer, murderer and rapist in the country." He pointed out the door. "We've taken your fingerprints. All I have to do is look them up and I'll have all my answers."

"I assure you inspector, you won't find me in any databanks you have. It's not like that."

"Is that a fact?"

"I'm not here to play games with you Garfield, I need your help," The Devil changed his own tone. His patience had finally run out.

"I beg your pardon?" said the inspector.

"I need all the information you have on the murder of Anton Baggio and I need it now."

Garfield looked about the room, as if searching for some inspiration. His gaze fell to the policeman by the door.

"Did I hear that correctly constable?" he asked. "I thought a suspect, a no-good-ned, was asking to see confidential police files."

The policeman gave a customary smile. He didn't want to disappoint his superior officer, nor did he want it implicated in anything unsavoury. The Devil had seen it all before and he was sick of wasting time.

"Look here Garfield," he said, standing up and pushing his chair across the floor. "We've fucked around in here for too long. There's a murderer on the loose out there and if I don't find him then I don't get to go on holiday. Is that understood?"

Garfield's bloodshot eyes widened as he clenched his fists. The officer stepped forward beside him, ready for action.

"Oh please," said The Devil. "Not this again. Honestly, you humans, you're always fighting. You love a good dust up, I don't know where you get it from."

"Just take it easy sunshine, nobody wants to get hurt," said the officer, holding out a hand. "Sit back down and everything will be fine."

"No I won't sit back down, I need your help."

"Don't make us restrain you son, you don't want that," said Garfield.

"What I want is some help from a local constabulary and for whatever reason, you're giving me a load of guff!"

The Devil banged his hand down on the table. Like a gun going off to start the race, the noise seemed to stir Garfield and his colleague. They leapt at The Devil in unison, grabbing both of his arms.

"Let me go!" he shouted. "Hell's bollocks let me go, I need help, not arresting!"

"Take it easy now!" Garfield said, breathing heavily. His massive frame was too big for The Devil to resist and his arms were brought about his back.

The officer clipped on a set of handcuffs and made sure he was sitting down. The two policemen were out of breath, satisfied their job was done.

"Now, where were we?" said Garfield, mopping his forehead with his hand. "Ah yes, Jenkins, would you go see what the computer thinks of our friend here?"

"Yes sir," said the constable.

"And bring me a cup of tea and a scone when you're coming back would you. I'm bloody starving."

"Yes sir."

Jenkins hurried out the room and closed the door behind him. Garfield rubbed his chest, his face still flushed.

"Bloody heartburn," he said under his breath.

"You're ill," said The Devil.

"You're a doctor now are you?"

"No, but my companion is."

"Ah, so that bird we brought you in with is your companion is she?" Garfield's eyebrows lifted as he smelled some new information. "Is it romantic?"

"Don't make me laugh," said The Devil. "Gideon is a little too skinny for my liking."

"So you like them big, firm?" Garfield squeezed the air with his hands.

"I'm not inclined to discuss my sexual preferences with a man I've just met. What do you take me for?"

"I've not got a lot to go on at the moment pal, you haven't told me a thing about yourself or why you were fighting with that bouncer."

"Shouldn't you be out catching murderers?" The Devil jibed. "This all seems a bit petty for a man of your rank and distinction don't you think?"

"I don't know, you tell me?" said Garfield, matching wits. "If it's nothing more than a tiff then tell me, I'll happily let a junior take over and get their first conviction. But if you've got some wider beef then I'll need to know. I can't turf you out and five minutes later you're kicking in some kid for what's in his wallet."

The Devil snorted. He shifted uncomfortably in his seat, the metal bracelets of his handcuffs digging into his wrists.

"Please," he said. "If I was going to commit a crime, you'd know all about it."

"Would we now?" Garfield smirked. "Well do tell me then, I never say no to a confession."

"I'll bet you don't," The Devil sighed. "Look, I'm being honest with you inspector. This really is a waste of your time and efforts. I've already told you who I am and I've told you what I want. The fight, that was a means to an end."

"How?" asked Garfield.

"I needed to get into a police station, specifically this police station to continue my investigations. This is the central Glasgow office, am I right?"

"You are."

"Yes, well, fighting, as much as I deplore it was the quickest method."

"Fighting was your quickest method?"

"That's right."

"Did you not think to just come and ask?"

The Devil thought for a moment. Garfield's suggestion had never crossed his mind. Spending a lifetime of dealing with the angriest, most hostile souls ever to exist must have warped his decision making slightly. It was only to be expected.

"Possibly," he said. "Although I doubt you would have listened."

"And brawling with bouncers is a better way of getting our attention is it?" Garfield jabbed.

"I'm here aren't I?" said The Devil.

Garfield made a deep growl from the bottom of his throat. He didn't trust the man in front of him, The Devil knew that. As well he shouldn't have, especially with the reputation he had on Earth. But that wasn't being discussed.

"Inspector Garfield, you must understand, this is much bigger than you, much, much bigger," he said. "You must help me with my predicament."

"And why would I do that?" said Garfield, leaning his massive frame on the table.

"Simple," smiled The Devil. "Your soul depends on it."

FIFTEEN

"Sign here," said the surly sergeant behind the desk. "And here, then here and then finally here."

Jill took up the biro with a trembling hand and signed her name on the forms. She had never been arrested before and was finding the whole situation thoroughly unpleasant.

From the moment she had set foot in the police station, it had been a total nightmare. Draughty and grey, the whole building seemed to pulse with a stern authority that she wasn't used to. This was, after all, how the other half lived.

She was from a middle-class Glasgow family. The closest people like her came to police stations was watching crime drama on television. And even then if it got a little too real, the channel could always be changed.

In her job, run-ins with the force had been limited to light-spirited affairs. Affairs, sometimes, being the preferred terms. Officers would frequent A&E departments, whether they were patient or on duty. During her career, she had stitched up quite a few and stood up the rest. Easy going flirtations over a bloody wound were all part of the NHS service.

Being manhandled into the back of a waiting squad car seemed altogether more realistic. Especially when she had been callously thrown into a slab grey prison cell that smelled suspiciously of urine.

"Here's your bag," said the sergeant, pushing her handbag across the counter. "Check everything's in it and you can be on your way."

"Thank you," she said feebly, taking her bag and holding it tightly against her chest.

She looked about the reception area of the station and spied a row of plastic chairs near the door. Hobbling in her heels, she sat down and began to rock gently.

"I said you could go," said the sergeant, peering over his glasses.

"I know you did," she replied. "But I'm waiting on my friend."

"Your friend," the policeman snorted. "Listen love, if that's what you call a friend, you'd be better off without him."

"Thanks for the advice."

"Do you want me to call you a taxi?"

"No, I'm fine, thank you."

"He might not be out for hours you know. The DI is a right ball buster, he won't let him go until he's got something on him."

"I'll wait," she said, more determined. "Thank you."

"Suit yourself," the sergeant shrugged and went back to his paperwork.

Jill had a thumping headache. Her feet were aching and she was frightfully cold. There was a bitter draught billowing in through the doors but she was determined to stick it out. She sat silently and stared at her good dress, the sequins sparkling in the hard light.

She remembered when she bought the dress. Her final year at university and there was a medical society ball. She had never really been one for formalities and, to no surprise, when she checked her cupboard, there was nothing but jeans and rugby jerseys.

The rough and tumble, not-washing-for-three-days look had always steered her well in the past. Heading to a black tie gala was suddenly a daunting prospect.

Egged on by her fellow soon to be graduates, she had splurged on a frock from one of Glasgow's premier boutiques. The thing had cost a fortune and, as she handed over the credit card, which was paid for by her parents, she had to choke down a little vomit. For the price of the dress, she could have lived in her own squalor for another two years.

Much to her surprise, her parents hadn't gone ballistic when they saw the price. She had put that down to them being grateful their only daughter was finally appearing feminine. A lifetime of short haircuts and grunge music had meant they had missed out on the Barbie and ponies phase. Not that it had bothered them, outwardly at any rate. But Jill had always known, secretly, her mother had wanted somebody to go shopping with or talk about makeup.

Ancient history now though, a fact highlighted by her surroundings. There she was, on a Saturday night, loitering around the foyer of a police station. At least there was a man to be waiting for. The thought made her even colder.

A notice board on the wall opposite her had brightly coloured posters on it. The faces of missing people stared back at her. Their eyes were dead, lifeless on the paper. Old people, young teenagers, it seemed there was a whole army of society who didn't want to be found. For one reason or another.

In the middle of it all was a neighbourhood watch advert. A smiling, happy family were stood outside their house, the details of the scheme all around them. Two-point-four children, a cat and a dog. Jill didn't think such a concept existed anymore. But there it was, staring back at her.

She wondered if she would ever have something like that. Or even something that closely resembled a family. All she had was a dingy flat, a broken down car and a bathtub in her living room. That was all there was to show for a two-year relationship with the man she thought she might marry and thirty years of existence.

It seemed almost laughable now. How things could change in such a short time. Once again sitting in a police station was testament to that. She had started the day as a doctor, now she was a hardened criminal.

At least she had the card from the flowers. She opened up her bag and found it staring back at her. She read the message, still disbelieving of what it said. How could that have happened? Why her? Was this what she was meant to be doing? She didn't even begin to contemplate understanding what was going on. She worried that if she did, some of the magic would disappear. And there had never been enough magic in her life, ever.

A loud voice sounded out from one of the corridors behind the sergeant's desk. The policeman looked up, gave a glance at Jill and then went to see what all the commotion was about.

She stood up, tucking the card back into her handbag and closing it. She peered over the desk and saw shadows on the wall.

"You're bloody lucky I'm not pressing charges," came the voice of The Devil. She would recognise it anywhere, loud, brash but somehow lethargic. "Honestly, I thought the constabulary of Her Majesty would treat its tenants much better than this."

He emerged at the front desk, tugging on his ill-fitting suit. His face was bruised and bloody and he lacked the normal colour of a human being. She supposed he was alright.

"On your way," said a huge, red-faced man with a bad comb-over. "And less of your cheek son or I'll come down on you like a tonne of bricks."

"Please," said The Devil. "That wouldn't be very hard would it?"

The large man threw him a scowl and sauntered off back into

the police station. The sergeant checked his paperwork and spoke directly to The Devil.

"You didn't have anything?" he said, more as a question than a statement.

"That's right," answered The Devil.

"No keys, no money, not even a phone."

"Why on earth would I have any of those things?" The Devil seemed genuinely perplexed.

"That's okay darling, I've got them in my bag," Jill interjected, turning him away from the desk.

"Darling?" The Devil screwed up his face.

"He must be a little groggy after the fight," she said to the desk sergeant. "Boys and their toys and all of that. I'll make sure he's alright officer, thank you for being so patient."

"Aye, well, just make sure he stays out of trouble," said the policeman. "Sign here."

He pushed another set of forms in front of The Devil. After a quick scan, he began scribbling something on the paper before turning it back to the officer. Jill watched as the colour drained from the portly sergeant's face. She could literally see the blood leaving the cells in his saggy cheeks.

"And that's all you're getting," said The Devil.

The policeman took the forms back and looked stunned. The Devil took Jill's arm and they hurried out of the station and into the night air.

"I thought you couldn't read," she whispered to him.

"I can't," he replied.

"Then how come you can write? Like you did on that form back there."

"Who says I wrote anything," he smiled.

"And what's that supposed to mean?" she snapped.

"Some things, my dear Gideon, are beyond the comprehension of the human brain. You don't have to be able to write to give somebody a message."

They stepped down from the front door and onto the pavement.

"What a nightmare," said The Devil. "Honestly, you Humans. You love your red tape more than I do."

"Shut up!" Jill shouted. "Shut up, shut up, shut up, just shut up!"

"You're angry," he said.

"Damn, bloody, shitting hell I'm angry! Do you have any idea how horrible all that was?"

"As a matter of fact I do," he said casually. "They didn't even offer me a cup of tea."

"Unbelievable," she said, clapping her hands against her sides. "You really don't get it do you? You really don't understand. I thought it was just an act, you know, pretending to be totally thick. But I see now, I understand. You're a total idiot."

"Sticks and stones," said The Devil, prodding his nose. "I've heard a lot worse from a lot better people than you Gideon, believe me."

She gritted her teeth. She was angry and confused, all at once. He was both infuriating and fascinating all in equal measure. She didn't know if she wanted to beat him senseless with a baseball bat or listen to him talk forever. And that frustrated her to no end.

"I'm going home," she said, storming off down the pavement. "I don't care what you say, I'm going home. This has been one big disaster after another."

"What do you mean you're going home?" he called after her. "Don't you want to find out what happened to Baggio?"

"I don't care!" she called back. "I don't know and I don't care."

"Come on, don't be like that," he jogged a little and caught up with her. "I made real progress in there."

"Progress!" she yelled. "You call that progress!"

She pinched his nose and he let out a scream. She was more than a little pleased that he was in pain. It felt like a slither of revenge.

"Bloody bollocks woman!" he moaned. "Why would you do that! Can't you see I'm in agony?"

"Good," she spat. "I'm glad."

She stood and watched him ease through the pain. She didn't know if it was her instinctive compassion as a doctor or just the exhaustion but she felt sorry for him. Despite who he was, he cut a rather pathetic figure in his rubbish suit and bloodied shirt. Even his hair was matted with sweat and grime, eyes dark and bruised.

"I'm sorry," she said softly.

"What?" he shouted.

The pity was gone in an instant. Replaced by an angry ambivalence.

"What do we do now?" she asked.

"Firstly, I'd like an apology," he said.

"What?"

"You heard me doctor. An apology, right here, right now."

"And why, in the name of all that's holy, would I apologise to you?"

"Ahem," he cleared his throat.

"Sorry," she shook her head. "The question is still the same."

"Because you didn't believe me."

Jill was confused. It wasn't difficult, given her current state. She closed her eyes tightly and waved her hands, trying to get a semblance of what he was talking about.

"No," she said eventually. "No I'm not getting it, not this time."

"Really?" said The Devil, goading her. "You don't know?"

"No, I don't."

"Well that's okay," he said. "Just apologise and we'll move on. I don't mind."

"You mightn't but I certainly do!"

"Why not?"

"Because you just… I mean, it's not… we don't go about apologising for things we haven't done you know," she said, getting flustered. "It's just not our style."

"Sure you do," The Devil smiled. "You do it all the time."

"In what way?"

"If somebody bumps into you, you're the one that apologises. If you're trying to get somebody's attention, you say sorry. Hell, you lot are so bloody polite to each other, it's almost sickening."

Jill couldn't deny that he was right.

"You should be a stand-up comedian," she said. "That could make a good crowd pleasing act."

"Hardly," he said. "You lot wouldn't know humour if it slapped you across your greasy faces."

"Either way, I'm still not apologising."

"You didn't trust me."

"You're The Devil, remember. I'm not supposed to trust you!"

"Pish posh, details Gideon, minor details," he dismissed her. "And as you'll see, you have every reason to keep faith in me. This little brush with the Gendarmerie wasn't all for nothing."

He lifted his arm and rolled up his sleeve. Ticking down with his finger, he looked at an imaginary watch on his narrow wrist.

"Right. About. Now."

On queue, a loud clank echoed down a nearby alleyway. A little astonished, Jill peered through the dark and filthy lane to see a crack of light coming from an open door.

A man appeared, wearing a policeman's uniform, ferreting about in the doorway. When he spied them, he beckoned them over.

"What's all this about?" she said.

"Connections my dear Doctor Gideon, never leave home without them." The Devil patted his nose with his finger.

He dashed down the alleyway and greeted the policeman. He slipped in the door and called on Jill.

"Come on love, we don't have much time!"

Looking about to make sure nobody would see her, Jill tentatively dashed towards the open door. She had just left the police station a free woman. Now she was breaking back into it. And all the while her strange, beguiling, unfathomably brilliant companion was treating the whole thing like a grand day out.

"You're going to be the death of me," she said, stepping into the brightly lit corridor.

"Don't be silly," said The Devil, closing the fire escape's door. "That's up to you, I can't go about interfering."

"Bit late for that pal," said the desk sergeant.

"Yes, well, shall we?"

The desk sergeant locked the door and shoved the keys back in his pocket. He pushed past the two of them and The Devil began to follow.

Jill didn't like where the evening was going. She didn't much care for where it had been either. But she followed on as she had done before. She was discovering that there was very little use in arguing.

When the door closed behind them, the world was shut out. It was a good thing too as there was something else in the alleyway. Something that neither Jill nor The Devil had seen.

Too large to be a man but not big enough to be a beast, there was a long, dark shadow lurking in the gutter. Moving away from the light, it seemed to hiss as it approached the locked door.

SIXTEEN

The Devil moved with a renewed urgency. The desk sergeant who had let them into the police station was furtive and cagey. He was overly cautious, hesitating every time he neared a junction in the long corridors. It was dreadfully annoying.

"How much longer?" The Devil asked impatiently.

"Not far, not far," said the sergeant.

"I didn't ask you how far, I asked you how long."

He felt an arm tug him backwards. Jill had a look of sheer terror etched across her very human face.

"What?" whispered The Devil.

"What do you think!" she said, wanting to shout but keeping her voice low. "What's all this about then? Are you going to tell me or should I start guessing?"

"Nothing, absolutely nothing," said The Devil.

"Nothing!" she shouted. "We've just been let into a police station through a back door and are now sneaking about, hoping not to get caught. That's hardly nothing."

"Yes, yes, trivial details," he tried to dismiss her.

"It is *not* trivial," she pulled him back.

"Would you let go of my arm!"

"Oi!" the sergeant shouted. "You two want to see this or not?"

The Devil smiled at Jill, happy that his point was proven. They marched up the policeman who stood by a large, blank door, keys in hand.

"Here," he said. "This is where we keep the records on file of all our active and inactive cases."

He turned a key in the lock and pushed the door open, stepping to one side. The Devil hurried in while Jill lingered a moment.

"And you're just going to let us in here?" she asked.

"What choice do I have?" said the sergeant, his forehead covered in sweat. "You know who he is as much as I do."

A chill went through her. She remembered The Devil scribbling something on the form and giving it to the policeman. She couldn't see what he had written but whatever it had been it had been enough. Like her, the sergeant had dropped everything he had, risked his whole career and livelihood for the mysterious man who appeared out of nowhere. The whole spirited ordeal was suddenly very real.

"I don't know what you're looking for," said the policeman. "But you don't have long. Hurry up, I'll stand guard."

Jill didn't argue. She shut the door behind her, leaving the sergeant to stand guard.

Inside was a labyrinth of towering, iron shelves. Large boxes and cabinets were stacked high, reaching all the way to the ceiling. Lights flickered on as she stepped forward, bringing the place to life.

As she walked down the narrow paths between the archives, she read the alphabetised names, numbers and labels on each of the boxes. Some were old, really old, dating back almost fifty years. She touched the old carboard, as if feeling the information would make it seem more real.

"I didn't think they still kept this stuff," she said aloud, hoping The Devil would hear her.

There was no answer. She stopped at a large cabinet, the labels on the drawers marked 1980. It was the year she had been born and thought it a good enough reason to have a nosey. Checking nobody was watching her, paranoia running high, she pulled open the middle drawer and smelled the stale, fuzzy scent of ageing paper.

She flicked through the files until one felt nice in her hands. She pulled it out and pawed through the notes inside. There was a photo, attached to a dossier by a paperclip. The man looked surly, mean, demented almost. He would have been imposing, had it not been for the dreadful perm.

Jill wondered what had happened to him. Had he ever been caught, ever gone to prison? Was he still in there now? Had he been able to turn his life around? Was he even still alive? Too many questions.

She closed the file and replaced it back in the drawer. Shutting it over, her breath was taken from her when The Devil appeared at her side.

"I wish you wouldn't do that!" she said, holding her panting chest.

"Do what?"

"That! That appearing out of nowhere! It's really quite disconcerting."

"Discon-what?"

"Never mind," she pinched the bridge of her nose, tiredness stinging her eyes. "Have you found what you were looking for?" she asked.

"No," The Devil sighed. "There was nothing under Baggio, certainly not from back then. It's like he didn't even report that he had been stabbed."

"Why wouldn't he?" asked Jill.

The Devil chewed on his bottom lip. In the buzzing light of the archives, she thought he looked almost angelic. Something about his features, the way his jaw curved, his cheekbones protruding from the scraped and dirty skin. He wasn't human, not when she really looked at him. He seemed more like what an alien would see as being a human being.

The thoughts hurt her head more and she decided to ignore them. She went to put her hands in her pockets then remembered she was wearing a cocktail dress.

"So we came here for nothing," she said.

"Looks that way," he drummed his fingers on his chin. "Still, plenty worse ways to spend an evening I suppose."

"You won't be saying that tomorrow morning when that fractured nose of yours feels like it's on fire."

"Lovely," said The Devil. "Thank you so very much for reminding me."

"So what do we do now?" she asked.

"Beats me," The Devil rubbed the side of his face. "Although I must admit, I'm feeling rather beat. Does this happen all the time?"

He yawned, stretching his arms. Jill had to laugh. He was like a child at times, totally innocent but completely mad. She supposed that was to be expected, all things considered.

"Maybe we should go home," she said. "Make a fresh start in the morning. How does that sound?"

"Sound?" said The Devil, narrowing his eyes. "Are you asking me to sleep with you?"

"What!" Jill shouted. "Good god, no! What gave you that impression!"

"I don't know, I don't know how you people do these things," he shrugged. "You lot are always going at it, worse than the bloody insects. I wasn't sure if this was how it all started."

"You mean…" she trailed off, unsure whether to progress with her question.

"I mean what?" he sprung on her hesitation.

"You mean you've never had sex?" she couldn't help but smirk.

The Devil rolled his eyes. Jill's smirk grew into a smile, then a grin and finally a fully grown beam.

"Really, we're going to do this, here, now?" he said. "In case you've forgotten Doctor Gideon, we're in the depths of police archives, in the middle of a police station, at night, having just been charged for breach of the peace. And you're going to ask me about my sex life."

"Well?" she shrugged. "I just figured that you being The Devil and all, you'd have been at it as much as we humans are. No?"

She felt justified in her question. She didn't think it was wholly unreasonable to tease him a little. Especially after the drama he had put her through in the past few hours. His face, however, told a very different story.

"Let's go," he huffed. "I don't have time to waste on schoolgirl chit-chat like that."

"Whatever you say," she said, following him towards the door. "Touched a nerve there I think."

He knocked once and the door opened a little. Outside, the desk sergeant was looking flushed, his face awash with sweat. His eyes were wild, a nervous panic making him jitter.

"We're finished," said The Devil.

"Good," replied the sergeant, his breath short. "There's some noise being made from upstairs, I think something big is going down."

"What do you mean?" asked Jill, slipping out the door.

"I don't know, they put out a call for all officers to head to the front desk," he said, wiping his brow on the back of his arm. "I need to go, they'll know that I'm missing. I need to go. You can see yourselves out. I need to go, need to go now."

"Why would they need all officers?" asked Jill.

The sergeant ignored her, breaking into a sprint and racing down the corridor away from them. Something nagged at her, something terrible. She went to ask The Devil but he had already started towards the fire exit.

"Shouldn't we see what that's all about?" she asked.

"Why?" he fired back. "It doesn't concern us."

"I know, but it could be serious, they might need my help."

"Do what you like Gideon, I'm not here to sort out the domestic affairs of planet Earth."

"But, I mean, don't you have a duty or something?"

"Duty?" he exclaimed, pushing open the heavy iron door of the fire escape. "In what possible way could a bunch of policemen getting into a tizz over nothing constitute my duty?"

"I don't know. It sounded pretty serious. Did you see the sergeant? He looked ill."

"He shouldn't eat so much refried dog shit then, should he? The Devil snapped, stalking the dark alleyway. "The man's a heart attack waiting to happen, anything would make him keel over if-"

The Devil was cut short by the sight that awaited them at the end of the alleyway. Yet again Jill found herself breathless and without words at what she saw. It was a nasty habit she was getting into.

The pair stood motionless, dumbfounded by the sight of a thousand moving figures, creeping through the shadows. Flaming torches highlighted just how many people had turned out into the streets.

Faces were covered by scarves and hoods, their hands filled with bottles, bricks, rocks and sticks. They were armed and angry, whistles, shouts and chants giving the whole street the feel of a football terrace. Jill had never seen anything like it, not in real life. A baying mob, on the march, trampling through the streets, looking for trouble.

"Sweet Holy Mother of God," she just about managed.

"No," said The Devil, equally astounded. "I don't think she's got anything to do with this one. Not this time, at least."

Somewhere in her peripheral vision, Jill caught sight of flashing blue lights. She instinctively cocked her head towards them, spying a fleet of police vans rolling out from behind the station.

But she wasn't the only one who had spied the arrival of the Force. Like a red flag being waved at a bull, the emergence of the police seemed to charge the atmosphere of the mob. The mood in the air changed in an instant, from angry to furious. The sound of breaking glass and shouting followed quickly behind, the whole group converging on the approaching vans.

"I think we should retreat," said The Devil.

"Where have they come from?" Jill asked, still taking in the sheer amount of numbers that had emerged, seemingly, from nowhere.

"What does it matter," said The Devil, his voice low and determined. "They're here now and they're looking for trouble. That's all we have to worry about."

"But why?" she asked. "Why now, I mean? What's it for?"

"All good questions doctor, but we can ask them in the safety of your lodgings. Now move."

He grabbed her hand and began to pull. She ran along with him, staring over her shoulder as the mob moved like a black ocean, filling up the street.

They hurried through the night, racing away from the police station and the impending battle. Something was wrong, Jill knew it. Roaming gangs and angry mobs weren't the norm in Glasgow. Not out of the blue anyway.

They rounded the corner and The Devil hailed a passing taxi. As they climbed into the back cabin, she wondered if the man she was with had anything to do with it. After all, violence and destruction were his modus operandi.

SEVENTEEN

"The riot broke out shortly after ten o'clock on Saturday night. Police all over the city of Glasgow were put on immediate red alert as they tried to confront the thousands strong force that was sweeping through the streets."

Even as he spoke, the newsreader found it difficult to maintain his composure. What he was talking about had never been seen in Scotland. Not since the Highland clearances.

"It is estimated that as many as two thousand people joined in on the disorder as it made its way from the city centre out to the west end. Windows were smashed, cars were set on fire and police were directly confronted as forces tried to subdue the protesting mob. Several smaller protests were registered in towns and cities across Scotland, however, the protests in Glasgow were the largest that the police had seen in the country's history. An investigation is now ongoing as to the whereabouts and how the riot started, with detectives believing there was a political motive behind the mass unrest. John Smith has more."

The screen cut away from the newsreader. A stiff looking man with greying hair appeared and he began to speak. The Devil didn't care and he turned the television off.

He was perplexed. That usually meant that something was bothering him. As a being of unimaginable power, knowledge and energy, feeling like a half-shut knife meant that something was deeply wrong.

He sat back in the empty bath and scratched his chin. Staring off at the pile of books he had tipped out of the tub, he tried to think. But as was becoming a nasty habit in his mortal life, he was interrupted.

"What did they say on the news?" asked Jill, drying her hair with a towel.

"Please," said The Devil, closing his eyes in frustration. "I'm trying to concentrate."

"Yes, I can see that," she said. "Your concentration has made a right mess of my living room."

"Excuse me Gideon, I'm not the one with a bloody bath in the middle of the floor. Don't you have a bathroom that this thing could live in?"

Jill didn't say anything. She grabbed the remote off of his lap and turned on the television. Resigned that he wasn't going to get his precious thinking time, he climbed out of the tub and sat down beside her.

"Is this what you people do?" he asked.

"What? Watch TV? Of course it is."

"But why?"

"How else are we meant to learn about the news?" she said.

"Don't you people have the internet yet?"

"We do, yeah, but that's not for everybody. What about old people and folk that don't like computers? Where do you think they get their news from?"

"Gideon," he said, clapping his hand to his forehead. "Why would I even bother to care about anything about what you've just said? I mean, honestly. Here I am, contemplating the murder of a man from four decades ago so I can take a long, overdue break and you're polluting my thoughts with the elderly."

"Sssh, they've got the First Minister on," she patted him down.

A woman appeared on the television screen. She was pale and curt, her lips a thin, red line across a flat face. She was wearing black and held herself with the reserve and respect in mourning politicians were expected to show on such occasions.

"Oh great," yawned The Devil. "Who's this?"

"Be quiet!" said Jill, turning up the volume.

"Today is a dark day for the city of Glasgow and for Scotland as a whole," said the woman, the flashes of cameras highlighting her crow's feet and bags beneath her eyes. "What we saw last night on these streets was absolutely barbaric. Nowhere in the country that I so proudly represent, should people feel afraid to walk freely in the place they call home. The violence and mindless, blatant thuggery that was on display will not go unpunished and I can assure the thousands of rioters who have ravaged Glasgow will be punished for their actions. And let me also express my deep-felt condolences to the families and loved ones of those who were injured in last night's atrocities. The finest care will be offered to you and once again this city's emergency services have outshone themselves, going above and beyond the care and duty expected of them. And for that, I'm grateful."

There was a pause as the First Minister adjusted her notes. She was flanked by city officials and other aides, all desperately trying to look more morose than the other. The Devil would have been impressed by the scene, had he not witnessed it a million times before. False gratitude and big words were all fine, it was the actions that followed them that stood for something.

He glanced over at Jill. She was transfixed on the television, engrossed by the First Minister's words. He believed that if he were to slap her across the face, she wouldn't even notice.

"Unbelievable," he said quietly.

"What's that?" she said, waking from her trance.

"Oh nothing, just making a little observation that's all," he feigned a smile. "Are you done with what's-her-chops there?"

"Please, try and show a little respect would you? It says there were three casualties last night with dozens taken to hospital."

"Hardly the crusades Gideon, come on." He folded his hands behind his head.

"Are you deliberately trying to wind me up or is it just your usual manner?" Her eyes were wide, face pointed in anger.

The Devil sat up. He pointed at the screen, ready to defend himself.

"What's going on here Gideon, is all part of His great cosmic plan."

"What do you mean?"

"I mean, He's up there, having the time of His life, letting all of this unfold. Don't you think He should have stepped in and made a difference last night. Don't you think He should be making a difference to the earthquake happening in the Pacific somewhere, or the forest fire in Australia or the countless other disasters befalling innocent human beings everywhere? But He isn't. He isn't doing squat."

"That's not how it works," she said.

The Devil let out a laugh. It was almost all genuine, to the point where he was surprised. He hopped up from the sofa.

"You're telling *me* how it all works are you? That's a new one," he laughed.

"Yes, I am, as a matter of fact," said Jill, standing up too. "I'm telling you that your endless scepticism and total paranoia are what makes you who you are. That's why you're always the underdog, that's why you're always beaten. Did you ever think of that?"

He was speechless. Actually speechless. The Devil could count on one hand, maybe even one finger, how many times he had been left without words. And this time had come straight out of the blue.

"Well?" she said expectantly, like her tirade hadn't been enough.

"I'm not quite sure what you want me to say," was all he could manage. "That's quite a claim you're making."

"That's all you've got to say for yourself?" she asked. "No apology, no nothing? People are dying out there and all you can do is sit on that couch and criticise them and Him up there."

Again, The Devil didn't really know what to say. He had witnessed some of the biggest atrocities in the history of human kind. He had played a part in most of them. He stood back with glee as Hitler rose to power, rubbed his hands when nuclear weapons had finally been crafted by human hands.

Yet here he was, in the body of one of Them, being lectured by a stroppy doctor who had woken up on the wrong side of her bed. The situation was almost hilarious, if he could remember how to have a sense of humour.

"Honestly Gideon," he began. "In all my many, many, many years of existence, I don't think I've ever been spoken to quite so frankly."

She didn't blink, her face still blazing with anger. She bit down on her lip, her wet hair stuck to her bare shoulder, skin quivering.

"I just think you should know that, that's all," she said. "I think you should know that while you're here, these things are important to us. They might not mean anything to you or to Him but they mean everything to us. To us!"

She bowed her head, the beginnings of a sob starting. The Devil didn't know what to do. Was this part of his test? Was he supposed to comfort her, tell her that it would all be okay? And if he did, would she even believe him? Would he believe him?

Before he could act, she wiped her nose and looked at him. Her eyes were a little redder but she had stopped herself before the tears began. She sniffed and threw down the towel for her hair.

They stood looking at each other for a silent moment, the television lost somewhere in the background. He could feel her breath on his face as she moved closer.

She stopped just short of him. Taking her hand, she laid it gently on his shoulder, her forehead touching his nose. She looked up at him before leaning in and kissing him on the lips.

She was warm, but not in a way that The Devil knew. The heat was powerful, alive, different from the blazing inferno of Hell. It was hard yet soft, a strange combination of feeling and passion along with sheer energy.

He couldn't do it though. He couldn't continue. While Jill's tongue pushed past his lips and deeper into his mouth, seeking out his own like a fleshy proboscis, he knew he couldn't continue. There was just something wholly unhealthy about it all.

"Blimey," he said, taking a step back.

She lingered a little longer, still kissing the air, before realising what had happened. Her pallid skin immediately flushed red, making her look like she had been badly sunburned from the forehead down.

"Sorry," she said quickly. "Sorry, sorry, sorry, I don't know what I was thinking."

She hurried to the couch, picked up her towel and raced for the door. On the way, she knocked over a box, spilling books and ornaments out across the floor. In a flurry of curses and panic, she reached the door and looked back at The Devil.

"Gideon," he said but before he could finish, she was gone.

He was left alone in the living room. The television was still on, the action on screen now turning to an impromptu memorial in

Glasgow's George Square. The First Minister was laying a wreath of condolence at the foot of a cenotaph. It joined an army of others already laid down by various dignitaries and passers by, all equally shocked by the violence.

The Devil knew he was right, he was always right. Humans weren't complicated creatures to fathom, they were animals. If he could work out the psychology of Him, then surely His creations would be a relative walk in the park. But it didn't seem to be going that way.

Jill's outburst then act of passion was testament to that. If that was how they all behaved, what chance did he have of catching the killer?

"Bloody humans," he said, cascading down onto the couch with a thump. He took up the remote and increased the volume. The same newsreader had returned, his overly made up appearance pressing all of The Devil's wrong buttons.

"The First Minister there at a press conference in the centre of Glasgow," he smarmed. "While there is no clear evidence that points to the cause of last night's riots, police are confident that they have a number of positive lines of inquiry. Early indications show that the unrest may have been due to the insurgence in the recent opening of the Hellcorp Institute in Edinburgh."

The name made The Devil sit up. He leaned forward, suddenly interested.

"Oh no," he said, panic stricken.

"In a statement released by the company, Hellcorp chief executive Creighton Tull was adamant that the corporation had absolutely nothing to do with the riots and that any suggestion of which would be absolute, quote, 'stuff and nonsense.'"

"No!" The Devil screamed at the top of his voice.

He shot to his feet and held his hands to his head. The whole statement appeared in a graphic on the screen, the stylised H in the top right hand corner. He read it quickly, every word making him sick as he realised then that his beautiful creation, the one he had worked on so hard, invested so much of himself into, was being torn apart at the seams in his absence.

There were PR disasters and then there was Creighton Tull. The statement was effectively painting the rioters as ill educated thugs, born in lower classes and totally void of any human decorum or thought. Be that as it was, they were still customers and customers were needed to pay the exhaustive bills that Hellcorp racked up every day.

He wanted to kick something, anything, just to release some anger. The closest thing was the cast iron tub. Without thinking, he took a short run up and swung his foot forward as hard as he could.

There was pain and then there was pain. In his short time on earth, The Devil thought he knew what real agony had felt like. That was until he booted the bath, the heavy metal ringing around the room.

He toppled over to one side, clutching his bare foot and watching it turn bright red then purple. He couldn't make a sound, he was totally paralysed. And all because of his temper.

The door swung open and Jill appeared, fully dressed. She saw him squirming on the floor and raced over.

"What happened?"

"Tull!" he shouted. "Bloody Tull happened! He's ruining my business, my lovely, beautiful business! He's calling the rioters a bunch of in-bred hicks!"

"But that's probably what they are," said Jill, trying to prize open The Devil's vice like grip around his foot.

"I know they are but you can't tell them that. They're our key demographic!"

Jill took his foot and fiddled with his toes one by one. He lay on the carpet, sweating profusely, his bloodied shirt sticking to his chest.

"Yep, you've broken them," she said, letting his foot drop with a thump. "You'll need to be careful you know. The rate you're going at, you'll be in a wheelchair before lunch."

"And dead by dinner," he said, breathing heavily. "Still, there's always a silver lining isn't there."

Jill didn't give an awkward silence a chance to take a grip of the conversation and she helped him back onto his feet. She passed him his shoes and socks and smiled.

"Come on, get dressed," she said.

"Why?"

"Because I think I've worked out a way we can find your missing murder."

The Devil took the socks and gave her a compulsory sneer. She didn't acknowledge it and instead slipped on her trainers.

"Alleluia," he said.

"Not yet," she replied.

EIGHTEEN

The Devil was still stewing when they pulled up at the hospital. He was plotting all the vengeful, vicious, most malevolent things he could do to the idiots he had left in charge of Hell. He felt like a teacher who had been called away for one moment, only to return and the class had descended into chaos.

Only this wasn't some childish primary school. This was the very economic, philosophical and metaphysical future of the afterlife. There were differences, huge differences, and it bothered him to no end that his minions couldn't see that.

Maybe they could and perhaps they just couldn't be bothered. That was certainly the case for Creighton Tull. The man was an idiot, raised to a position of power greater than any of his peers. There was even an argument to say that he was the most powerful human being ever. The Devil couldn't really blame him, not when it came to his humanity. It was like an illness and an incurable one at that.

He couldn't stand laziness though. Being unintelligent could almost be forgiven. Ignorance was an excuse that, thin as it was, could get most off the hook. Laziness, on the other hand, was totally unforgivable. And The Devil suspected that without his ever present iron fist to crack the whip, the whole business was falling to pieces.

That certainly looked the case with the way Hellcorp was handling the riots. The thought of that public statement gave him chills. He wondered how such a dreadful mistake could have gotten past Alice. Normally she was all over these things with her usual ruthless ease and bad humour. The faintest pang of what could loosely be described as worry flickered somewhere in the depths of his soul. Locked away, in a dungeon, chained to a wall so that nobody would ever see it.

"What's wrong with you?" asked Jill.

"Pardon?" he said, blinking and turning away from the window.

"You look like you've got the weight of the world on your shoulders."

"Gideon, if you've ever said a truer word, I doubt anybody, anywhere, has ever heard it."

"What's wrong then?" she asked.

"What does it matter," he sighed loudly. "Makes no difference anyway, I doubt I'm ever going to get a rest."

"Why the sudden lack of optimism?" she asked, glancing back and forth between him and the road. "Is this because of what happened earlier. Because, you know, that was a mistake I didn't mean to-"

"Please," The Devil held up his hands. "Don't bother. I've seen you lot try to explain away mistakes a dozen times, I don't need to be put through it again. The awkward apologies, the tense silences, you should really just try and avoid it. Makes for such boring conversation and, worst of all, it drags on and on and on. Get over it."

He adjusted his seatbelt, still unsure why he needed it in the first place. His human body was shivering and its skin looked grey in the morning light. His stitches were itching, his face was on fire and the nagging headache that had been dull but constant was altogether driving him mad.

"Aren't you happy that we're making progress with the murder though?" she ventured.

"Progress?" he blurted. "I hardly think retracing our steps is progress Gideon. We're driving back to the hospital, where we've just came from. The police have no record of what's going on, you have no idea medically what happened and I doubt the body is even still there. It's totally useless."

He rubbed his eyes and was tempted to gouge them out. The sheer agony would have been a pleasant change to the numbing irritancy he was being subjected to.

"At least here we can find out where his next of kin lives," she said. "Maybe they'll be able to shed some light on what happened."

"Maybe," he conceded. "Maybe. But I'm starting to think that this whole thing is just a wild goose chase designed to wear me down so much that I give up and skulk off back to Hell with my tail between my legs."

"I thought you said you didn't have a tail."

"I don't, I'm just…"

He trailed off when he caught sight of a smirk on her face. She was joking again, or at least trying to. He didn't have the energy to argue and come up with a witty retort.

"Nothing?" she asked. "Nothing for that one? I thought I might have gotten *something*."

"Doctor Gideon, if I'm ever in need of humour, I'll simply take a stroll through one of your human nightclubs and listen in on the dreadful process you lot call 'chatting up'. Maybe then I'll be able to muster a smile. But until then, no, you're getting nothing."

"Fair enough," she said, her smile still there.

The car pulled around the corner and the huge Victorian building of the hospital loomed large up ahead. The traffic was queued all the way down the road and an army of flashing blue and red lights illuminated the whole street.

"What's going on here?" asked Jill, leaning forward onto the steering wheel.

The Devil tried to focus, battling his ailing eyesight. There appeared to be two large, articulated lorries near the entrance to the hospital. Police vans and cars were flanking the huge vehicles, officers patrolling the streets in their luminous jackets.

"Something's happened," he said. "They're pulling something out."

"Out of where?" asked Jill, sounding panicky.

The traffic began to move and slowly they edged closer to the hospital. The nearer they drew, the more apparent it became that the building had not gone unscathed throughout the previous night's riot.

Jill switched on her indicators, signalling that she was pulling into the hospital. A policeman waved her to stop and came up to her window.

"Good morning," he said in a gruff Glaswegian accent. "The hospital's closed to visitors this morning love."

"I'm not a visitor," she said, flashing her identity badge. "I'm a doctor, I'm here for my shift."

"Oh aye?" said the policeman, taking the badge. "And who's he then?"

Jill looked quickly at The Devil. He leaned forward, nudging her out of the way so he could see the policeman clearly.

"Professor Yegor Titov," he said in a Russian accent. "I'm a visiting academic here to learn about Scottish hospitals and their best practices. And I must say constable, I'm not very impressed by this lack of access to a major, metropolitan emergency centre."

"Sergeant," sneered the policeman, tapping the chevrons on his shoulders.

"Yes, forgive me, sergeant," said The Devil. "Tell me, why is the hospital closed?"

"Because of that," the policeman pointed over to the two huge, articulated lorries.

They were towing what remained of a double-decker bus out of the ruins of an old stone guardhouse within the hospital's grounds. The twisting metal shrieked as the vehicle was pulled free, bringing with it a huge cloud of damp dust and broken rubble.

"A group of rioters thought it would be funny to crash a bus into a hospital last night pal."

"Where there many hurt?" asked Jill.

"A few cuts and bruises. One woman's water broke. The driver was killed, but that was before the crash," said the policeman, tipping his cap back a little. "A group of the rioters thought it would be funny to cut his throat and drag him through the bus first before they smashed the thing into the building. So no, not a good night here doctor."

There was a roar from the crash site as the recovery trucks began to arduous task of removing the bus permanently. Several workers were propping up makeshift buttresses in an attempt to keep some of the guardhouse's structure.

Amid the constructional chaos, The Devil spied a familiar face. Inspector Garfield was navigating his way across some rubble, a half eaten bacon roll in one hand and a cigarette in the other. His face was flushed, brown sauce all around his lips. The Devil shuddered at the thought of the policeman and just how vulgar he could be.

"That's what we're dealing with at the moment," said the sergeant by the car. "So if you don't mind, would you hurry up and clear the way for the diggers, we're in a bit of a rush to clear this mess up before the press get here."

He waved the car on and Jill didn't argue. She rolled into the car park and found a space near the main entrance.

"Bloody hell, this is just terrible," said Jill. "I mean, it's like the end of the world or something. How can people be acting normal one day and then this happens. What drives them to do that kind of behaviour?"

"It's said that your society is only three square meals away from anarchy," said The Devil. "I'm inclined to believe that it's probably a little less."

"And I'm inclined to agree with you," replied Jill. "It's certainly the case on a Saturday night in Glasgow. Although that's probably more to do with the booze and drugs. Who said that again?"

"I don't recall," said The Devil. "It was either Plato or someone from Red Dwarf. It's difficult to distinguish them at times."

"Quite."

The pair left the car and headed into the main building of the hospital. As they were expecting, the place was utter chaos. The Devil's predictions about anarchy had proven to be right. One quick view of the accident and emergency department and it was clear to see that society had lost its way. Perhaps for good.

Jill weaved her way expertly through the trolleys, wheelchairs and hobbling patients. The Devil stuck close behind her, determined not to get caught up in this wave of ill health. From coughing elderly to young men clutching bloodied wounds, the effects of the riot were beginning to take their toll. And still he couldn't fathom out its origins.

While Jill plotted a way to the wards, he let his mind slip into a state of waking thought. None of the computer models had predicted much backlash from the opening of Hellcorp. And these weren't the off the shelf models that humanity was still messing around with. Technology that set Hell and The Devil above even the concept of the gods.

There had been plenty of resistance met by various religious groups, that was only to be expected. The Devil had begrudgingly complimented The Pope and his Catholic legions on their attempts to shut the programme down before it started. Despite The Devil's best efforts and olive branch of sorts, the Bishop of Rome had still seen it fit to utter a call-to-arms for all of his faithful followers to boycott anything and everything to do with the project.

The result had been a constant battle of wills with protestors during the construction of the headquarters in Edinburgh. The London, Berlin and Los Angeles branches had been slightly easier. But there was something about the Scots that really turned them out in great numbers.

The Devil wasn't really surprised. The people of Scotland loved a good moan and something to rally behind. They trailed only the Germans in that respect.

Thankfully, the boffins in Hell had managed to work their magic. Somehow, some way, Hellcorp had been legitimised and opened to the public. And the public were opening their hearts, minds and more importantly, souls, to the corporation.

The Devil afforded himself a little smile as he stepped into the elevator. No, the riot couldn't have been anything to do with Hellcorp. If it had been, he would have known about it. Wouldn't he?

"Here we are," said Jill, stepping out of the lift.

He chose to ignore her chirpiness as they headed into a ward. A nurse's station met them at the head of the huge room, large windows from the building's original architecture letting in floods of damp light to the beds.

"Good morning," said Jill, announcing herself to the gaggle of nurses. "I was wondering if you could help me."

"Hold on!" snapped the nurse closest to the desk.

She was big, too big, poured into her standard issue uniform, the faintest of stains still visible on the belly. The Devil took an instant dislike to her and could feel Jill getting tense.

"I don't need to take up much of your time," offered the doctor. "I just need some notes from a patient that died yesterday."

"Listen hen, can't you see that we're up to our eyes in it at the moment?"

Both Jill and The Devil stared at the nurses. One was carelessly pawing through a paper file, another was on her mobile phone and the third was picking something out of her teeth with the cap of a pen. Even their leader, the big one, appeared to be doing nothing. The Devil's laziness alert was almost fit to breaking.

"Yes, I know, but I can do it myself, if you point me in the right direction," said Jill.

The nurses' leader sighed loudly. If she had been acting any worse, The Devil would have arranged some scenery she could chew on. He clenched his knuckles, contemplating punching her in her fat face.

"Fine," she moaned. "Who are you looking for?"

"Baggio," said The Devil, stepping in. "Anton Baggio, he was brought in yesterday afternoon but declared dead shortly after in theatre. Where's his file?"

The nurse's face seemed to tighten from the lips outwards. She didn't like his tone but he didn't care. Authority was best left to those who knew how to handle it. In the hands of an idiot, it made life so much more difficult.

"Over there," she thumbed at a stack of files that had been left carelessly on a trolley. "Anybody that croaked it yesterday will be in there. We haven't sent them down to medical records yet."

"Why not?" asked The Devil.

"Excuse me?" said the nurse, looking totally offended.

"Why haven't you done your job? It's a fairly easy task and basic requisite of you being paid money in the first place."

"I beg your pardon?" Her face began to flush.

"You heard me Mother Theresa. I asked you why you weren't doing your fucking job. Instead you're sitting here on your fat arse giving grief to this doctor here. There was a riot last night, woman! Shouldn't you be caring for the sick and the needy!"

"That's been very helpful, thank you," said Jill, stepping between the two. "I think we can manage from here. Can't we?"

She pushed him backwards, away from the nurses. The Devil tried to resist but she slipped her hand under his armpit and pinched the skin.

"What are you doing!" he said, leaping a little in pain. "Get off, I'm putting that awful woman in her place."

"No, you're going to come with me to check on Anton Baggio's next of kin details and then we're going to leave. Got that?"

She twisted her grip and he let out a little scream. Nodding, he conceded defeat and she let him go.

"Has anybody ever told you how much of a bitch you are?" he asked, rubbing the skin she had gripped.

"Yes, frequently, but I don't listen anymore."

"Maybe you should, it might make you a bit more attractive to me. Or women, come to think of it."

They reached the trolley and Jill began pouring over the papers until she found Baggios. The Devil didn't even try to understand, the disorganisation was enough to make his head swim.

"Did you see our friend downstairs?" he said quietly, keeping a lookout and one eye on the nurse's station.

"Who?" asked Jill, engrossed in paperwork.

"Inspector Garfield."

"Who's that?" she asked.

"You mean you weren't introduced? What a pity. He's the nice policeman who decided he didn't like me very much and that I was little more than trouble. Still, he played ball eventually. Everybody has their price."

"And what was his?"

"I can't say," The Devil smirked.

"Why not?"

"I would have thought a doctor would understand patient confidentiality. No, no my dear Gideon, some secrets are best kept up one's sleeve."

"Whatever."

She examined the spines of the beige folders until one jumped out at her. Heaving a pile onto the floor, she found what she was looking for. Throwing it open, a picture of Anton Baggio stared back at them, his face puffy, eyes closed, dead.

"That's our man," said The Devil, his interest re-sparked.

"Good," she drew a line with her finger down his past medical history, the whole record on file.

"Anything interesting?"

"Nothing we didn't already know," she said. "He was diabetic, had a heart attack about fifteen years ago. Smoker, little exercise, high blood pressure. He was lucky he got as long as he did."

"Yes, yes, all very good," said The Devil. "I'll mourn later. What about an address?"

Jill flipped the file to the index page. She stopped midway down the page.

"Says his next of kin is a Francesca Baggio, stays in the west end. Address is here."

"Good," he pushed her out of the way and pulled the page out of the file, the inner binding popping open and with it the pages instantly became loose and began cascading out.

"What are you doing?" she asked, appalled.

"Taking the address," he said, shoving the sheet into his pocket.

"I could have written it down."

"No time, come on." He lifted her by the arm and forced her towards the main door.

They passed the nurses and headed out into the corridor before they could comment. The Devil quickened his pace, Jill trotting along beside him.

"You do know this looks mightily suspicious," she said.

"Really?" he asked, his head swivelling around to make sure they weren't being followed.

"Well, yes. A strange man, covered in bruises and a broken nose, ushering a doctor, a female doctor at that, out of a hospital quickly. You're attracting more attention to yourself doing this."

"Nonsense," said The Devil, mashing the buttons for the lift.

The elevator arrived and they hurried in. There was an old man there, being helped by a nurse. The smell of stale urine coming from him was pungent and The Devil had to choke back some sick. Jill seemed unperturbed.

When the doors opened, he hustled her out quickly and they headed for the door. But before they could reach the outside world, three brutish looking security guards stepped in their way.

"Excuse me doctor," said one of them. "Is everything okay here?"

"Oh great," said The Devil. "Here we go again."

"Not now," said Jill sternly.

"Is everything alright here doctor?" said the same guard. "We got a call from ward thirteen saying that you were seen with this man leaving rather quickly. The nurses up there seemed to think that something was wrong."

"Really? Why's that?" She tried to smile, aware that The Devil was still holding onto her arm.

"They said that this gentleman here was aggressive towards them, started calling them names."

"That's a lie!" shouted The Devil. "I bet it was that fucking bitch nurse, you know the one I mean, tell them Gideon. The fat one with the face like a mangled sofa."

"Please," she said, willing him to be quiet.

The guards were getting restless. They started to fidget, hands flexing in and out of fists. It was clear to see they were in the mood for a fight.

"Okay, okay, let's stop beating around the bush," he said, taking a step forward. "We all know you're looking for a dust up so let's just get on with it, shall we?"

The guards looked at each other in turn. Their elected spokesman was the first to crack.

"Excuse me sir?" he said.

"I said-"

The Devil swung his fist around like a pendulum. It clattered into the guard's shoulder hard, sending a shockwave of pain down The Devil's arm. The guard staggered a little, more surprised than injured, his colleagues equally dazed.

"Oh fuck!" The Devil shouted. "That was sore!"

"Grab him!"

"Look out!" Jill screamed from behind.

The Devil swivelled to see an empty wheelchair come barrelling towards him. He rolled out of the way as it clattered into the security guards, splitting them like skittles. The Devil straightened himself, spying the open door a little further down the corridor.

"Nicely done," he said to Jill, grabbing her by the wrist and breaking into a sprint.

They charged past a collection of patients and staff, all astounded by what they had just seen. The shouts and cries from the trio of security men sounded in their ears as they broke out into the car park.

The Devil was running hard and he didn't see what hit him. All he knew was that something was wrong. The strange, almost unearthly grace with which he was taken off of his feet was a pleasant if odd sensation.

Everything came crashing back down to the ground quickly, as did he, and he learned to feel pain again. He made a groaning sound, or something close to it, and peeled himself off the wet tarmac.

"Jesus Christ, are you alright?" said Jill, helping him to his feet.

"I told you," he said, cracking his neck, "stop calling me that, you've got the wrong man."

When his senses returned to their normal, dulled selves, he saw that he had been hit by a car. The owner was climbing out of the seat but already The Devil could see who it was.

"Jesus Christ," barked Inspector Garfield. "I could have killed you there son are you alright?"

"Would you stop calling me that, please!" said The Devil, closing one eye at a time in an effort to clear his head. "He's probably tucked up safe in bed somewhere, away from lunatic policemen in their second-hand cars."

"Wait a minute," said Garfield. "I know you! You're that arsehole that tried to beat up a Polish waiter last night. Hey! Come here!"

"Run!" The Devil shouted and pushed Jill forward towards her car.

She unlocked the doors from a distance and they both shambled into the cabin. She fired up the engine and reversed the car quickly.

"Shit, shit shit," she said, slamming on the brakes as Garfield came speeding towards them. "Shit, now we're running from the police!"

"We haven't done anything," said The Devil. "Just bloody drive would you. Drive!"

Garfield banged on the roof of the car. He was shouting and cursing, his big red face beaming in the rear window. Jill did what she was told and pulled away as quickly as she could. The Devil watched the irate guards join the inspector, their yelling get fainter the further they drove away.

"Shit, shit, shit, this isn't good," said Jill, hopping up and down in her seat. "You know what this means, I'm going to be sacked. You've gone and got me bloody sacked, do you know that?"

"Relax," said The Devil, producing the crumpled death certificate from his pocket.

"Relax? How can I possibly relax? They'll be coming after us now, sending police cars to chase us down. I'm not a criminal, I'm a doctor for god sake."

He went to correct her but she beat him to it. She wagged her finger in his face.

"Don't say it!" she snapped. "Just don't!"

They sped through the morning traffic and started towards the western district of the city. The Devil was feeling smug again. Progress was being made.

His arrogance was such that he didn't notice the impossibly black spot in the rear-view mirror. Something was following them at a safe distance.

NINETEEN

Suburbia, where Humans went to die. Row after row and row of pristine houses, leafy avenues and a swarm of luxury cars and well manicured lawns. If The Devil hadn't been so sure he was still on earth, he would have thought he was back Upstairs.

Glasgow's suburban havens rolled past his window. Each abode looked prettier than the last. Some had apple trees in the front gardens, creepers climbing up the pebble-dashed walls and driveways wide enough to park double-decker buses. Every street was identical, almost down to the exact detail. He wondered how anybody found their way home at night.

It wasn't that The Devil was hugely opposed to this idea; he just hated the lack of creativity. And then there was what went on behind closed doors. Hypocrisy was all the way down there with laziness and a lack of responsibility.

As the keeper of the underworld and therefore privy to more secrets than most, he was never shocked by what went on in the suburbs of humanity. Newspapers and websites might have been filled with the appalling nature of housing estates and ghettos. If they only knew what was going on in the front rooms, kitchens, backyards and basements of the mock Georgian villas and mansions on the outskirts of every major city.

The Devil's surprise wasn't exhaustive. Every time a new case came across his desk, he always had to laugh a little. Businessmen caught with prostitutes in their wives' beds. Lawyers and doctors strangled at sex parties gone awry. Even drug barons and gangsters, hiding like wolves in sheep clothing among their middle class brethren, shot dead in their double garages, blood staining the monoblocking.

The list was endless. And he really meant it was endless. The sordid little lives of those who tutted at inner city crime knew no limitations. The only difference between them and the junkies on the street was trust. After all, who would believe a highflying attorney could be capable of being a heroin addict. The sharp suit and cognitive functioning just didn't match up with the image humanity had painted for its wasters and leeches.

But The Devil knew. The Devil always knew. The worst part about the whole pretence was that The Devil would always know. If there was one person in all of existence that shouldn't know about dark little secrets, it was him. Knowing that They didn't know made him feel good about himself.

"Here we are," said Jill, bringing the car to a halt.

A huge, red sandstone building stood at the end of a gravel pathway, obscured by eight-foot high hedges. The Devil resisted rolling his eyes, knowing he was right.

"You sure?" he asked.

"Yeah, here, look." She showed it to him.

"I can't read, remember." The Devil sucked on his tongue.

"Oh, yes, right. Sorry, I forgot about that."

He suspected that she hadn't forgotten. In the short time he had known Doctor Jill Gideon he was aware of a cruel streak within her. How far that streak went was anybody's guess.

"Hold on, wait a minute," she said, climbing out the car. "If you can't read, how come you knew that Anton Baggio's file wasn't in the police station?"

"I didn't," said The Devil, fastening his top button and dusting off his ill-fitting suit.

"But you said the file wasn't there. You told me we had wasted our time."

"I had to say something, didn't I?"

"Wait, what? You mean you had us break into the police station for nothing? Do you know how much trouble we could have gotten into?"

They started up the gravel driveway towards the front door. A large, black Range Rover sat near the garages, flanked by two colourful sports cars and a moped. The Devil quickly calculated how many could be in the large house.

"News flash Gideon," he said. "You're not exactly in the police's good books at the moment are you?"

"Fair enough," said Jill. "But that still doesn't answer my question."

"I had to double-check, to see if the cops had anything on Baggio before we did anything else," he said.

"How do you know they don't?" asked Jill, irritated. "You can't fucking read!"

The Devil rang the doorbell and fastened his jacket. The sound of footsteps thudded from behind the door and he smiled at his companion.

"Watch, shut up and learn," he said, his crooked face and yellow teeth looking slightly creepy.

The door swung open to reveal a tall, slender woman with long, black hair. She was wearing a figure hugging dress and matching heels, giving the impression she was towering over the two strangers at the door. She blew her nose politely and dabbed her eyes, makeup unscathed.

"Yes?" she said, voice hoarse.

"Good morning," said The Devil. "Inspector Garfield, Iain Garfield, I'm from the police archives department. May we come in Miss?"

The young woman blinked. She was unsure what to say or do. The Devil could see her mind working, the glint in her dark eyes enough to show him there was imagination there. She was grieving, mourning even, but she was still sharp, still suspicious. That let him know there may have been guilt somewhere within her skinny depths.

"Archives?" she asked, obviously buying time to think. "What do you want here, we've just had a family bereavement, I'm not sure we're up for helping the police at this tim-"

"Please, Miss…" The Devil interjected.

"Baggio," she said. "Therese Baggio."

"Miss Baggio, we understand that a gentleman from this house, a mister Antonio Baggio, has recently died," said The Devil. "We understand that there may be some records from our archives missing to do with a case some years ago involving the gentleman in question."

Therese rubbed her nose again. She looked back in the house and then to the pair standing on her doorstep. The Devil willed her to cooperate. He might have been human but he was certain there was still some of the old charm, wit and guile from his old self left in him.

"We would like to ask you some questions about your father was it?" he asked.

"Yes," she nodded. "Anton was my father."

"Then please, we promise we won't take up too much of your time. Just a few short questions and we can leave you be."

The young woman took another look back into the house. She was weighing up the possibilities, every eventuality. The Devil surmised there was more family in the house, she was wondering what they would say if a couple of police came traipsing in. But she needed to show she was honest, a good citizen, clear her father's name perhaps? The Devil wasn't sure, he couldn't be just yet. Just yet.

"Okay," she said, standing to one side. "But you must be quick. My family is here, we want to mourn in peace."

"Of course," said The Devil, stepping through the porch ahead of Jill.

The pair let Therese lock the door behind them and followed her down the long hallway of the house. A huge table sat in the middle of the hall, fresh lilies sending out a strong aroma from a vase on its surface. The Devil took a long, hard sniff and leaned in closer to Jill.

"Who's the ignoramus now?" he asked with a smirk.

"Yeah, yeah," she replied. "It's about bloody time you started pulling your weight. Up until now it's been me doing all the talking. You just do the fighting. And you're not very good at it."

"Please, this way," said Therese, extending a long, thin hand and arm towards an open door.

The Devil entered first, Jill close behind him. Inside, half a dozen people, all dressed in black, were sitting around in comfortable looking chairs and seats. They all had the same look about them, similar features, dark hair and matching eyes. The family of the deceased Anton Baggio had come together in the family home. As had the man himself.

The Devil took a microsecond to compose himself when he noticed the coffin in the middle of the floor. Inside, the trussed up figure of Baggio lay perfectly still. His face was the same as it had been on the operating table and in the morgue. Only this time the gory gizzards of his insides were not on show. Instead they were locked up safely inside an expensive looking black suit, shirt and tie.

"Who are you?" asked a chubby old woman, her curly hair silver beneath a black veil.

"Mama, these people are from the police," said Therese, moving to be by her mother's side.

"The police!" said the old woman. "What do you want? Can't you see my husband has just died."

"Yes madam, I can see that, quite clearly," said The Devil.

"Gently, gently," Jill said quietly, squeezing his forearm.

The Devil cocked an eyebrow. Reluctantly, he observed Jill's criticisms and took her advice. He put it down to shock. The sight of human bodies, lying in state, was still new to him. And he found the whole ceremony perplexing.

"Pardon our rudeness," he said, bowing a little. "My associate and I are from the records division of the police constabulary. We're here to talk to you about the deceased Mr Baggio."

The old woman began to sob again. Therese rubbed her shoulders while two men, sons or grandsons, looked awkward and stiff in their store bought suits.

The Devil took the opportunity to look about the room. There were photographs everywhere. Old, new, the same faces repeated time and time again. This was a close knit family, he surmised, typically Italian in almost every way.

He contemplated avoiding the necessary questions but remembered how difficult it had been to get to this stage. Running around, breaking into police stations and stealing from hospitals. If this was detective work, he didn't envy Garfield in the slightest. Not that he did anyway. Only the molluscs clinging onto damp rocks on damp beaches envied that man.

"I understand this is a very difficult time for you," said Jill, stepping forward and taking the old woman's hand. "But it's imperative that we find out a little bit about your husband's background."

She was very good. Even by The Devil's standards, Jill Gideon was proving to be useful. Resourceful and insightful, he was staggered that He had delivered such a productive assistant. And The Devil knew that her involvement was His doing. He just couldn't figure out why that was the case.

The old woman stared into Jill's eyes, her own awash with a deep, dark sadness. The last time The Devil had seen anything close to that level of morose was when he welcomed those do-gooders into Hell who thought they were destined for the Great Golf Course in the sky. Their misery was usually complete when he revealed to them that all the gossiping, back stabbing and false altruism were actually really bad for the soul.

"My poor Antonio, look at him," cried Francesca. "He is dead, he is dead and there's nothing I can do."

The two men beside her shifted uncomfortably. One of them choked back his own tears, desperate to retain at least some semblance of machismo.

"I know, this is a dreadful time for you, for all of you," said Jill. "We can't express just how sorry we are for your loss. You have to take time to remember Mr Baggio, to mourn him. That way you'll be able to cope and, eventually, through time, you'll be able to move on."

Francesca nodded glumly. Her daughter Therese did the same, the pair alike in so many ways, only decades distinguishing them from each other. The Devil's suspicions about it being a tight family had proven correct.

While he congratulated himself, his gaze slipped from the two women and fell on Anton's pale face. The sight of the dead human was making his skin crawl. He couldn't fathom why, it just seemed dreadfully unnatural. The stillness, the lack of noise, even the absence of movement. It was all incredibly odd.

"Mrs Baggio, I know this can't be easy for you, but I need you to think for me," said Jill, distracting him long enough to tear his eyes from the corpse. "My colleague and I understand that your husband may have been involved in an altercation."

"An altercation?" said Therese, pushing away her sadness. "What do you mean? My dad wasn't a trouble maker if that's what you're talking about."

"No, no, quite," said Jill, trying to diffuse her anger. "This altercation, it wasn't recent. It was quite some time ago."

She looked at The Devil for some help. He licked his lips and thought about how best to approach the matter.

"What was Anton Baggio doing forty years ago?" he asked.

Jill rolled her eyes again. She was making a habit of it. No sooner had he asked the question did The Devil realise he had gone in all guns blazing once again. Tact wasn't his strong point. On Earth at any rate.

"I don't understand," said Therese. "Forty years ago, what are you talking about?"

There was a hint of anger in her voice now, The Devil could taste it. The human psyche was a strange device. Evolution had sharpened it so finely, it could switch emotions quicker than anything else in existence.

"Forty years ago, what was he doing?" he asked again.

"What do you mean, what was he doing?" Therese fired back.

"I mean, where was he, where did he go, who did he kick around with?" asked The Devil. "That is what you people say isn't it?"

Jill shook her head disapprovingly. He shrugged, unperturbed.

"I'm sorry, what has this got to do with anything?" asked Therese, rising from her mother's side. "You can't come into our home and ask questions like this. I thought you were from the police. This can't be allowed surely."

"Miss Baggio, please," pleaded Jill. "We just want to get to the bottom of something."

"The bottom of what?" she shouted. "What are you trying to say?"

"Forty years ago, your father was stabbed!" shouted The Devil. "We want to know who bloody well did it. Alright? Happy?"

The sound of a grandfather clock ticking back and forth took over the sound of the room. The Devil and Jill stood beside Anton's coffin while his family remained dumbfounded. The two men were slack-jawed and Therese, their sister, looked equally shocked. Her face was a mixture of anger and fear, smudged with grief and stress.

"I don't believe what I'm hearing," she said breathlessly. "Really, I don't. This is unbelievable, literally unbelievable."

"Miss Baggio, please," said Jill again.

"I mean, you come in here, to my family's home and start asking questions about my dead father," Therese's voice was growing louder. "Then you say these things, these terrible, terrible things about him and expect us to help you. This can't be happening, seriously, it can't be. I'm going to wake up in a moment, aren't I? Get out! Get out of this house!"

"Madam, if you would just listen-"

"Get out of here!" her voice screeched loud enough that the window panes rattled a little. "Get out before I call the real police!"

"If we could just-"

"He never told anybody," came Francesca's brittle voice.

Immediately, the room fell silent again. Every pair of eyes fell on the old woman in the chair.

"What did you say?" asked The Devil.

"Mama, you don't have to say anything," said Therese.

"He didn't tell anybody, about what happened," said Francesca again. "He was too proud, too stubborn more like."

She smiled a little and wiped her eyes again. Lifting the black veil, she stared hard at The Devil and Jill. Her sadness was easing and she looked determined, more determined than anybody of her age should have.

"What happened?" asked The Devil.

"I'll tell you," said Francesca.

TWENTY

"Ah, love the dancin', I love it," said Anton, doing a few steps as he shuffled down the pavement. Beside him Francesca hurried along, her coat wrapped tightly about her, trying to keep out the November Glasgow air.

"Hurry up Antonio, hurry up," she said.

Anton wasn't listening to her, he had had too much to drink. Saturday night, out and dancing, that was how it had been since they first arrived in Scotland.

It was what everybody else did and, as immigrants, they didn't want to paint a target on their back. Go along with the crowd, that was what she had insisted. If they all went dancing, so should she. If they all talked about each other behind their backs, so would she. If they all jumped off a cliff, so would she.

Francesca wasn't stupid, she knew the score. She only hoped her young husband was just as bright.

"Would you come along," she said, her accent still hinted with twangs of the old country.

Anton smiled at her. The sulphuric orange of the streetlights made him look dangerous. But he wasn't, not her Antonio. He was the warm, loving husband who tried to earn as much money as he could for her and their children. He worked all hours of the day and night, just to keep them above the bread line.

It was hard, it was damn hard. Saturdays were the only day he ever took off. She hated dancing but she knew he loved it. That and appearances were all that drove her out of their home each and every week.

"I love you Franny," he said, his accent a little more ladened with Italian than her's. "I love you with all of my heart."

He ran after her, took her in his arms and spun her around. She let out a little giddy scream, her voice echoing off the old stone tenements that loomed overhead. He could still make her laugh, still make her scream. She was still in love with him too.

Their journey had been a long one, even though they were only in their twenties. Italy was on the decline and there was no work in their hometown of Sorrento. Even in Naples, the work for men and women had dried up. The whole place just wasn't the same, not after the war.

Anton had learned that Scotland was thriving. Britain, in a new age of freedom and wealth, was welcoming all sorts from the continent. Houses, business, the freedom to do what you liked. It was almost too good to be true. At least, that's what Francesca thought.

His father had been to Scotland, during the war. He had visited Glasgow, had said it was a city like no other. He had kept a biscuit tin with a piper painted on it under his bed, where the money was kept. Anton always knew where it was, although he dared not go near it.

He had always been a dreamer. It was up to her to keep him attached to the ground. Like a ball and chain around his ankle, she was the sense and sensibility to his wild fancy.

He had begged her to go, literally begged her. She had never known him to be so convinced of anything in all of their long years together. But she was pregnant with their first child. She wanted the child to be born an Italian, in Italy, in Sorrento, like she had been.

It wasn't to be. He was too ambitious, too impetuous. They boarded the ship and left their homeland, bound for a city called Glasgow. With no foothold on the language, no idea where to go, they landed in the city known as the Dear Green Place with next to nothing.

The years that had followed were tough. Setting up shop and a home in the Gorbals area of the city, three children down, they were starting to look and feel like natives. The kids even spoke like the Glaswegians, Italian a second language. If she had had her way, things would have been different. But that's not how it had gone, she had to accept that.

Now, as another Saturday night drew to a close, all she wanted was her bed. A cup of tea, a slice of toast and into bed. Up early for Mass in the morning, then back to work in the shop. Eat, sleep, worship and repeat. That was what a good wife did.

"I love you," he said again, whispering in her ear.

"I love you too," she smiled and they kissed, beneath the streetlights.

They started off again, down the Saltmarket and off home. Hand in hand, they walked in a happy, contemplative silence. That was, until another set of footsteps joined them.

Francesca didn't know what made her frightened first. Either the new arrival or the sense of impending disaster. It was a question that would plague her for five decades and one she would never get an answer to.

"You!" came a coarse voice from behind them.

Francesca tightened her grip on her husband's arm. Her heart sank and lifted all at once when she felt him stop.

"Don't," she said quietly. "Keep walking Antonio, keep walking."

"Hey, ah'm talking to you!" the voice shouted.

Anton turned around slowly, Francesca joining him. There, standing a few yards away, was a mountain of a man. Huge shoulders spread out like eagle's wings from beneath a tiny head. Hard light shone down on an even harder face, a permanent scowl etched beneath a heavy growth of stubble.

"You okay there pal?" asked Anton.

"Aye," said the stranger, breath disappearing away into the night in a cloud of condensation. "You alright?"

"Come on Antonio," said Francesca. "He's drunk, we don't need trouble."

"We'll leave you to it then pal," said Anton.

"Pal?" said the man, stepping forward a little, revealing more of his face. "I'm no pal of yours Baggio."

Francesca peered through the night and realised who she was facing. Tommy Rafferty, a local lunatic. The man was trouble, big trouble. When he wasn't in prison, he was doing everything in his power to get back in there. His family were just as bad. His wife was the talk of their street, coming and going at all hours with a face full of makeup. And the children were hoodlums, more than once had she caught them lingering about outside their shop.

"He's drunk Antonio, leave him," she said, hearing the fear in her own voice.

"Listen Tommy, I've got no problem with you, alright," said Anton, still standing his ground. "Me and the missus are heading home, you should too."

"Don't you tell me whit ah should and shouldnae be dain'!" shouted Rafferty. "You hearin' me?"

The thug took a step forward. Francesca felt her pulse quicken. She tried to pull Anton away but he wouldn't budge. Whether it was fear or bullish pride, her husband wasn't back down.

"Antonio," she said. "Come on, let's go home. Ignore him, ignore him."

"Hiding behind yer wife noo?" laughed Rafferty.

"You watch your mouth," said Anton. "Leave us in peace Tommy, I'm serious."

"Or whit?"

Rafferty's eyes were wide with a wild desire. Francesca saw anger in there, a sheer unquenchable rage that she knew would never be satisfied. This man was a lunatic and she wanted nothing to do with him.

But running away was not an option. Not anymore at least. Before she really knew what was going on, Anton had let her go and was charging towards Rafferty. All she could do was watch as her husband tried to get his retaliation in first.

There was a clatter and a thud and then Anton dropped. He lurched violently to the side and began to shake. Only then did Francesca's breath come back to her long enough for a shriek.

She raced forward and cradled Anton in her arms. She was crying but she had no time to acknowledge the tears. She turned Anton over and felt something wet touch her hands.

"What have you done to him?" she shouted at Rafferty.

The big man didn't answer. He simply turned and began walking the other way, head down, collar upturned, a shadow in the night.

"What have you done!" she screamed after him.

Anton made a groan. He was still alive, still breathing, still with her. She couldn't see his face, the light was too dim. She had to get him up and home, as quickly as she could.

"Come on," she said. "Come on my darling, come on."

Helping him to his feet, they began to stagger in the direction of their flat. They passed beneath more streetlights but Francesca was too afraid to look at her wet hand. She focussed on the street ahead, counting every step they took, scratching it off of the list.

Her world became a series of simple tasks. It started with every footstep, then it would be the stairs in their close and finally seeing what had happened to Anton. If she thought like that, she might stand a chance of saving her husband. Entertaining what might have happened wasn't an option. Cold, hard, clinical facts were what was needed.

They reached the front door of the tenement. Juggling her husband in one hand and her handbag in the other, Francesca somehow managed to salvage her keys. She unlocked the door and they tackled the challenge of the stairs.

Four storeys up, they clattered into the darkness of their hallway. Francesca took Anton into their bedroom and laid him down on the bed. With a trembling hand, she switched on the bedside lamp and prepared for the worst.

"I love you," he breathed. "I love you my darling."

She ignored him, concentrating on the large pool of blood that had stained his shirt around the abdomen. It was clear to her now that Anton had been stabbed. Rafferty must have been carrying a knife, unsurprisingly. The city was full of blade carrying lunatics and Rafferty was one of the worst.

She pulled off her coat and raced into the kitchen. The house was dark and cold but she was glad. The children were staying with a neighbour, she didn't want them to see their father like this. And it meant she could work quickly, quietly, with precision.

She boiled a kettle, took a pile of towels from the airing cupboard and opened a bottle of Dettol. Her makeshift medical kit was complete with her sewing box.

"Right," she said, mopping her brow of sweat and blood. "Let's get you fixed up."

She opened Anton's shirt and took in the wound. It wasn't big but it looked deep. Dark, almost black, blood oozed from it, running down the side of his gut. She said a quiet prayer, looking at the crucifix above their bed, and got to work.

The ordeal was painful for her but not nearly as agonising as it was for Anton. At one point she thought he was going to pass out. She had never seen him writhe in pain so badly. She had never seen anybody take such punishment. Her respect for her husband grew and grew with every passing moment of the operation.

When she was finished with her impromptu treatment, the clock had just struck two-thirty in the morning. She was exhausted, physically and psychologically. Never had their wedding vows, sickness and health, been so appropriate. Or literal.

She clapped her hand against Anton's forehead, hushing him to sleep. The wound was sewn together with black thread, the skin puckered and red. He would have a scar but it could be hidden.

"Rest my darling," she said to him quietly. "Rest now, you'll be better in the morning. Then we can go to the police."

Anton's eyes opened quickly. Like a man possessed, he sat up, holding Francesca's wrists.

"No," he said, over and over again. "We can't. We can't tell anybody anything."

"What? Why not? He should be in jail Antonio, that bastard Rafferty deserves to rot for this!"

"We won't tell a soul," he said. "We can't, we can't risk it."

"Risk what?" she asked, confused.

"I can't be known as a grass," he said, a sadness coming over him as he lay back down. "We would never have another customer Franny, we'd go out of business. We can't tell anybody, not even the children."

"And that bastard gets away with it!" she shouted. "You could have died Antonio, you could have died in the street if I hadn't got you back here…"

She trailed off as the tears finally got the better of her. Sobbing into her hands, she felt her husband's arms wrap about her.

She was beaten, at last, the emotion too much. The adrenaline was wearing off and she was glad it had lasted as long as it had. Without it, she didn't know what might have happened. She didn't want to know, ever.

If Anton didn't want to report Rafferty, then she would accept that decision. Like every other choice he had made that she had followed, she would be the good wife. He was her husband and the light of her life. Whatever he wanted, she would give to him if she could.

The Baggios fell asleep in each other's arms that night. Neither was sure what the future held for them. But for now, they were content and relieved that they still had each other.

Across the city, Tommy Rafferty made his way home too. He had already forgotten what had happened to him that night.

TWENTY-ONE

The Devil had to stop himself from yawning. He felt a nudge in his side and he sat up, blinking.

"He never wanted to let anybody know, ever," said Francesca. "He never told me why, not really. He never wanted to be known as a snitch but I always thought there was more to it than that. I guess I'll never know now."

The Devil didn't care, not really. He was hoping that Jill had been paying attention enough throughout the whole story. He had no time or patience for sentiment; it was almost as unbearable as pity.

The old woman blew her nose for the thousandth time and stared down between her feet. She was shaking her head, her face contorted with grief. Jill was looking at her. Her children were looking at her. Even the pictures on the mantle and tables seemed to be looking at her.

She was the centre of attention. The Devil wondered if she knew or even cared. He certainly didn't. Was he a little jealous? No, that couldn't have been it. So what was the odd grumbling in the pit of his stomach? Surely he wasn't emotionally empathising with this woman. Sure, her husband had just died but it happened all the time.

From the mightiest king to the lowliest peasant, Humans were born to die. For a species that had such great morals and high standards, they were killed all too easily, he thought. Add to that no concept of the wider nuances of time and space and the whole thing was like watching a child try to calculate Pi using only their fingers and thumbs.

He had had enough. Pushing himself up from the couch, his head spun a little. When he got his bearings, everybody was looking at him. That was more like it.

"I think we've probably been polite for long enough," he said. "I think we should be getting out of here, don't you Gideon?"

Jill drew him a disgusted look. He clapped his hands against his chest.

"What?" he said. "I'm only telling the truth. I thought you lot liked all that. You certainly never shut up about it."

"Excuse us, just for a moment please Mrs Baggio," said Jill, touching the hand of the old woman. "It's just a little stuffy in here for my colleague. We'll be right back."

She got up and began shoving him out the living room door. Down the corridor, she pushed him onto the front porch, her face scarlet with anger.

"Why are you being such a prick?" she spat. "Can't you see they're all really upset in there?"

"What? Why am I getting nailed to the cross for this, pardon the expression," protested The Devil. "We've got what we came for so let's go. What's the point in prolonging the agony for both of us any longer, she's just going to sit there and make herself feel worse. And then you'll feel worse for watching her, the family will feel dreadful for having let their mother get in such a state and I'll be so bored I'll have tried to gouge out my eyeballs."

"You're some piece of work, you know that?" Jill shook her head in disbelief.

"So you keep saying."

"I mean, honestly, you really are. We're brought up on stories about you, how you're bad, the worst person in the world. How you do terrible things to innocent people and that you're totally devoid of love and compassion. I'll be honest with you, I never really believed it. But meeting you, speaking to you, seeing what you were like in there with that grieving widow, it's pathetic. Family means a lot to some people, to most people in fact. You can't just go stomping around on people's memories. What gives you the right to do that eh? You ought to be ashamed of yourself."

The Devil puckered his lips. Jill was serious, he could see it in her eyes. She was passionate, aggressive, like a cat with its back up. How he kept angering her was nothing short of a miracle. He had tried for eons to get under the skin of people as badly as he was with her and failed miserably. He wished he could bottle it.

"Firstly, I'm not totally devoid of love and compassion, as you so eloquently put it," he said. "I love lots of things."

"Like what?" she snapped.

"Well, I like women with round, fully formed hips for one thing."

"What?" she squeaked.

"Oh yes, a nice Human female with big, round hips and a rump to match. Nothing gets me going more."

"Why are you telling me this?"

"You asked. You should see my secretary, you know, downstairs. My goodness what an arse that woman has on her. A murderer, she stabbed her husband in the neck with a kitchen knife. Unfortunate really, but hey, them's the breaks as they say. She's ruthlessly aggressive with her job and she has a rump steak to die for. Not literally of course but you get the picture."

Jill squeezed her eyes tightly together. She waved her hands about either side of her head. He was still getting to her, even by telling the truth. This was brilliant. Typical though, of Him, to let him do his best work when there was no way of capturing it for further use.

"I don't need to know," said the doctor. "I just don't want to know, okay. Whatever floats your boat, that's your problem, I've got enough of my own."

"Oh come on Gideon, don't act all innocent with me," smiled The Devil. "You're telling me you've never had a quick glance at the same sex, thought about it, maybe even, dare I say, fantasised about it? Come on, I know you."

"You most certainly *don't* know me, mate," she said, crossing her arms.

"Oh yes I do. I reckon you had a quick peak in the showers at school, just to see if it was something you might like, a little sampler from the *other* menu. There's no shame in it, it's just Human nature to be inquisitive."

Jill closed her eyes until they were like slits. She put her hands on her hips and sneered at him.

"How do you know that?" she asked.

"Know what?"

"Know that I used to look at other girls in school and ask myself the question."

"What question."

"*The* question. How could you *possibly* know that? I mean, surely you had better things to be doing with your time than what one Glaswegian public school girl was thinking."

"As much as it pains me to admit it Gideon, I didn't," laughed The Devil. "I just took a wild stab in the dark, an educated guess.

All the signs are there right enough, the nervous tension, the folded arms, the reluctance to accept your past. So I suppose it wasn't that much of a shot in the dark. Simple psychology my dear doctor, look it up sometime."

"Psychology, ha. Don't make me laugh," she said. "You don't know anything about me and I'd like to keep it that way."

"Of course I do," he fired back. "I know that you've obviously got a problem with families, that's as clear to see as a banana wearing a tropical shirt."

"What do you mean, *family issues*? I don't have any family issues."

"Yes you do," he remained firm. "The way you were acting in there, holding that woman's hand, being all sympathetic and such. It's the classic signs of somebody who either hates their own family or never had one. Overcompensating I think you lot call it. And that's before I even start with the whole medic thing."

"What medic thing?" she almost laughed. "What does me being a doctor have to do with anything."

"Really? You're going to deny that? Come on, don't insult both of our intelligences. Caring for others, trying to stave off death, making a difference to your fellow man. It's a cry for attention, a way of blotting out the past, whatever that may be. You don't have to be The Devil to work that one out Gideon. You're broadcasting on all channels with that one."

Jill was about start shouting at him when the front door opened. Therese Baggio appeared, looking concerned.

"Ah, Miss Baggio, good to see you," said The Devil, clapping his hands. "Thank you very much for letting us speak to you and your family, I'm sure it wasn't easy but your help has been greatly appreciated."

He reached forward and took her hand. Raising it to his crusted lips, he kissed her skin once, gently before taking a step back. The young woman looked equal parts surprised as she was beleaguered.

"I'm glad we could help," she sniffed. "But I still don't really know what all of this is about Inspector. I mean, surely this could have been done at a later date, over the phone or something. You didn't have to come to our house."

"Personal touch Miss Baggio, the personal touch," The Devil bowed. "Anyway, we'll be leaving you and your family in peace now. Please accept our deepest condolences at this time. Thank you."

"But I-"

"Thank you!"

The Devil turned Jill around and began marching her down the gravel path. He took three stops and stopped. Stroking his forehead, he shook one finger in the air.

"Actually, before you go Miss Baggio, there is one more thing," he said. "Nothing hugely important, just a confirmation really. The man who stabbed your father all those years ago. What was his name again please?"

Therese's nose wrinkled at the bridge. She couldn't tell if he was joking or being serious.

"Rafferty," she said. "Tommy Rafferty."

He clapped his hand to his forehead. Giving Jill a quick dart with his eyes, he smiled again.

"And whereabouts was Mr Rafferty from, you know, when he, well, had some black business with your father?"

"I don't know, I never met the man," said Therese. "But my mother always said he was local so I assume, the Gorbals, where they stayed."

"Of course, of course, Tommy Rafferty of the Gorbals, it makes perfect sense now," laughed The Devil.

"What are you doing?" whispered Jill. "Why are you doing this?"

"And just one more time please Miss Baggio, nice and loud, so we can all hear."

Therese was getting angry now. Her brow had lowered, the Italian blood in her veins getting fired up with a thousand generations of quick-fire temper. She snarled at The Devil.

"Tommy Rafferty from the Gorbals!" she shouted.

She hurried back into the house and slammed the door closed hard. The Devil was in hysterics, staggering about the driveway, clutching his sides. He wiped away a tear and looked up at the sky.

"Did you hear that?" he shouted. "Tommy Rafferty from the Gorbals! There's your killer! Easy, peasy, job done! Let me pack my bags and jet off to the sunshine!"

"Who are you talking to?" asked Jill, trying to calm him down.

"Who do you think?" he laughed. "I've done it, all done, sorted. Case closed, this Rafferty bloke, he's the one who killed Anton. All be it he wasn't exactly aiming to do so and it took him forty years to die but there you go, swings and roundabouts."

"Come on!" Jill said, dragging him down the pathway.

They got out to the street and she tried to force him into the car. He resisted, insisting on staying on the pavement. He was still laughing, his hands outstretched, head tipped back, a contented grin on his face.

Jill watched him the whole time. A young man walking his dog tried to get past but The Devil was in the way. He rounded the car, gave Jill a dirty look and then cursed under his breath.

"Wanker," he said, before carrying on up the pavement.

It was enough to break The Devil's hilarity. He dropped his arms to his side and stared up the street after the young man.

"What did he just call me?" he asked.

"He called you a wanker," said Jill.

"What's that?"

"Never mind, would you get in the car please?"

"I'm not getting in the car," he said.

"Why not?"

"Because I'm not for this earth for very much longer, that's why."

"Oh no?"

"No, I'm not. You see, that's the crime solved, case closed, the murderer found. That's all He wanted from me, I've done it now so I can go on holiday. And the sooner I'm allowed out of this monkey suit the better, it's beginning to smell."

He shrugged and smiled at Jill. The doctor wasn't quite as convinced. She leaned on the roof of the car and cocked an eyebrow.

"You sure that's you finished your shift?" she asked. "Only I was expecting a train of angels to come down and put a Hawaiian shirt on you and give you a grass skirt. You know, like they do on cruise ships."

"I wouldn't be seen dead on one of those bloody cruises Gideon, please," he snorted. "No, I don't think I'll be getting the whole majesty of Heaven treatment but something, anything would be nice."

He stared longingly up at the clouds. It was a normal day in a normal street. Nothing was happening. This wasn't right. Something had to happen, anything.

The Devil began to panic. He paced back and forth in front of the car, his feet slapping against the pavement. He trundled his fingers on his chin, pawing at the bristly hairs.

"This can't be right," he said. "This can't be right at all. I did what He asked, I found out who the killer was. You heard her, the old cow in the house, what she said. It was Tommy Rafferty, from the Gorbals, yes, that's who did it. It makes sense, it adds up, the wounds, the wounds Anton had, they match up with that, with what killed him, don't they?"

"Yeah, it seems pretty watertight," said Jill.

"You hear that!" The Devil shouted at the sky. "She's corroborated, she's a doctor! She knows what she's talking about! You heard the old woman in there! She said Anton was stabbed by Tommy Rafferty! T-O-M-M-Y R-A-F-F-E-R-T-Y! Now come on! Let me out of here, I've done all that you asked for, everything, down to the last detail! Let me go!"

All that answered him was the chirping of the birds in the trees. The quiet suburban avenue was unperturbed, uninterested. Even Jill, after all they had been through, looked quietly unbothered by his little outburst.

"I don't believe this," he said, clenching his fists into little balls. "I really don't believe this is happening to me, to *me*, of all people! What am I supposed to do now! I've done all that He asked of me. We had a deal, a bloody deal! He's not supposed to go back on deals, *I'm* the one who is meant to do that! Not only have I been right royally screwed in the arse with this, He's stealing my ideas! Can you believe it?"

Jill lifted her head from her hand. She blinked and shrugged, much in the same manner as he had done.

"What do you care what I believe or don't," she smirked. "I'm only Human after all."

She opened her door and climbed into the car. She started the engine and waited for him.

That was all he needed. Now the Human was scoring points off of him. Would the indignity ever end?

The Devil took one more glance up at the sky. A fleet of clouds blotted out the sun, drenching him in shadow. It was poignant and strangely relaxing. He felt like somebody was giving him a shoulder massage. Oh how he longed for simple little pleasures like that.

Instead, he had to go on suffering the ineptitude of the Human race and its dreadful transport vehicle. He pulled open the door and threw himself into the seat. Folding his arms, he made a loud huffing sound as Jill turned on the radio. The caterwauling that came out of the speakers was enough to make his ears bleed.

Everything was against him. And he knew who was responsible.

TWENTY-TWO

The light in Garfield's office was flickering. Ordinarily, he would have put this down to an electrical fault. The bulb's filament was probably ready to go. A quick change and everything would be back to normal.

Only things weren't normal, not anymore. Detective Inspector Iain Garfield was spooked and he didn't like it at all.

There had been days throughout his career where he had wondered if there was no end to the atrocities people would commit. From violent murders to rapes and molestations, being a policeman meant acting as a filter between different parts of society – mainly the good and the bad.

When he was a rookie, uniformed officer, he thought he had seen it all. Eighteen years old, fresh out of the academy, he had been thrown straight into the deep end. Given the east end of Glasgow as his beat, he had been mentored by some of the best coppers the city had ever known.

This was the seventies, when there were still ex-military men in service. They had captured machine gun nests in Normandy before tackling drug traffickers and drunks in civilisation. To them, shaking down a knife wielding skag-head in Easterhouse was breakfast. Garfield hadn't just looked up to them, he had idolised them.

Combined with his youth and exuberance to make a difference, he felt almost indestructible. Then the murders had started to filter in.

One by one that confidence was quickly stripped away. Responding to calls in housing estates where some of the worst acts of humanity were conducted did that to a young man. In his first six months he had seen more entrails, brain tissue and bodily fluid stained carpets than he cared to count.

But there was always a reassuring pat on the back. The old guard would be there to tell him it was alright, that he had a job to do. Seeing a man who had been ripped in half by a lunatic was child's play to them. When you had witnessed your friends get blown up by tank shells, it was easy to see how mundane a thing death could become. Garfield always understood that. And, more importantly, he respected it.

After the first year on the job, he learned never to be so cocksure ever again. It had stuck with him throughout his climb through the ranks. One by one as the old guard were pensioned off into retirement, he came to embody their ideas and toughness. He made sure he passed that on to the new recruits. It had steadied him when he needed it the most.

So why was he suddenly so frightened? He was in his own office, the door closed, the blinds down, nothing could get at him. Beyond the walls was a station filled to the brim with at least fifty officers. Then there were the cleaners, the canteen staff, the top brass of Scotland's law enforcement. He was no more alone now than he had ever been.

Yet something about the air didn't feel right. Something was wrong, the atmosphere, the temperature, the way the light was flickering. As a cop, Garfield had learned to trust his instincts. And right now, they were telling him he had to go.

He was blaming that strange pair who had been in the night before. The doctor and the yuppie. Something about them wasn't sitting correctly in his mind.

What was it he had said to him again? He was The Devil. No address, no belongings, nothing. Just the terrified looking woman who he had been brought in with. The whole thing smacked of strangeness but he had nothing to hold them on. The Polish bouncer wasn't going to press charges, that was certain. Opening up the books on an illegal migrant wasn't the best for anybody.

Then there was what the man had said. That made Garfield shiver.

"Your soul depends on it," he said aloud.

He had hoped hearing the words again might make him feel better. It didn't. If anything, he felt much worse.

The light flickered above his head again. He watched it settle and then leaned on his desk, his face in his hands. He had been at work for too long. Not just today but in general.

Nutters like this were always being pulled in off the street. Babbling about the end of the world or how Jesus loved them, Glasgow was full of modern day saints and sinners. So what was so different about this one? Why couldn't he get him out of his head?

A knock at his door almost made him faint. When he had started breathing again, Garfield stood up, heaving his gut over the lip of the desk.

"Yes?" he said loudly.

The door opened and Constable Jenkins appeared. He looked haggard, tired, without any sleep. His normally clean shaven face bristled with stubble.

"Jesus Jenkins," said Garfield. "You look like you've been dragged down Copland Road wearing a Celtic scarf."

"Aye sir, very good," said Jenkins, breathless. "We've got a man at the front desk who's asked to see you."

"Asked to see *me*?" said the DI, surprised. "Who is he?"

"Don't know sir, he wouldn't give us a name."

"Why does he want to see me then?"

"Don't know that either sir. He was pretty insistent though, kept asking for Iain Garfield."

"What do you know then constable?"

"I think he's foreign sir, speaks with a funny accent and he's… well…"

"Well?" probed Garfield.

"He's very tall sir, very large. I don't know, there's something about him that's, well, not quite right, if you know what I mean."

The alarm bells were going off in Garfield's mind. First had come that strange couple, then his paranoia, now this. The first thing he had learned at the academy was never to believe in coincidence. Do that and there would be trouble.

Every fibre of good sense was screaming at him to get out of the office, the building, the city. Whoever this was asking for him, they weren't good news.

But he couldn't refuse. In forty years of loyal service to the law, he had never backed down. This would be no different. It couldn't be.

"Alright," he said. "Send him up."

"Aye sir," said Jenkins.

"And Jenkins, don't let him out of your sight. I want you outside that door when he arrives and I don't want you moving until this stranger is gone. Is that understood?"

"Crystal clear sir. I'll fetch him just now."

The constable disappeared and left Garfield alone. He rounded his desk and stared blankly at the door.

He had never been a religious man; the notion had never taken him. His parents had both been Protestants, although they only behaved that way at three o'clock on a Saturday.

Yet he suddenly had the urge to pray. Not full blown down on knees and clasped hands praying. Just a little word with anybody who would listen. Before he could act on this desire, another knock at the door came and interrupted him.

"Come in," he said, retaining some authority in his voice.

Garfield had seen plenty of big people in his time but this man took his breath away. Stooping to get beneath the doorframe, the stranger cut a frighteningly imposing figure as he entered the office. The whole room seemed to shrink when he straightened up, extra space vanishing all around him like a black hole.

His attire didn't help. He wore a long, thick woollen black cloak and a wide brimmed hat that covered most of his face. He stood staring down at Garfield in silence while Jenkins floated around behind him.

"That'll be all constable," said Garfield, his voice barely louder than a whisper.

"Aye sir," said the policeman and quickly left the office.

Garfield then made his brain work again. He offered his hand out to the stranger who didn't budge.

"Detective Inspector Iain Garfield," he said. "Police Scotland; I understand you were looking to speak to me Mr?"

"My name isss Norman," said the man.

"Norman?" repeated Garfield as he reached for a pen and a scrap of paper on his desk. "And your last name Norman."

"Sssmith."

"Norman Smith, I see."

The inspector made sure to add a question mark at the end of the name. He wasn't buying it; this man didn't look much like a

Norman. In his experience, Normans were short men who wore knitted sweaters and cardigans and read the Telegraph. The giant clad in black standing in front of him wouldn't have looked out of place at a séance.

"Alright, glad we've got the introductions out of the way," he said, trying to keep the mood light. "What is it I can help you with Norman? My colleague informs me that you were looking for me in particular. But you'll forgive me for not knowing your acquaintance."

Norman didn't move. His head was bowed just enough that Garfield couldn't see his eyes or nose. All that appeared around the lip of the hat was a pointed chin that creased when he spoke.

"I have travelled a very long way to be here Inssspector," he said, his voice controlled but loud. "Those who I ssseek were here not two nightsss ago. You were visssited by these two peoplesss. A man and a womansss. Thisss isss true?"

A chill went down Garfield's spine and then raced back up it again. He let his mind wander from his guard and he could suddenly feel fear. A terrible, almost death-like fear strangled him and he had to lean backwards onto his desk for support.

"We get a lot of visitors Mr Smith," he said, sweating. "We're one of the busiest police stations in the country I'll have you know. What does your business concern with these two people?"

"You were visssited by them yesss?" Norman hissed.

Garfield knew exactly who this man was talking about. The Devil and Doctor Gideon. It made too much sense. He could hear his tutors at the academy screaming at him through time that there was no such thing as coincidence.

"Like I said, we get lots of visitors," he tried to make his voice sound firm but knew it was a losing battle. "Now if you want to tell me what this is all about, maybe I can help you son. But until then

I don't think -"

"I am not your ssson Inssspector," barked Norman. "And you sshould pay heed to my wordsss, they could be the lassst thing you ever hear."

"Are you threatening me sir?"

Norman took a huge step forward. Suddenly he was pressed against Garfield, his huge, black cloak smelling distinctly like rotten eggs. The inspector looked up at the face towering over him, the black hat still pulled down low.

"I do not deal in idol threatsss," said the stranger. "I am looking for a man and a womansss, they were here the night before lassst. You know who I want Inssspector Garfield, do not wassste anymore of my time."

A hand appeared from inside the cloak. It was deathly white, the same pallor as the man's chin. It reached forward, fingers like claws, moving slowly towards Garfield's throat.

The inspector panicked. He could hear his heart thumping in his ears. He was convinced then that this was the end. And if he was going to die, he wasn't dying in his office, at work, away from his family. A lifetime of duty was suddenly thrown to all abandon. Some things were more important than professionalism.

"Gideon!" he shouted.

Norman's hand stopped in mid-air. His head seemed to twitch beneath the brim of his hat.

"What?" he spat.

"Gideon, the woman's name is Gideon," said Garfield, eyes still trained on the claw.

"Where doesss thisss Gideon live?"

"I don't know."

"Where!"

"I can find out for you. But you have to let me go."

Norman considered Garfield's request. When he was ready, the huge man took one step back, giving the inspector room to breathe. He quickly rounded his desk and logged onto his computer.

Rattling on the keys, he accessed the fingerprint records of recent arrests. To his relief, he found who he was looking for.

"Here, I have her," he said, pointing at the screen.

Norman stalked around the desk and took his place beside Garfield. He leaned down to examine the screen, the sound of metal clanking and creaking leather coming from somewhere deep within his cloak.

"Doctor Jill Gideon," said Garfield. "She was brought in with an unknown man. We took her address and fingerprints. Looks like she lives in the west end."

The stranger leapt quickly over Garfield's desk and moved straight for the door. Without thinking, he called after him.

"Mr Smith," he said. "Don't you want to know about the man she was with?"

"No," hissed Norman. "I know him already. He isss who I ssseek, who we all ssseek and who will ultimately judge you for your actionsss here today Inssspector Iain Garfield. You ssshould never forget thisss."

Norman opened the door, ducked beneath the frame and was gone. Garfield sat for ten minutes, staring mindlessly at the walls. When he awoke from his trance, he had trouble remembering what had happened.

He looked at his computer screen and saw that it was blank. He could have sworn he had opened some files on recent arrests or something.

Putting it down to his lack of lunch and too much caffeine, he closed down his computer and packed up. He was going to go home, to his wife, to his family, his professionalism done for today.

"Jenkins, you there?" he shouted.

The constable appeared at the door and sniffed. He remembered where he was and who's company he was in and straightened his face.

"You smell that too?" asked Garfield.

"Aye sir, I do," replied Jenkins. "It smells like rotten eggs in here."

"Aye, that's what I thought too. Bloody strange, I don't eat eggs."

TWENTY-THREE

The Devil sat in the bathtub that took up most of Gideon's living room. He was livid, fuming, angrier than he had been in a long time. He steepled his fingers in front of him and stared out of the large bay window at the far side of the room.

The world was changing. One season was passing into another before his very eyes. The leaves that had once been vibrant and green were withering away, all of their colour replaced with a bronze crispness.

A wind was blowing through the branches, lifting the leaves from their homes, carrying them far away. Soon they would end up in the gutter, clogging up a drain. The rain would come and flood the street, causing all kinds of traffic chaos. Blood pressures would be lifted, tempers pushed to boiling point and it wouldn't take long to snap.

The Devil wondered why Humans put themselves through it every year. In this part of the world in particular, there seemed to be an underlying masochistic tinge to everybody. And he was the one who was supposedly sick.

The brief foray into future events had only distracted him from his anger. It hadn't totally dissipated it. In all his long years of service, he had never known betrayal quite like this. Even he thought He was incapable of something this underhanded.

What more did He want? All the boxes were ticked, he had even gone as far as making a bereaved daughter name her father's killer in the street. If that wasn't convincing enough then he didn't know what was.

And that was the real problem. If what he thought was the solution turned out to be nothing more than a red herring, then where could he possibly go next?

He had been extremely vague, as usual, when it came to the details of the mission. If The Devil had to spend an eternity confined to one human body, he was certain he would go insane. Or even more insane, depending on who he asked.

It made for a huge headache that he could do without. He let out a long, frustrated sigh and started grinding his teeth again. That was one aspect of his human form he didn't mind. There was something quite satisfying about hearing that crunch.

"Are you hungry?" asked Jill, coming in behind him.

"No, thank you," he said, pinching the bridge of his nose. "I don't much care for the cuisine here, it disagrees with me."

"Everything disagrees with you," she said, sitting down on the sofa. "I see you've made yourself at home in my bathtub."

"What? Oh this, yes, it's oddly comfortable. Once you get rid of the pulp fiction and trashy literature that was lining it, it's actually quite pleasing."

"Pulp fiction!" said Jill, lifting up one of the books The Devil had flung to the floor. "This is Jackie Collins I'll have you know."

"I'm sure it is," he raised an eyebrow. "But that doesn't make it any easier on the eye. Or the arse for that matter."

"Says the man who is illiterate."

He was going to retort with a barb but he didn't have the energy. Instead he slumped further into the tub and began drumming his fingers on his chest.

"What's the matter?" she asked, flicking through the pages of the book.

"Nothing," he said.

"Oh come on now, that's a little porky pie."

"Porky pie?" he sneered.

"A lie, a fib, an untruth," she smiled. "I suppose I should expect it from you but I have a feeling you're not exactly in the mood to be playing games right now."

"That may be the first observation you've made correctly all week Gideon."

"I try," she bowed. "So come on, tell me, what's wrong. Is it something to do with that little outburst at the Baggio's house?"

The Devil couldn't really blame his human companion for trying. In her world, what she had already done for him was already over and above what was necessary. While he didn't understand her motivations, he doubted he ever would, she was still entitled to ask him what was the matter.

But how was he expected to answer? How could he possibly put into words the cosmic battle he was raging against, forces she could never comprehend? Where to begin, first and foremost? Did he start at the very beginning, at the singularity point where existence simply blinked into life? Or should he fast-forward a few million years to when he was unceremoniously dropped into the body of a human being and told to solve a murder case.

Just thinking about it made his brain hurt. He was certain there was something medically wrong with him, regardless of what Jill said.

Instead of throwing his rattle from the pram he simply shook his head. He had a dreadful taste in his mouth too that was incredibly annoying.

"Yes and no," he said.

"How ambiguous," she laughed.

"When you get to my age Gideon, you learn that everything is ambiguous I'm afraid. There are always two sides to every story, sometimes more. I suppose that's what the problem is really."

"That there are more sides to the story?" she asked.

"Not necessarily more, just the right one."

He pushed himself up from the bottom of the tub and let his arms drape off the sides. He stared up at the ceiling and counted the spider's webs that clung to the large light directly above him. There were six.

"When you say the right one," said Jill. "Do you mean the right solution to your little arrangement with, you know, Him Upstairs?"

"That's *exactly* what I mean," sighed The Devil.

"Well, why don't you work through it logically, retrace your steps, outline your problems one by one and go through them individually and work out a solution. That's what we're taught to do at work."

"Don't you think I've tried that?" he asked.

"Well," she said expectantly. "Have you?"

The Devil went to answer. He could have lied but somehow he didn't see the use. Lying was only helpful when you could get something out of it. He might as well come clean.

"No, not exactly, not as thoroughly as you've put it," he huffed.

"There you go, now we're getting somewhere," she leaned forward with renewed energy. "So what's the problem? Start at the beginning; what's the biggest issue that's bugging you?"

He tilted his head so he could see her. Her eyes were bright in the dying sun. She looked almost childlike, her whole body quivering with excitement. Was this how Humans got their kicks? Revelling in the misery of others.

"You're enjoying this, aren't you?" he spat. "You're enjoying seeing me like this, like a half-shut knife. It's making you happy, isn't it?"

"A little bit," she smiled. "But come on, it'll help you, I promise. If we get it all out in the open then you'll be able to come up with something."

She bashed the side of the tub. The hard iron sound made his head hurt. He licked his lips and decided to play along. If for nothing else it would distract him for seconds.

"Very well," he sneered." The problem, my dear doctor, is that as far as I'm concerned, I've held up my end of the bargain with Him. We retraced Baggio's steps, found out what killed him and how it was inflicted and even got a name from the man's wife, telling us in great and boring detail what happened all those years ago."

"Right, so?" she asked.

"So? I'm still here!" he shouted. "I'm still here, sitting before you in this stupid bathtub of yours instead of lounging around on a beach somewhere sipping tropical cocktails that are full of sugar, eating copious amounts of red meat and being surrounded by half-naked women with dubious morals."

"And large bums," she added.

"And large bums, exactly," he sighed. "So there you have it, my problem."

Jill seemed to examine this for a moment. The Devil could see she was enthusiastic, he couldn't really fault her there. Although why she was so committed to his cause was still beyond him.

His scepticism was running rampant, as he had expected. She must have been looking for something that he could offer. Perhaps an easier trip in the afterlife when she inevitably came knocking at his door.

Not for the first time did he curse being unable to draw on his powers. Had he the ability, he would have called straight into the office and checked up on her file. There had to be something in there he could use. Shoplifting, not giving to charity, anything that would put her in the bad books just enough to earn a trip Downstairs.

The mysterious other half that she spoke so lowly of was a possible option. He had noticed that there were no photographs of this Geoff character. For a woman who was in the midst of a messy breakup he thought she would still have the odd image dotted about.

Now that he thought about it, there weren't a great deal of photos of anybody in Jill's flat. No family portraits, no nights out with friends. If he had been suspicious, and he was *always* suspicious, he would have thought she was hiding something. Perhaps that was where he would turn the screw.

Humans, he had always been led to believe, valued their relationships. It was what set them apart, supposedly, from the other animals in creation. Holding onto beliefs that were so far from the truth had become engrained in the Human condition. So why was Jill Gideon acting against that grain?

The Baggio household was like a museum. Hardly any wall space was free. If The Devil had been forced to look at one more ugly relative, he thought he might have exploded. But not here, not in Gideon's flat. Here it was barren, bare, like the thieves had been in and gutted the place.

"So what you're telling me is that you think you've done your job but you haven't been paid yet," she said, interrupting his train of thought.

"Yes, if you want to put it so bluntly, that's exactly what's happened," he replied.

"Well, what if you haven't done your job?" she asked. "What if, and bear with me on this one, what if the job you were supposed to do isn't in fact what you've done up to this point. Maybe there's a part of it you've still got to do?"

The Devil tried to work out what she was saying. When he thought he had a grasp of it, he snorted.

"But surely it's *all* been done now Gideon, I can't think what else there is left to do."

"Let's be honest here, He doesn't strike me as the type who would try to trick you, come on now. Even you would admit that."

"You don't know Him like I do."

"But still, it's not really in his CV to do something like that, even to the likes of you."

"Charming."

"Well, it's not, is it? Which makes me think that there's more to this than you've been thinking."

"Like what?" asked The Devil. "What else could possibly need doing?"

Jill squinted at the carpet. She was deep in thought again. The Devil considered getting up, teaching himself how to play piano and then come back to the conversation. These brainstorming sessions, he had noticed, were likely to take a long time.

"It must be something to do with this Rafferty chap that stabbed Anton," she said eventually.

"How did you come to that conclusion?" he asked.

"He's the only part of this equation that we're yet to speak to," she said. "It makes sense really, if you think about it. It's all very well finding out how Anton was murdered. We know how and when it happened. What we don't know is why."

The Devil could feel the energy returning to him. He was like a car being refuelled, the liquid revitalising his joints, his bones, his muscles and his brain. He stood up quickly from the tub and clambered out, racing for the door.

"Wow!" shouted Jill. "What are you doing? Where are you going?"

"To find this Rafferty man," said The Devil. "I think I might have cracked it!"

"I might have cracked it?" she asked. "Don't you mean me?"

"Yes, yes, whatever, semantics Gideon, semantics. If we lounged about in here arguing about all that tripe then we'd never get anything done now would we?"

"True, but I'd still like the credit."

"Is that pride I detect in you there doctor?" The Devil smirked. "Because that's one of the classics you know. That'll get you a first class ticket straight down into the lower levels."

"Bastard," she said.

"Thank you," he cackled. "I do try."

He raced out of the living room, Jill not far behind. She locked the door and headed down towards the street and her car. The light of the day was beginning to slowly ebb away. Only things were a little darker overhead than anywhere else.

TWENTY-FOUR

"Surely there must be an easier way of doing this Gideon. I mean, what is this, the dark ages?"

A severe looking woman with crescent moon spectacles whispered something inaudible at The Devil. He feigned apology and cursed under his breath.

Since the dawn of time, Humans had been obsessed with cataloguing. Libraries were an embodiment of this traditional obsession. Some of the greatest buildings that had ever been created were used to store dusty old books and out of date computers. It was a testimony to just how much the Human race loved to keep things in order.

This building in particular was as gaudy and triumphant as they came. High ceilings, marble floors, grand looking windows. It was a cathedral to law and order.

The Devil had no time for any of this. It was yet another example of how they focussed on all the wrong things. Now he found himself amongst miles and miles of paper, intricately stored away so that nobody could ever find anything.

"Do you have any idea how many trees needed to be cut down to create something like this?" he said, pointing at the large stack of files Jill had pulled from a mahogany cabinet.

"Would you be quiet please," she said.

"You're talking hundreds of acres. And you wonder why nature goes bat shit crazy with hurricanes, earthquakes and famine. You're chopping its lungs down tree by tree all so you can keep a track record of who voted for who in some bygone election."

"Actually, if you let your mouth stop moving and your brain start thinking, you'd realise that this is the best way to go about getting our job done."

"Oh really?" he asked. "And how's that?"

Jill stood up. She pushed her hair from her face and sighed. Keeping her voice low but firm, she was losing patience with her companion's loss of patience.

"This is an electoral register," she said, waving a stack of papers in his face. "It has the full names, addresses and telephone numbers of people who registered to vote for the general election a few years ago. Following me so far?"

"Despite the poor attempt at sarcasm, yes I am, unbelievably," The Devil sniggered.

"Now rather than breaking into police stations and getting into fights with Polish bouncers, this will provide all the answers we need when it comes to finding our Mr Tommy Rafferty."

The Devil had stopped following. He thought he was disguising his confusion well but Jill saw through it easily. She sucked on her tongue and ran a finger down the lengthy list of names.

"What age was Anton Baggio?" she asked.

"Seventy-something," replied The Devil.

"Alright, so that means we're looking for a man roughly around the same age, yes?"

"Yes."

"That means he would be a pensioner now, just like Baggio, that make sense?"

"Perfect."

"And what social demographic are the highest represented when it comes to registering to vote?"

The Devil could feel his Human tendons flexing in his cheeks. He hated being slow on the uptake. That was why the Renaissance happened when it did and not two thousand years earlier.

"Well, have you found him?" he folded his arms across his chest.

"I would have if you gave me a chance to look."

"Well get cracking then, we haven't got all night."

"Fine then."

Jill bent back over the desk. The Devil watched her, took one look at all the papers she still had to check and grew bored. He began to wander, whistling as he went.

"Sssssshhhhh," said the severe woman again.

The Devil ignored her. Librarians deserved the very worst of his treatment. Unfortunately they were somewhat of a guilty favourite of Him. A lifetime dedicated to filing and bureaucracy seemed an unlikely path Upstairs. But that was how it was.

He was convinced that it was a slight dig by Him. Upstairs ran smoother than clockwork, all the paperwork filed neat and tidily on time. Unlike in Hell where it all seemed to be laid at Alice's desk. She did a valiant effort in getting on but there was only so much she could do.

"Ah Alice," he sighed quietly. "I could be doing with you right now."

He stopped at a bookshelf and began peeling off the coloured labels on the spines. Mixing them all up, his mind drifted back to his home.

Missing Hell was reserved to him and him only. It was part of his professional prerogative, being its overlord and ruler. Any demon or escaped soul that claimed to miss Downstairs was quite obviously lying. That was probably why they were there in the first place.

But The Devil did genuinely miss the place. It wasn't up to much and the equipment was mostly faulty but he had grown accustomed to it over the eons. His office, his desk, Alice, it all added up. Maybe he was getting nostalgic in his old age. Or maybe he had spent too long as a Human. Either way, he had developed a longing to be back amongst the fire, brimstone and wonderfully cutting edge technology.

"Found him!" shouted Jill, her voice echoing around the draughty library.

The Devil snapped out of his daydream and raced over to the desk. The doctor was smiling, pointing at the name on the sheet.

"No use asking me to check it Gideon," he said. "I can't read."

"I know that, just a force of habit," she said.

"Well? Where does this man of the moment live?"

"Looks like it's still in the Gorbals," she answered. "In one of the high-rise flats. Unless, of course, he's moved since he registered."

"There's always a chance I suppose but it's all we've got to go on at the moment."

He leaned forward and ripped the page from the file. Scrunching it up and looking around to make sure nobody had seen him, he stuffed the paper into his ill-fitting suit pocket and grabbed Jill.

"Let's rock and roll, as you lot say."

"I don't say that," she said.

"Well maybe you should start to."

They hurried past the severe librarian and across the large lobby towards the main doors. Before they could reach the exit, a loud bang stopped them.

"What was that?" asked Jill.

"I don't know, come on."

They took another step forward and there was a second bang. A third step and a third bang. With their fourth step, the main doors ahead of them slammed shut, completely of their own accord.

"What's going on?" she asked, looking about the expansive library.

"Oh shit," said The Devil. "I had a feeling something like this might happen."

"Something like what?" she was panicking now.

A dark cloud blotted out the light that was pouring through the tall windows. One by one they were overcome with shadow. Only the dim electric strip lights dangling from the roof kept the place illuminated. It appeared as though night had fallen in a matter of seconds.

"You have to tell me what's going on here," said Jill, grabbing The Devil by the lapels. "If this is something to do with you, you *have* to tell me."

"Everything has to do with me Gideon, don't you understand? I'm the ying to His yang, we're anything and everything all at once."

"I mean *this*!" she shouted. "Why's it suddenly gone dark? What's happened to the doors? It's like something doesn't want us to leave."

"Yes," said The Devil. "You could say that."

A low rumbling began beneath their feet. Jill took a step back as a huge, jagged crack formed in the marble floor. She screamed and reached out for The Devil.

"Don't move!" he shouted. "Just stay where you are!"

Pillars of dust began to drop from the ceiling. The severe librarian was running around, her hands waving in the air.

"Madam, if you would get underneath a table or something, you might feel a bit better!" he shouted.

"How is that going to help?" shouted Jill.

"It won't but she'll think it will, false hope and all of that."

The librarian ran as fast as she could and disappeared

somewhere into the back sections, lost among cookery and self-help. The Devil had no time to worry about her, there was a more pressing problem.

The rumbling grew louder and louder until it was deafening. The ground was shaking violently, the crack widening enough that a huge gulf had parted between the two companions.

Taking a short run up, The Devil leapt across the gap and skidded to a halt beside Jill. She helped him back to his feet as they cowered from the falling dust and masonry.

"What's happening?" she asked. "It's like there's an earthquake or something? But we don't live on a fault line; Glasgow's nowhere near a fault line! What's going on?"

"I can assure you Gideon that this is no earthly doing," said The Devil, shielding his eyes from the grit and dirt.

"Then what is it?"

The rumbling continued for a few moments, shaking the foundations of the library to its core. Then it began to ease a little before stopping altogether. The tremors beneath the cracked and broken floor also halted and The Devil and Jill were left to look about the ruins.

"Bloody hell," she gasped. "That was terrible."

"Yes," said The Devil coyly. "It was."

"You know what this is and you won't tell me," she said. "I thought we were partners."

"What on earth gave you that idea Gideon?" he said, edging his way around the outer wall, his eyes locked on the gaping chasm in the floor.

"Well, I thought, you know, after all that we've been through."

"Please, don't get sentimental with me just now Doctor, it's hardly the time or the place."

"But the earthquake has stopped."

"I told you, that wasn't an earthquake. In fact it was pretty much the furthest thing from a natural occurrence as you could imagine."

"What?"

He grabbed her hand and moved them both slowly towards the main doors. Carefully choosing his steps, he eased himself and Jill over broken stonework and tributary cracks in the marble.

They reached the huge, mahogany doors and he tried to open them. When they wouldn't budge, he tried again a little harder.

"They're locked," said Jill.

"I know," he dusted off his hands. "But I thought I'd better try anyway. I think we should be going now, in fact, I insist on it."

"Why? What's happened. Who locked these doors? You have to tell me."

"I don't *have* to tell you anything and believe me when I say that you really don't want to know what I think might be coming."

"Why not?"

"Because if I'm right, which I *always* am, then something rather nasty is going to be spewing out of that hole in the floor very, very soon."

An odd gargling noise emanated from the chasm. It grew in strength until it sounded like a voice. It wasn't a human voice, Jill could tell that straight away. It was too deep, too low, too powerful. It sounded like it was groaning or even yawning.

"Oh shit," said The Devil.

He furiously started thumping the door, shouting for help. Jill was watching the hole, transfixed by the sound coming up from its depths. She started walking towards it, shoes crunching on the debris littered about the lobby.

The nearer she got the more tempted she became. It was like she was being drawn in against her will. But she wanted to go, she couldn't help herself. Every ounce of good sense was telling her to turn away, help The Devil, escape the library. Yet she couldn't resist, the pull was too great.

When she was about a yard away, a fountain of black liquid began gushing out of the crack. Like an oil well, it sprayed up to the roof but didn't come down. Instead it spread over the damaged stone and carvings, wet and shiny but impossibly dry.

Jill held out her hand. She wanted to touch the fountain, to feel it, to hold it, to make it seem more real. The closer she got, the more detail she could see. It had tiny fragments within it, all shooting up at a great speed towards the ceiling. It was like dark silk, smooth and soft. She could see her reflection in its surface. All she wanted to do was hold it.

Her fingers were only an inch away when something grabbed her. The force was strong enough to pull her back. The spell was broken and she returned to the room.

"What... what happened?" she blinked.

"Nothing, thankfully, although it might have had I not been here," said The Devil, panting.

"What is that thing?" she asked.

Long tendrils were stretching out from the top of the geyser. They looked organic, the ends probing at the stone, the walls, the columns that supported the ceiling. It appeared as if the mass was learning about its surroundings.

"It's beautiful," she said.

"Oh yes, very beautiful, now come on."

"What, no, I want to know what that is. I've never seen anything like it, what is it? Tell me!"

"We have to leave right now Gideon, trust me. If that thing touches you then you'll know all about it."

"Why, what happens if I touch it?"

The Devil ground his teeth. Humans could be so difficult sometimes. Their ingenuity and curiosity were what set them apart from all the other animals. But it made them almost impossible escape partners.

"Look, if you can imagine the worst hangover you've ever had multiplied by a million, that'll about sum up what the first thousand years will be like for you if you touch that thing," he said, frustrated.

"Really?" she almost sounded enthusiastic.

"And there won't be a day when the hangover is finished, that's for certain. After the first few millennia, it really kicks in and you'll know all about it."

"But it's so beautiful," she said.

"Famous last words Gideon now help me with this door!"

While she continued to watch the fountain consume the room, The Devil hauled her to her feet and dragged her back to the main doors. He started lifting the handle, trying to raise it as far as it would go. Sweat was pouring down his forehead and cheeks, his bruised face crimson with strain.

"Help me!" he screamed.

Jill began doing the same with the other door. She kept looking over her shoulder at the blackness. It was stretching out across the floor now, long tentacles probing and feeling diagonally from the chasm.

"It's coming towards us," she said.

"Oh shit!" said The Devil. "Help me with this one, if we can break the handle we might be able to get into the lock!"

"Wait a minute, I might have an idea!"

"Hurry up Gideon!"

She felt around her ponytail. The Devil's eyes got wider.

"What are you doing?" he bellowed. "This isn't the time to be fixing your hair. We're going to die!"

"Would you just calm down!" she barked.

Pulling a Kirby grip from the back of her head, she kneeled down and started fiddling with the lock. The Devil kept trying to jar the handle but it was no use, the old brass knob too robust and secure.

He stopped and knelt down beside Jill. Trying to peer into the lock, she pushed him out of the way. She pulled another Kirby grip from her ponytail and forced it into the lock hole. Clicking and scratching, howling and moaning, The Devil felt like he was inside a washing machine.

He glanced back at the black mass. It was getting closer, edging agonisingly close to them. He kicked bits of rock and broken masonry towards it, hoping to slow it down. If anything, it sped its progress up.

"Now would be a good time to open the doors Gideon. Now would be a really good time!"

"Hold on, hold on, I think I've -"

The lock clicked and the door swung open. Bundling his companion out into the street, he slammed the door behind him, narrowly avoiding the black mass.

A terrible howl erupted from inside the library before the rumbling started again. He leaned against the door, his eyes closed, gasping for breath.

Outside, the sky began to get lighter. The concentrated darkness around the massive, ornate structure of the library began to retreat. When the early evening embers returned, the howling, rumbling and tremors beneath their feet stopped.

"That was close," said Jill, fixing her hair. "Now do you want to tell me what the hell that thing was or will I just have to guess?"

The Devil ran a hand through his sweaty hair. He snorted and pushed himself off the door, dropping down the steps that led to the main road.

"Well?" she shouted after him.

"Wait a minute!" he snapped. "I'm checking something."

He stopped at a large bronze plaque that had been turned green through time. He spotted a small, ornate cross in the top right hand corner, above the inscription and date. He shook his head.

"I should have known better," he shouted back to Jill. "I should have bloody known better."

"Known better about what?" she asked, joining him.

"Consecrated ground," he said. "This library, it was built on ground that's been blessed. That's why it almost got us."

"What was it? You still haven't told me."

"I think the more important question is why Gideon, try to keep up."

"I'd keep up if you bothered to tell me things!"

The Devil put his hands on his hips and stared up at the huge library ahead of him. That had been a close call, he had endangered them both unnecessarily. The closer he got to completing his task, the riskier it was becoming. He had to stay sharp, stay alert and most importantly stay clever.

"I know how you Humans like metaphors so I'll give you one right now," he said, turning from the library and marching towards the car. "When you were younger and you went out for a night out with whatever spawn you call your friends to a discothèque or whatever."

"A nightclub," Jill scoffed. "They haven't been called discotheques for about a million years."

"And your mother always wants to know where you are," he continued, ignoring the jibe. "It's only natural that she'll start to worry if you haven't been in contact for a while. So she'll, understandably, grow concerned and look for as much information as she can."

"You're trying to tell me that that black thing in there was your *mother*?" she sounded shocked.

The Devil groaned and rolled his eyes. This was why he hated speaking like a Human. It was far too ambiguous and needlessly complicated.

"No, not exactly," he said. "But the principle is still the same. It seems that my friends in low places are growing ever more concerned about my whereabouts and they want me back. Only I think if it continues this way then we're all in very, very big trouble."

"How big?" she asked.

The Devil looked at her. He didn't smile, he didn't smirk and he certainly didn't laugh. His lopsided face was as grave and serious as he could make it.

"You don't want to know," he said.

TWENTY-FIVE

The Devil and Gideon sat in their car. From there, they had a clear view of the whole street. It was late and the whole place was dark and damp.

The smell of fried food clung to the air of the cabin and The Devil choked back a little sick. In his time on earth, he had very quickly come to hate Humanity's obsession with frying. Any goodness that the food they ate was totally drained, replaced by the same, concrete taste. He sucked on his tongue loudly and lowered the window a little.

"What?" said Gibson, tucking into a fish supper.

"Nothing," said The Devil glumly.

"No, seriously. What is it?"

"That food," he nodded down at the takeaway box. "You shovel that into yourselves every day and don't think about its consequences."

"Of course I do," said Jill, licking her fingers. "I'm a doctor, I can't help but think about it. But you'll forgive me if I treat myself just this once, it's been a bit of a long day and I think I deserve it."

"Savages," he shook his head.

"Oh come on," said his companion. "Are you trying to tell me that all cuisine in Hell is better than this? I don't think so somehow."

"It couldn't be much worse," said The Devil casually, watching the darkened entranceway of the tower block across the street. "Then again, eating raw sewage wouldn't be as bad for you as that garbage."

"I disagree," said Jill. "Here, why don't you try some?"

She offered the box but The Devil wasn't interested. He flinched clumsily and a handful of chips scattered into the foot well.

"Shit," said Jill, scrambling for her food.

"Leave it would you, come on, focus," said The Devil.

"I'm just trying to pass the time, that's all," she said. "I've heard stakeouts can take forever. And besides, we don't even know if this Tommy Rafferty is still alive."

They fell into an uneasy silence. The case was beginning to get on The Devil's nerves. More accurately, it was his inability to solve it that was driving him mad.

Having powers that were beyond the comprehension of most creatures in existence was one thing. Being unable to use them was another. And to make matters worse, he was trapped in a vessel that itched, stank and made everything ten times more difficult.

"So what's Hell like then?" asked Jill, drumming her fingers on the steering wheel.

He looked across at her. She seemed genuine enough. Her experience in the library hadn't left any residual trauma. Sometimes when Humans came into contact with beings from other realms, it left their minds like scrambled eggs. Not Jill Gideon though. If anything her curiosity had been peaked by the experience.

"Don't ask," replied The Devil sullenly.

"Honestly?"

"Honestly."

"What, is it one of those situations where if I ask, I'd die or something?"

"No, nothing like that," he sighed.

"Then what is it then?"

"I can't be bothered," he said flatly.

"Eh?"

"I can't be bothered going through it all with you Gideon," he shrugged. "If you want to talk about inter dimensional transportation, philosophical and moral dilemmas beyond that of anything you're ever likely to even comprehend then sure, I'll happily chat away. But if not then shut your pus, as they say up here."

"Suit yourself," she huffed.

The Devil was unsure if he had offended his human companion. He wasn't sure if that bothered him at all. Ordinarily he wouldn't have thought twice about shooting somebody down, quite literally sometimes. But this whole experience was leaving its mark on him. Whether he liked it or not.

"Do you mind if I put on some music?" she asked, reaching for the radio.

Before The Devil could answer, the human had flipped the switch. The car suddenly came alive as the speakers cranked into operation. It didn't take long before Gideon was thumping away on an imaginary drum kit.

"Yes, yes, yes!" she said. "That's more like it, a bit of Led Zeppelin. I used to love these guys growing up. My mum, she met my dad at one of their concerts, my step-dad that is. Good times."

The Devil rolled his eyes. He counted down the seconds until the inevitable question was raised. In five, four, three, two.

"Hey, is it true?" she asked, the guitar solo of *Black Dog* squealing out of the darkness.

"Is what true," groaned The Devil.

"That, you know, Led Zeppelin sold their souls to become rich and famous."

"What do you think?"

"I don't know," said Jill. "I guess so, maybe. I didn't give it much thought until, you know, I met you."

The Devil could have been cruel and ignored her. He could have reverted back to his old ways and toyed with the doctor. She wasn't dim, far from it. But he still knew how to get her. He always knew how to get Them.

Yet, bizarrely, and for reasons he didn't quite comprehend, The Devil was feeling sentimental.

"You asked about Hell," he said, clearing his throat and sitting up a little. "Well, I've got better music playing for one thing."

"Better music?" asked Jill.

"Yeah, all the hits," smiled The Devil. "Zeppelin, AC/DC, a bit of KISS, it's a hard rock and heavy metal music festival all the time Downstairs."

"Really?" her eyes shone in the darkness, like a child on Christmas morning. "All of the time?"

"Twenty-four hours a day, seven days a week. We never close, on the airwaves morning, noon and night."

"Bloody hell," Jill whistled. "Now *that's* my kind of place. What about, you know, the alternative?"

"Alternative?" The Devil asked.

Jill tilted her head towards the ceiling. The Devil puckered his lips, he wasn't going to lie, not this time.

"It's pretty quiet," he said. "There's this whole country and golf club vibe going on. I don't know where He got that from but it really pisses me off. Everybody so keen to help. They flap around you, make you feel even more uncomfortable. It's like having to be on your best behaviour *all* of the time."

"And that's a problem for you is it?" Jill smirked.

The Devil looked at her through the darkness. Was that some

attempt at humour from his companion? If so he didn't recommend her giving up the day job.

"So you've been up there then?" she probed.

"More times than I care to remember," he answered. "That's another thing Humans can't understand. The fact that me and the Big Man are actually on good terms, relatively speaking. We're just two heads of departments on the opposite sides of the building."

"That's an odd way of looking at it. I can think of more than a few groups of society who would disagree with you."

"Human society, Gideon, Human society. Everybody else is fine with it, it's just you lot that can't quite grasp the concept that good and bad aren't so diametrically opposed."

He wondered if he believed her. He wondered if he was telling the truth. Like so many questions in the universe, The Devil couldn't ever be certain that what he was saying was being understood fully. Miscommunication had led to the downfall of so many for so long. One wrong word and it was game over.

"Anyway, Upstairs, yes, it's calm and peaceful but it's all a bit too quiet for my liking. Makes my tinnitus flare up."

"You have tinnitus?"

"I do."

"So what, they don't have any music playing Up There then. What if you're mad keen on your music though? Like, what does Beethoven do all day up there?"

The Devil let out a raspy laugh. He smiled, broadly, touched by Jill's innocence.

"Firstly, old Ludwig is Downstairs with me and he's a right good laugh. Loves the darts, can't get enough, always knocking on doors going 'Come out for a game of darts, just a quick frame.'"

"No way," said Jill, her mouth hanging open. "I don't believe that for a second."

"It's true, keeps everybody up at night with it," The Devil continued. "But secondly, and most importantly Watson, you've got to remember that music has never been on His agenda, not really. It's a distraction, something that you humans have busied yourselves with over the eons."

"But what about hymns and that?" she asked, pointing a finger. "Surely anybody that wrote a hymn gets a ticket in. No?"

"Occasionally, maybe," said The Devil, thinking. "But it's usually because they've been extra good somewhere else in life. Enough to eclipse any financial or anti-altruistic gain they've received from the music."

"Blimey," breathed Jill. "The more you know eh?"

"Why do you think so many musicians 'find religion'? Compared to other industries you lot have got going. The percentages per head must be through the roof. Don't ask me though, I'm not very good with numbers."

"Six, six, six is about the level of it then," she nudged him in the ribs.

"Quite."

"So, if making music is bad, that means you must have a kick-arse line-up down there then yeah?"

"Yup."

"And it's on all the time?"

"All the time," said The Devil. "Forever."

"What do you mean *forever*?"

"I mean *forever* forever."

"As in, all the time?"

"All the time."

"What if you don't want it to be on?"

"That hardly matters Gideon," smiled The Devil. "Remember, it's supposed to be punishment, it's not a jolly-up to Magaluf or wherever you philistines go to these days. It's on all the time, day and night, sober or hungover. In fact, I like to crank up the speakers in your room when you're hungover, you know, just to make you that little bit more uncomfortable," he cackled.

"Hungover? Is there booze?"

"Gallons of the stuff," said The Devil. "Remember, most of the original brewers are Downstairs too."

"Bloody hell fire," said Jill, shocked.

"Well, that's the point," said The Devil.

"So all you do is have one big party, am I right?"

"It's not quite as simple as that," The Devil eased himself a little, his buttocks numb from the sitting around. "You see, it's sort of like a prison down there, but more of a prison of the mind. After a while, quite simply, people get used to the same old same old. You can have a raven peck out our liver every day and sure it's a bit painful, but after the thousandth time it happens, it's no big deal right? The trick is being able to continue that misery for all of time."

Jill looked confused. The Devil wasn't surprised. The human mind was a talented creation and it had come on leaps and bounds over the centuries. However, being able to conceptualise its own demise was still beyond it.

"I see," she said bravely. "A grim future then."

"For some," The Devil stretched and rolled his shoulders and neck. "Not everybody has to end up Down There. Some people deserve it, others don't. Some people have a great time, ironically, but what are you going to do eh?"

"You said it."

The Devil turned back towards the main entrance of the tower block. There was a gang of youths loitering nearby, their dialect too strong for him. He realised that they could be there all night waiting for who they thought was Rafferty, only to be disappointed.

He unfastened his seatbelt and pushed open the door. Jill jumped a little beside him.

"Where are you going?" she asked.

"I'm finished with this waiting game," he said. "I'm going up to his flat. You can stay here if you like, I'm not hanging around here any longer."

"Wait, hold on a minute."

She quickly followed him, making sure she locked her car. Skipping across the road, she kept her head down as they passed the gang.

"That your burd mistur?" shouted one of them. "Tell her to giese a pictur."

"Don't fancy yours much!" yelled another.

"Oi, giese some change for fags would ye?"

The Devil stopped but Jill kept him going. It wasn't until they were in the lobby, the light flickering above them, that he got a chance to speak.

"Why did you keep us moving?" he said. "Those little shits were spouting off at you."

"Because they're just that, little shits."

"Exactly! They need to be taught some manners."

He went to leave but she stopped him. Pulling him back into the lobby, she tried to explain the nuances of Glasgow culture.

"Just leave it," she said. "Believe me, they're not worth the trouble."

"I know but -"

"No buts this time! You don't know what you're dealing with there."

"Oh come on," he laughed. "How dangerous can they be?"

"Did you see how many there were? Six, seven maybe, and that's just the ones we can see. I've worked enough shifts in A&E

to know that every single one of them will be carrying a knife, a blade at least six inches in length. And these little idiots aren't scared of using them on each other so what chance do you think you would stand eh? You'd be cut to ribbons."

"I really don't think it's that -"

"And do you know why?" she squeaked. "Because they don't have anything else. They don't have a future, they have nothing to get up for tomorrow. So what's one more stranger stabbed in the chest, the back, the eyeball. It happens, believe me. You think us Humans are just a bunch of apes running around here with no clue. Well trust me buster, we're capable of some pretty dark shit too when we put our minds to it."

The Devil had no answer for that one. She was exactly right. That was why he had been in business for so long. That was why *Hellcorp* was thriving. Humans were fickle and a little slow but they knew what they wanted. And they would stop at nothing to get there.

He took one last look out the door and nodded. Maybe he wouldn't try his luck, not this time.

"Fine," he huffed. "If my safety means *that* much to you. Let's go see what Mr Rafferty is up to tonight, shall we?"

Jill nodded her thanks and pushed the door open that led into the tower block. The Devil stayed close behind and made sure they weren't being followed.

TWENTY-SIX

The lift doors opened to reveal a dark, dingy landing. The lights weren't working properly and some of them flickered badly. A drip echoed off the greasy, peeling paint walls from a broken pipe somewhere. The doors on either side of the corridor looked sad and worn out, dim glows coming from their depths.

The Devil stepped out of the elevator first. He was hit with the smell of damp and stale air. His face contorted automatically as Jill joined him. She didn't fare much better.

"How awful," he said, pinching his nose.

"Yeah, it's not great is it?"

They started across the landing, the lift doors closing behind them like a rusty set of jaws. The flickering bulbs made the whole place seem distorted, out of shape. It reminded The Devil of Hell a little bit. Nothing appeared to be normal, everything had a warped, mutated tinge to it.

"This is quite bizarre," he said.

"What is?" asked Jill.

"This, this place, it's uncanny."

"Uncanny for what?"

"The smell, the lighting, the overall sense of entropy. It's just like being at home."

Jill shivered at that. She rubbed her arms and walked steadily beside him, counting down the numbers on the doors.

"I don't know about you but it's giving me the creeps," she said. "If this is what Hell is really like I'm glad I won't be going."

"How do you know you won't be going?" he asked.

She stopped. Realising that she was looking at him, The Devil caught her gaze.

"What?" he asked, perplexed.

"Do you know something I don't?" she asked.

"My dear Gideon, I know *lots* more than you, it's just a matter of what parts."

"Do you know about my afterlife?"

"No," he said.

"You're lying."

"I'm not, I can't, not in this body anyway. If I tell lies I do it in style, not wearing a shaved monkey suit."

She didn't believe him. He didn't care. They were here to do a job. He pulled out the crumpled piece of paper from the electoral register and handed it to his companion.

"Here, which flat is it?"

She snatched it from him. Holding it up to one of the flickering lights, she nodded down the corridor.

"Come on," she said.

They pushed through a set of double doors into a second chamber of the landing. The smell was stronger in here, the dripping louder too. The lights, however, worked a little better and The Devil could see more. Not that there was a great deal to see. Poorly maintained corridors in blocks of council flats were about as dull as it got.

Jill stopped at the door furthest from the lift. She folded up the paper and handed it back to The Devil.

"Here we are," she said. "Number thirteen."

"Thirteen?" he laughed. "You've got to be kidding."

"Believe me, I'm not. That's what it says on the register."

He looked up at the damp covered ceiling and smiled.

"Now you really are pushing me," he said.

"What do we do now?" she asked.

The Devil blinked. He frowned and drummed his fingers on his chin. He hadn't thought that far ahead yet.

"I suppose we knock," he said.

"I know but once we've knocked. What do we do then?"

"Just ask him if he stabbed Anton Baggio in 1975. Simple."

"Simple?" she scoffed. "You think he's just going to answer us, like that? Are you mental or something?"

"Why wouldn't he?"

"If he's not told anybody for forty years, why would he suddenly start blabbing to us, two complete strangers who have turned up in the middle of the night. You really don't get us Humans at all, do you?"

"Well why do you think I keep you around Gideon? For the company? Don't make me laugh. I'd have a better time with a trained dolphin."

"Fine," she stomped her feet. "If that's how you feel I'll just go then shall -"

The door of the thirteenth flat swung open. A surly, brutish old man appeared wearing a string vest, trousers and braces. A gnarled cigarette drooped from his thick lips, two beady little eyes poking out from a thick, scarred brow.

"You want to shut the fuck up!" barked the man. "Ah'm tryin' tae sleep in here!"

The Devil glanced at Jill. The doctor nodded her head a little. They had found their man.

"Mr Rafferty?" he said. "Mr Thomas Rafferty?"

"Aye," said the old man, squinting. "Whits it tae ye?"

"Garfield, Iain Garfield, from the council, very nice to meet you Mr Rafferty, would you mind if we come in?"

"Cooncil?" he said, defensively. "Whit are you daein here at ma door at this time o' night? Because if it's aboot ma rent arrears, the benefits office huv told me they're sortin' it oot!"

The Devil looked at Jill. He hadn't understood a word the old man had said. Part of his deal with Him meant that he had a universal translator in his head. But this was beyond any Human communication he had ever heard.

To his relief, Jill seemed to get a grasp of what Rafferty had said. She stepped forward and shook his hand.

"No, no, nothing like that Mr Rafferty, we're here for the drip," she said.

"The drip?" yelped Rafferty.

"The drip?" repeated The Devil.

"That's right, the drip," Jill nodded. "That drip, can't you hear it? We understand it's been going on for some time."

Rafferty frowned. He took a long drag from his cigarette before blowing smoke in The Devil and Jill's face.

"Aye, so what?" he said. "It's no ma problem is it?"

"No, it's not sir," coughed Jill. "Turns out it's been a leaking drainage pipe and it's quite close to your property. We were wondering if we could come in to discuss a package of compensation, you know, just to make sure you've not been put out at all while this mistake of ours has been going on."

At the sound of money, Rafferty's beady eyes lit up. He coughed, wiped his hand on his vest and stood to one side.

"Oh aye, aye, come on in, come on in," he rasped.

"Thank you Mr Rafferty, greatly appreciated," she said.

Jill took the lead, The Devil staying close behind her. They stepped into the flat while Rafferty shuffled about behind them.

"Livin' room is straight through there," he said.

"Thank you," said Jill.

The companions moved down the narrow hall and into the living room. The whole flat was a tip. Plastic bags crowded the corners, old newspapers were stacked up against the walls, some piles almost reaching the roof. An old electric fire provided little heat and the only light to the place, a sagging arm chair placed directly in front of the television.

While the landing outside smelled like damp, Rafferty's flat had the odour of dry urine about it. The Devil was regretting jumping to the conclusion that the tower block was just like home. Hell wasn't nearly as bad as this grotty little place.

"Can I get you two a drink?" spluttered Rafferty, shambling up behind them.

"Yes, please Mr Rafferty, that would be lovely," said Jill.

"Ah've got lager. Do you drink lager?"

"Good grief no," said The Devil.

"Eh, yes, thank you sir, that would be grand," Jill nudged him in the ribs.

The old man gave them a distrustful look before hobbling into the kitchen, leaving them on their own. The Devil clasped his hands together, making sure he didn't touch anything with his bare flesh. Jill did the same.

"Blimey," he said. "How the other half live. How did you know he would let us in if you offered him money?"

"Think about it would you?" she sneered. "He's hardly living the high life. I've seen enough old Glasgow tough guys like him, I know they'd sell their right arm for cash to buy a six pack and a packet of fags. And he's not exactly living in the lap of luxury here, is he?"

The Devil couldn't argue. Once again Jill had surprised him. He congratulated himself on keeping her around.

"Here you go," said Rafferty, emerging from the kitchen with six cans of cheap beer.

He handed a half-pint glass to The Devil and Jill before opening up a can for himself. The Devil watched in horror and disgust as he drank the entire can in one gulp. The belch that came afterwards was equally revolting.

"So," he said, sitting down in the armchair. "Whits this aboot compensation?"

The Devil placed his glass down on a nearby stack of magazines and wiped his hands. He nudged Jill and nodded to her.

"Mr Rafferty, we have a confession to make," she said.

"Confession?" he asked, opening another can of lager. "Whit kind of confession?"

"Well, you see, we're… how can I put this," she was fumbling for words.

She kneeled down so she was beside him at his chair. Running her hands through her hair, she called on all of her diplomacy and tact, just like she did when she was delivering bad news to relatives of patients. It was a valuable life skill, especially when the situation was tricky. She couldn't think of anything trickier than this.

"I suppose, I should start at the beginning with it all-"

"Did you stab Anton Baggio?" blurted The Devil.

"Jesus Christ," groaned Jill, letting out a sigh.

"Whit!" shouted Rafferty.

"Did you stab Anton Baggio? Forty years ago, did you stab him?"

"You just couldn't help yourself, could you?" said Jill, standing up quickly. "You just couldn't keep your mouth shut for ten seconds while I tried to handle this. What's your problem man? Have you lost your mind?"

"Who the fuck ur you two?" coughed Rafferty. "Get oot of ma hoose! Right noo!"

"Mr Rafferty, please, we don't want any trouble," said Jill, trying to calm the old man down.

"Get oot! Or ah'm phonin' the polis!"

"Go ahead!" shouted The Devil, pushing Jill out of the way. "Go ahead and call the police. You'll save us the bother Rafferty. And while you're at it you can explain to them why there's a corpse in the city morgue with a healed up stab wound that you gave him four decades ago!"

"Whit?" said Rafferty.

His eyes had widened. His scarred brow seemed to retreat, his weather beaten face going slack. The huge bag of fat that hung beneath his chin seemed to quiver with fear. The Devil sensed his opportunity and went for the proverbial jugular.

"That's right, he's dead. Anton Baggio is dead Rafferty, and you caused it!" he snapped.

"Whit do you mean?" said the old man. "You mean he's deid? Like proper deid? When?"

"A few nights ago," said Jill. "He was brought into hospital and passed away from a bowel obstruction. It had been caused by ventral hernias we reckon came from an old stab wound."

"You hear that Rafferty? You stabbed him all those years ago and he's dead because of it. You're going to jail me laddie-oh, you're a murderer. And when the inmates are through with you, I'll get to enjoy myself."

"Ah don't believe it!" shouted Rafferty. "Ah don't believe you, either of you. Get oot of ma hoose!"

"Oh spare us your dramatics you old bastard," spat The Devil. "Don't sit there and pretend like this never happened. We know it was you that did it, Baggio's wife has told us the whole story. You stabbed him, you were drunk, you were coming onto his missus and you bloody stabbed him. He was innocent, you were guilty and you've lived for forty years getting away with it. Well time's up Rafferty, it's judgement day!"

"Nonsense!"

The old man folded his arms in front of his chest. He was defiant, he was lying and he was making The Devil angry. Throughout the ages, he had seen men like Rafferty before. They never failed to amaze him but they could also bring out the very worst in him.

He had never really known if they were lying or they genuinely believed they were innocent. Faced with insurmountable evidence, the guilty always pleaded otherwise. That made The Devil angry beyond even his comprehension.

He stormed forward and grabbed the old man by his vest. Clawing chunks of flabby, loose flesh, he pulled Rafferty to his feet and began shaking him.

"Admit it!" he shouted. "Admit what you've done or so help me I'll cave your head in right here with that beer can!"

"Get him aff of me!" Rafferty bleated.

"Let him go!" Jill tried to prize the two men apart.

"Do you have any idea who you're dealing with here Rafferty? Do you?" asked The Devil. "I'm your worst nightmare friend, the very worst, and you're jerking me around like some two bit whore in the street. Admit what you've done! Don't be a spineless shit worm all of your days! Admit it!"

Rafferty spat a huge glob of phlegm in The Devil's face. He let the old man go and stumbled backwards, blinded. When he cleared away the gunk, he prepared to charge at Rafferty. But Jill was in the way.

The doctor slapped the old man hard, the clap echoing about the whole flat. Rafferty fell backwards into his chair. A thin trail of blood dripped from his bottom lip, his right cheek turning red. He looked up at Jill, fear in his eyes.

"You bastard," she said, breathless. "You absolute bastard."

Rafferty said nothing. He looked up at her, cowering in his seat. The Devil cleared away the remainder of the spit from his face and joined his companion.

"Nice shot Gideon," he said. "I didn't think you had it in you."

"Shut up," she said. "Just shut up!"

He was confused. He looked at her and saw two lines of tears streaking down her cheeks. She was shaking, her whole body quivering. The Devil furrowed his brow.

"What's the matter?" he asked.

He noticed something in her hand. It was a picture frame. The glass had cracked beneath her thumb, broken with pressure from her grip.

"Gideon?" he said. "Let me see that."

She didn't move. Her chest was moving up and down in short, sharp bursts. He bent down and took the frame from her. She didn't move, her stare locked on Rafferty but somehow looking beyond him, beyond the flat, beyond everything.

The Devil shook out the broken glass onto the carpet. There was a photograph inside the frame, a picture of a young girl in a school uniform, posing for the camera.

She had the same dark hair, the same dark eyes, the same face. She was years younger, still fresh, untainted by the rigours of life on planet Earth. There was a spark there, of intelligence, hidden within the concerned smile. It was a smile The Devil had seen before. The girl in the photograph was Jill Gideon.

TWENTY-SEVEN

Jill's heart was thumping against the inside of her chest. She knew what was happening, what her brain was doing. In an effort to cope with the psychological trauma she was going through, her body was filling with adrenaline. It would keep her conscious, sharpen her senses, make sure she was ready to run or fight or both.

Hundreds of thousands of years of evolution were fuelling her now. As a doctor she thought it was quite remarkable. As a human being, she didn't know if she was coming or going.

She stared down at Rafferty, cowering in his chair. He hadn't moved since she slapped him. She wished, almost instantly, that she had hit him harder. He was bleeding, his face bruised but it wasn't enough. Not after what she had been put through by him. No amount of bleeding, no bruising or wounding could account for that.

Somewhere beside her she was aware of The Devil. Had he been part of this the whole time? Was this some sick, twisted joke that he had been playing on her? Maybe she was nothing more than a punch line, something to play with. If he was who he said he was, and she had no reason to doubt that, not anymore, then this was exactly what she should have expected.

None of that mattered though. The journey wasn't what was important. The destination, the final destination, where she had arrived now, was. There she stood, towering over the man she had spent her entire life hating, in some dingy Glasgow flat in a run down tower block.

"Do you know what you've done to me?" she asked, her voice hoarse. "Do you know what you have *done* to me?"

Rafferty said nothing. He was staring at her with fearful eyes. His gnarled, mangled face was the picture of terror. He looked like he had been caught red handed, with no route of escape. It was good, she wanted him to feel that way. It made her strong, while he was weak.

"Answer me!" she screamed.

The old man flinched. He sat up, wiping away blood from his chin. He looked at the sliver on the back of his hand and then back to her. Smiling, he shook his head.

"That's a fair ol' punch you've got on you lassie," he rasped.

She reached down to him and began scraping at his face, his arms, his shoulders. She was shouting, screaming, tears flooding down her face. She could hear him pleading for her to stop but she couldn't, she didn't want to. Thirty years of bottled frustration, curiosity and shame were being released all at once. How could she ever be expected to stop that?

Something grabbed her from behind and pulled her away. She tried to fight it but it was too strong.

The past few days had been so confusing. More than once she had thought she was having a break down. She had questioned her own sanity, resisted the temptation to check herself into a hospital with psychotic tendencies. Her therapist could retire with what she would tell them.

She had questioned the reality of her situation over and over and over again. This strange man who seemed to haunt her like a ghost, the one who claimed to be The Devil. Did he even exist?

Was he maybe a ghost from her subconscious? Seeing a geyser of black venom break through the floor of a library meant she would believe anything.

He couldn't be a ghost, he was wrestling her away from Rafferty. She could see that now as he bundled her over towards the windows of the grotty flat.

"I think you should probably calm down," he said, tired from fighting her. "And maybe, just maybe, you can tell me what's going on here."

The Devil was holding the picture. She snatched it from him, stared down at herself. She remembered when it had been taken. A rainy Tuesday afternoon, she was in primary school, no older than seven. The photographer had been a friendly old man with the patience of a saint. She remembered thinking he had to in order to deal with her classmates. Even at that age she was conscientious.

She touched the face, as if feeling through time itself. Little did she know then that over twenty-five years later she would be looking at that image again, from the other side. How could anybody ever know that?

Two tears dropped from her chin onto the picture. They ran down the cheeks of the smiling seven-year-old. How many times had that happened back then? How many times had it happened since? Too many to count. And most because of the man across the room.

"It's him," she sniffed. "It's him."

"Him who?" asked The Devil.

"Him," she nodded at Rafferty. "He's my father."

The word burned in her mouth. She felt hot, like her head was on fire from the inside. She wanted to douse herself in ice water. She wanted to run out the door and never look back. She wanted to fly away to the other side of the world and be away from all of this.

But she couldn't. She couldn't do any of those things. She was stuck, in her reality, facing three decades worth of consequences, all brought together in one room.

"Your father?" asked The Devil. "Him? Tommy Rafferty? He's your dad? No Gideon, you're confused. You're not thinking straight, this is the man who stabbed Anton Baggio, remember? The case, the stabbing. We're here to bring him in. Remember?"

Jill detected the slightest hint of sympathy in his voice. It must have been a mistake.

She wiped the photo clean of tears and sniffed again, clearing her throat. She looked at him through bleary eyes, unable to stop crying.

"Rafferty is my father," she said again.

"But I don't understand," said The Devil. "I thought you said you grew up in the south side, you told me who your parents were. You didn't know Tommy Rafferty existed until earlier today? What's going on here?"

She walked across the cluttered living room and handed Rafferty the picture frame. He took it and looked up at Jill. His face was stoic, missing of any emotion.

"I found it," she said to him. "Over there, behind those newspapers. It's the only one you've got."

"Aye," he said. "So it is."

"Why?" she asked. "Why have you got it? Why have you got a photograph of me from when I was at school? What gives you the right to have that? And I swear to god Rafferty, if you don't start talking I'll let him loose on you."

The Devil sidled up beside her. He licked his dry lips and cracked his knuckles.

"And believe me pal, you don't want that," she continued.

Rafferty shrugged his shoulders. Jill wanted to hear what he had to say. She wanted answers from this man she knew nothing about. She wanted the truth.

"Your mother gave it tae me, after it was taken," he said. "She told me that it was aww ah was gettin' of you and that ah couldnae' see you ever again."

"Lies," Jill spat.

"He's not lying," said The Devil. "Not anymore. I know a liar, I've seen enough. He's telling the truth Gideon."

Rafferty dabbed his swollen lip on his vest. He fixed the back of the photo and placed it gently on the table beside his chair.

"She didnae' want me to hiv anythin' to dae wae you. She thought it was best if ah stayed away from ye. So that's whit ah did. Ah stayed away."

"She never told me," said Jill, her mouth curled downwards. "She never told me who you were. But she told me what you did to her. She told me what you did!"

She leapt forward but The Devil stopped her. He pulled her backwards before she could hit Rafferty again. She clawed at the air, desperate to get at him but he was out of reach. Like he had always been.

"Take it easy!" said The Devil. "Just take it easy Gideon."

"Ah'm sorry!" Rafferty croaked.

Jill stopped her lashing out. She pushed the hair from her eyes and batted The Devil away.

"What did you say?" she whispered.

"Ah'm sorry," the old man repeated. "Ah'm sorry for whit ah did tae yer maw. Ah'm sorry."

"You're *sorry*?" she scoffed. "I don't believe I'm hearing this. You're actually apologising for what you did?"

"Well whit else dae ye want me to say?"

"You're actually apologising for raping… for raping my mother?

That's what you're doing to me?"

"Jill, ah don't know-"

"Don't call me that!" she shouted. "You don't have the *right* to call me that! You never will. Do you hear me? Do you *understand*? You'll never have that right. Ever!"

She turned away from him. Her head was light and she felt dizzy. The adrenaline was wearing off. She leaned onto the door that led to the balcony, the taste of sick filling her mouth.

A hand fell on her shoulder. It was cold, clammy, almost without life. She looked at it and saw The Devil, his lop-sided face staring back at her in the gloomy light.

"He raped my mother," she said firmly. "When she was sixteen. She fell pregnant, she never told me who he was but she told me what he had done to her. She always knew who he was but she never said, she never told me. He was nothing to me, he was the pig who brought me into this world, that's all. Now I'm here, now I'm in his house. Do you have any idea what that's like?"

She broke down, her resistance finally giving way. The tears streamed from her eyes and she felt like she was going to die. Her whole body went numb, limbs suddenly heavy. She could feel herself tipping over.

But The Devil caught her. He held her in his arms, pulled her in tight to him. She cried and cried and cried. Her hands were clenched around his shoulders so tightly that it hurt. The fabric of his ill-fitting suit was sodden with her tears. She felt so ill, so weak, so tired.

She had to know though, she had to ask. It might have been a kick while she was down but she had to know the truth.

Peeling herself from his shoulder, she looked up at him. He met her gaze coolly.

"Did you do this?" she asked, her voice hoarse, throat raw. "Is this your work?"

The Devil let out a long sigh. He helped her back to her feet and made sure she was stable. He rubbed his forehead and sucked air through his teeth.

"You have to understand Gideon, this sort of stuff happens for a reason," he said.

"Did you do this?" she asked again. "Tell me the truth. Did you make this happen? Is this one of your tricks, one of your little games, the way you like to play with us apes? Have you set me up here? Have you let me walk willingly into this to bring me face-to-face with this man, this monster? Because if you have, I need to know! I *need* to know!"

She was shaking with anger, fear and fatigue. She had to know and she wouldn't stop until she was told.

"Yes," said The Devil.

He was quiet, humbled, almost defeated. Gone was his swagger, his self assurance, his presence. The man who had kidnapped her from the hospital, who had fought with bouncers and taxi drivers, who had broken into police stations and spoke of impossible things. He was just that now, a man. Nothing more, nothing less.

"Yes?" she repeated. "Is that it? Is that all I'm getting."

"It's all you'll ever understand," he said sadly. "I wish I could tell you more but it just wouldn't make sense I'm afraid. And believe me, I take no pride in saying that."

He walked over to Rafferty, the old man bowed over with shame, and lifted the photo. Holding it up to the light, The Devil laughed weakly.

"Sometimes things turn out the way they do because they are supposed to," he said. "No matter how much interfering or non-interfering me and the rest of them try, circumstance always seems to find a way of getting the job done. It's just a fact of life, nothing more. I can spout out about it until my heart's content but I'll never get to the bottom of it. Sometimes, the shit is always going to happen. And there's absolutely nothing that you, me or even He can do about it. It's a little clause in the small print of existence. And you should always read the small print. The machine keeps on ticking over."

She was tired of his talking, of his words. She was drained, emotionally and physically.

"Small print, machines, existence, it means nothing," she said, her shoulders slumping. "It means nothing, when you think about it. I mean, really think about it. What are we? Bags of organs with emotions, that's all. We're here to create more of the same and then pop our clogs. You lot think you're so great because you know what's happening but you don't really, not really. You, Him, you have no idea what we go through? And you know why? Because you're not us. You've never been us. You've never gotten your hands dirty, you've never seen fear in a man's eyes before he's about to die. You've never felt the joy and love of being in a room when another life is born. All of that is nothing more than paperwork to you and Him and everybody else. That's why you don't get it. That's why you don't understand us. We're Humans and we live, every single day of our lives. You, you're nothing. Because you don't feel anything. Anything."

She was finished. She was finished with The Devil, she was finished with Rafferty, she was finished with everything. She wanted to go home, go to bed and maybe never wake up. The world could end for all she cared. She wanted nothing else to do with it.

"I'm going home," she said. "I've had enough of all of this shit."

"Jill, please," said Rafferty.

Jill clenched her fist into a ball and swung her arm as hard as she could. She caught the old man square on the chin and sent him flying back into his chair. He slumped to one side, a broken tooth dropping from his mouth in a dribble of blood.

"I've had enough," she said, shaking away the pain in her hand.

She turned to The Devil. He cowered a little, his eyes shifting between her hands and her face.

"And as for you, I don't want you anywhere near me, do you understand?" she said firmly. "I don't care where you go, what you do or who you do it with. I don't care if by ignoring you my soul is condemned to an eternity of Hell, damnation and corporal punishment. Do you know something, it's just not worth it anymore. I might have found this whole thing fun at first, maybe even exhilarating. To have a man in my life who showed me a good time, that was a first. But it's come at too high a cost. This, this whole episode, here in this flat, nah, I can't handle that kind of shit. Not anymore. I'm done."

"But where am I suppose to go?" asked The Devil.

"Go to Hell," she said and pushed passed him.

She took a deep breath as she stalked down the hallway. She kept her head high, determined to walk out of that flat and to never return. She was going on her terms and only her terms. It was a victory she deserved and she owed it to herself.

As she approached the front door, three knocks came from the other side. She stopped dead in the hallway. A strange sensation went though her whole body, like she had been struck by a bolt of lightning. She couldn't tell what it was, there was no medical explanation. All she knew was that it felt dreadful, like her head was in a vice.

"What was that?" whispered The Devil, scurrying up beside her.

"I don't know," she whispered back. "I think it was the front door."

Three more knocks made them both flinch. The dread was

growing, pressure tightening on both of her temples. She took a step backwards, The Devil moving with her.

Another trio of knocks thudded against the door. Whatever it was, Jill knew it wasn't good. Whoever, or whatever, was outside, was looking to get in.

"Maybe Rafferty is expecting guests," she said quietly.

"No," said The Devil. "They're not here for Rafferty."

Like clockwork, three knocks again echoed down the hallway. She felt The Devil tighten his grip on her shoulders.

"They're here for me," he said.

"Who're *they*?" she whispered.

"Our worst nightmare."

TWENTY-EIGHT

The Devil darted back down the hallway and into the living room. Rafferty was still knocked out cold, his unconscious body slumped over the side of his chair. He had no time, there was none left. He had to act quickly.

"Gideon!" he shouted. "Gideon! Get in here, I need your help with him!"

Jill came back into the living room. She looked petrified, her skin the shade of a corpse's. The Devil thought that was wholly appropriate, given their situation.

He bent down and felt his back click. His human body wasn't able to keep up. It was slow, lethargic, unable to move as quickly as he wanted or needed. He cursed it for the millionth time.

"Help me with his arms," he said.

"What is that out there?" she asked.

"Just grab his arms! We need to get out of here."

"No!" she shouted.

"No? What do you mean no?"

She folded her arms over her chest, legs spread apart. She looked like a schoolchild who wasn't getting their own way. The Devil despaired.

"I'm not helping you and I'm certainly not helping *him* until you tell me what's going on," she said firmly.

The Devil clenched his fists in anger. He thought about punching her, throttling her, doing something terrible. It felt like he hadn't done something truly ghastly in decades, although it was most probably just hours. Surely he could be afforded a little misdemeanour.

No, there wasn't any time. Murdering Gideon would only slow him up. And he needed to move, think, act as quickly as he could.

"If I tell you what's outside will you help us escape?" he said.

"I'll think about it."

"No good, I need guarantees Gideon, this is, where they say, the shit hits the fan."

Three knocks filtered down the hallway. Jill's head snapped towards them, her eyes widening.

"That's fifteen," said The Devil.

"Fifteen what?" she asked fearfully.

"Knocks, fifteen knocks. There are only three more to go."

"Why only three?"

"That'll be eighteen then," he said with a dry gulp.

"So what?" asked Jill, more in hope than anything else. "What's so special about eighteen."

"Do the maths Gideon, three knocks, eighteen of them in total, that's -"

"Three sixes," she said, turning back to him.

"Congratulations," he said. "You win the prize."

"What... what is it?"

The Devil dropped Rafferty's legs with a thump. He crept up to the living room door and peered down the darkened corridor. The front door stared back at the companions with an ominous silence. Consumed in shadow, the whole flat seemed to be getting darker.

"To tell you the truth, I'm not exactly sure," he said. "This has never happened before, in all of the time existence has, well, existed. I've never been away from Hell for this long."

"You must have some idea though," she whispered.

"I do, but you wouldn't want to know. I suppose I can only describe it like being an automated system. When there's something wrong, a series of measures clicks into place to stop everything from falling to pieces. Whatever it is out there, it's not going to stop until it's found me."

"A bit like *The Terminator*."

"What's *The Terminator*?" he asked.

"You've never heard of *The Terminator*?"

"No, do forgive me Gideon, I haven't heard of *The Terminator*. You see, I've been busy dealing with the punishment and torment of souls since the dawn of time. Somehow finding out what *The Terminator* is somehow never made it onto my To Do list."

He was interrupted by three final knocks. The pair retreated from the door and hurried over to Rafferty. The Devil gathered up his ankles and pointed at his arms.

"Time's up Gideon," he said. "Let's get out of -"

There was an almighty crash from the corridor. The sound of splintering wood was accompanied by a low, ominous growl. Jill stood perfectly still, staring down the hallway at whatever had just forced itself into the flat.

"Gideon!" The Devil shouted. "His arms!"

She didn't move. She was paralysed with fear. Her mouth hung wide open, eyes popping from her head. She began to shake uncontrollably.

The Devil dropped Rafferty's legs again and rushed around the chair. He grabbed her but was stopped by a blood curdling hiss from behind.

Slowly, he turned. Stooping to get into the living room, a huge figure of a man in a black cloak and wide brimmed hat arrived. The smell of rotten eggs beat out the damp and dry urine of the place, making The Devil cough. He backed away, pulling Jill with him.

"Your Majesssty," said the man, his face obscured by the rim of his hat. "I have come to take you back to the Kingdom of Hell."

"Kingdom of Hell? I've never heard it called that before. You sure you've got the right place?" said The Devil, trying to be flippant.

"Your wordsss are not your own," hissed the man. "You ssspeak with the tongue of the Humansss. You must be purged of their sssinsss and reclaim your rightful place on the thronesss."

The man stepped forward but The Devil and Jill were too quick. They passed by Rafferty, still slumped in his chair. Noticing the old man, the cloaked figure stopped.

A long, white arm appeared from inside the creature's cloak. It's claw like hand reached down towards Rafferty. Grabbing the old man by the throat, his eyes sprung open, his mouth gaping and short, sharp breaths escaping his lungs.

"Thisss man hasss committed many sssinsss in his lifetime," said the stranger. "He mussst be punisssshed for all that he has done."

"Yes!" shouted Jill. "He should be! Are you the one to punish him?"

"Gideon," mouthed The Devil. "Don't, not now."

"What? No, he's right. Rafferty is a crook, a lowlife, he raped my mother!" she was shouting at the stranger. "He needs to be punished! Punish him!"

The man in the cloak looked at The Devil, like a dog would its owner. The Devil had no answer for him, how could he? He was Human now, he had no remit, no jurisdiction, no authority.

Whatever happened next would have to happen of its own accord. Those were the rules.

"This womansss," said the stranger. "Ssshe ssspeaksss the truth, I can sssee it in her sssoul."

"I do!" Jill said. "I do speak the truth."

"Then the human man mussst be punisssshed!"

Rafferty's face whitened, his eyes bulging further out of his head. The stranger's grip tightened around his throat. As he did so, he began to make a low growl, as if drawing from some unknown power source.

The old man's arms and legs began to twitch and shake. His body convulsed, like he was having a fit. Then the skin on his arms and chest began to peel away. Like an onion, he was stripped down to his muscles, then his bones and then finally to nothing.

All that had once been Tommy Rafferty was gone, save for a puff of black ash that frittered away to nothing in the air. The stranger turned back towards The Devil and Jill, straightening himself up.

"The deed isss done," he said. "The mansss hasss been sssent for punisssshment to the Kingdom of Hell."

"You shouldn't have done that," said The Devil. "You shouldn't have taken his life like that."

"I am here to ssserve your purpossse My Lord," said the stranger. "I am here to return you to your rightful place in the Kingdom of Hell. I am-"

"I wasn't talking to you!" The Devil barked.

Immediately, the stranger was silent. His head bowed a little, the rim of his cap covering his pale white chin. He looked scalded, like a child who had been told off.

"I was talking to you Gideon," said The Devil, turning to his companion.

She looked confused. She was crying again, her face and eyes wet. In the gloom of the dingy flat, she looked haggard and beaten up. The past few days had been rough on her, The Devil could see that now. Never before had she looked so human.

"You shouldn't have done that," he sounded angry.

"Why not? He was a bastard," she remained defiant.

"That's not the point," he said, taking her by the shoulders. "Don't you understand? Haven't you figured it all out yet? Please Gideon, please just tell me you're on the right track. Just tell me."

Her brow narrowed as she stared into his eyes. She didn't know what he was talking about. She was so blinded by her hatred, so consumed by her lust for revenge that she had strayed from her path. And The Devil knew it. But more importantly, he knew what came next.

"Please Gideon, I can only give you one last chance," he said.

"One last chance for what?" she asked. "I don't understand what you mean? Help me understand, I want to understand? Tell me!"

"I can't tell you!" he shouted. "I can't, that's not the point. You have to work it out for yourself!"

The stranger took a step forward, pale arm still reaching out from his cloak. Jill's look of terror intensified. The Devil could see her mind working, the gears clicking into place. The stranger took another step forward, his growl getting louder.

"You've got to see!" The Devil shouted over the din. "You've got to understand!"

"I don't… I can't think…" she was panicking. "Is he… why is he coming towards me?"

She recoiled, but The Devil held her firmly in place. The stranger was getting closer, only a few feet away. He was almost out of time.

"Just think Gideon! Just think! Just think about what you've done, that's all. You'll get there! You'll get there!"

"But… but I can't think! Oh god! Oh god what's going to happen to me!"

"You have committed sssin," hissed the stranger. "You mussst be punissshed, like all othersss who defy the laws of creation. You mussst be punissshed!"

"Oh no!" she screamed.

"Think Gideon!" The Devil yelled. "Just think!"

"Oh no! Oh god! Please, no! Just give me another chance! Another chance that's all I want! I'm sorry! I'm sorry!"

The claw was almost at her face. The Devil was panicking. A cruel wind had whipped up and about them, the terrible roar filling the whole room. Everything was getting dark, the gloom consumed by shadow.

He wanted to save her, more than anything else he had ever desired. Why though, he thought. Why this human? There must have been millions of souls down the millennia who were more deserving.

People lost in car accidents, plane crashes, robbed of precious years of loyal service due to illness, famine, incompetence. Why now? Why this one? Why Jill Gideon?

He couldn't explain it and he didn't have the time to think. So, like everything he had ever done before, he acted. All guns blazing, head first, without a care in creation.

He pulled her away from the stranger's claw and dived towards the balcony door. Shouldering it open, the billowing gale washed over them both. The stranger stumbled but quickly got back to his giant feet.

"Do you trust me Gideon?" he asked her. "Do you trust me to do the right thing?"

It was a question he thought he would never ask. Since when did he need approval from Humans? Yet here he was, asking, begging this woman for endorsement, for justification, for hope.

"I trust you," she said, her voice quivering.

"Then let's hope I'm right," he said.

The Devil hopped up onto the safety barrier of the veranda, Jill doing the same. He took a quick look back at the stranger, ducking beneath the doorway of the balcony.

With one deep breath, he pulled Jill into his chest as close as she would go. He shut his eyes tightly and hoped for the best.

They teetered for a second before gravity took control. The weightlessness of free fall was almost pleasant, soothing, gentle. The world around them melted away, the wind in their ears vanishing as silence took over.

The Devil thought that he could hear birds somewhere, in the distance. He wasn't sure if they were really there or it was his Human brain preparing to cope for the worst.

Like all things he had found on the earth, anything pleasant tended to last a very short time. And before he knew it, the free flight had come to an end.

The ground slammed into them hard, fast and with a relentless lack of forgiveness. Strange, thought The Devil, that it was just that simple. Life could be snuffed out instantly, in less than the blink of an eye. He had never thought about it like that before. He could understand where Jill was coming from.

Then everything went black. That was that.

TWENTY-NINE

Everything went white. A wave of bright light had engulfed him, knocking him backwards onto his rear end. It was all painfully familiar.

When the disorientation cleared, he looked about his surroundings. He was amongst rolling fields of primly cut grassland. The sun was sitting high in a clear blue sky, beating down with a comforting warmth.

Jill was nowhere to be seen. He was on his own, the world desolate all around him as far as his eyes could see. He patted his chest, his arms, his legs. He felt his face. He wasn't Human anymore.

Everything felt sharper, less dull. He brushed his hand across the lawn, feeling every blade of grass like it was a burning knife's edge. He could smell that it had been freshly cut, the familiar odour mixing with the breeze air. Even the sun on his skin was more real somehow, like it hadn't been filtered through smudged glass. He could taste the freshness on his tongue.

"Curious," he said to himself, hearing his voice for what felt like the first time. "Very curious."

The time The Devil had spent in Human form had been a trialling and tiresome one. He hadn't quite realised how dulled their senses were until now. He felt positively liberated, freed, glad to be back in his own skin. But there was something else too, something he hadn't counted on. He couldn't quite place what the sensation was but he knew it was there, like there was something, or someone constantly in his periphery.

He ignored it. There would be plenty of time for dissection when he got home. At least now he was that little bit closer.

Standing up, he stretched. Gone was the fatigue and pain of the Human body. Instead he felt flexible, nubile, back to full fitness. It felt good and he found that he was smiling.

There was a gentle thud beside him. A golf ball rolled passed his scuffed brogues. The smile was wiped from his face instantly. The boss had arrived.

"Fore!" came a voice from behind.

The Devil turned to see a tall, lean, athletically built woman striding over the nearest ridge in the grassland. She waved a golf club in his direction, a large smile on Her face.

"Great," said The Devil. "That's all I need."

"Good morning," She said, tipping back her golf visor and leaning on her club. "Good to see you old boy."

"Really?" asked The Devil. "You're appearing like that and expecting me to give you my fullest attention?"

"What?" She asked, twirling.

The Devil tried his best not to look at the short skirt, the tanned legs, the enlarged rear end. Temptation was meant to be one of the aces up his sleeve, not His. And despite the pleasing form, The Devil was in no mistake that he was in His presence, although He now appeared to be a She.

"I thought I'd test drive this new model," She said. "What do you think? Not too shabby, great for walking, running, everything really. Yes, I'm quite pleased with it if I do say so myself."

"Oh and don't you just *love* to say so yourself. Who do you think you are eh? Coming around here in these sexy new bodies?

I may not be flesh and blood but I still feel you know. You make my teeth itch."

She laughed politely. The Devil scratched the back of his head and looked about the golf course. The blue skies, the rolling fairway, already it was giving him a sore head. He pinched the bridge of his nose.

"Would you mind awfully?" She asked.

The Devil stepped back, allowing Her to take her shot. He deliberately didn't look at Her rump as She wiggled it in front of him. There was something not quite right about looking at it, as much as he wanted to. Even he had to draw the line somewhere.

She took a long, calculated swing that hit the ball with a satisfying snap. However, rather than shoot off straight into the distance, as it always did, the ball veered off to the left.

"Drat," She said. "Shanked it."

"You?" laughed The Devil. "You shanked a shot? No way, I don't believe it."

"You had better believe it," She said. "It's gone off that way. Blast."

"If I didn't know better, I'd say you were a little angry," he smarmed. "Old chum."

She didn't rise to the bait. The Devil wasn't surprised. Instead, She began striding off in the direction of the ball, swinging Her club around in Her hand.

"I don't mind admitting to you that I've had a pretty rough time of it actually," She started. "That's probably why my shot is off. Can't concentrate you see, too much on my mind."

"Hazards of the profession," he said. "It gets to us all. Only, I thought you were on top of the game, ahead of the curve. Anything that could ever cause you problems you usually snuffed out before it got a chance to give you a headache. Remember the Ark?"

"Ah yes, the Ark," She said sadly. "That was most unfortunate. I didn't go into that lightly, let me tell you."

"No, bloody right you didn't. You went in with a planet's worth of water and purged the whole place clean."

"Like I said, unfortunate."

They walked on in silence for a while. The Devil wasn't sure what She wanted with him. As far as he was concerned, he had completed his task, to the letter. The fact that outside influences had complicated matters was hardly his fault.

But there was still that nagging in the back of his mind. It wouldn't go away and it wouldn't reveal itself. He was beginning to think that She had something to do with it.

"I found out who the murderer was," he said, hoping that by speeding up the conversation, he would get his reward quicker.

"Yes, I know, I saw that," She replied. "You did a good job, a great job in fact."

"You sound surprised."

"No, no, not at all. I knew you would, I knew you'd keep going until the very end, see it all out and bring everything to a close. That was partly why I chose you for it in the first place."

"*You chose me*?" he said. "I think you'll find I was the one who got the ball rolling old bean. I'm the one who wanted a holiday, remember?"

"Details," She said. "Ah, here we go."

Out of nowhere, the golf ball appeared sitting on the lawn. She lined up another shot, took aim and swung. This time the ball rocketed off in a straight line, disappearing over the horizon.

"It's what happened afterwards that I'm more concerned about," She said, turning to face him. "That business with the Demon, that was all a little unfortunate."

"You know I hate to agree with you but yes, I agree," said The Devil, putting his hands in his pockets. "Still, nothing to be done. My lot don't like to be without me for all that long, they panic you see. They just love me that much."

"Yes, quite," She said, taking off her golf glove and adjusting her visor. "You see, that's where it's complicated things a tad. You know me, I don't like to interfere. This exercise was meant to be untouched by forces not born on the earth. That's why I gave you a Human body, so you wouldn't go rushing about causing mischief."

"I didn't, by the way, if you had been watching. Anything I did was strictly by the book."

"Oh yes, I know, I know," She smiled. "Surprised a fair few back at the Club House with that, I should say."

"And what about you?" he asked. "Were you surprised?"

"Nothing surprises me old sport," She smirked.

"I should have known."

"But that's not the point. And I think you know what I'm getting at, namely Doctor Jill Gideon."

The Devil winced at the mention of her name. He knew this was coming. He had tried to put it off for as long as possible. His companion had interfered in an interference and it had cost her her life. There were going to be repercussions.

"Yeah, about that," he started. "Look, I know she was a bit vengeful towards the end there but I don't think that should be held against her. I mean, she's a doctor after all, she does the best she can with a bad lot."

"No?" She asked.

"Sure. Have you seen what they're dealing with down there? It's like they haven't learned a thing since the Dark Ages. Cutting each other up, shouting, swearing, bumping into each other. It's like they get off on being bad to one another. No wonder Hellcorp is doing as well as it is. But she's not like that, not really. She was just caught up in circumstance, that's all."

"You tried to help her," She said. "You were interfering."

"No, I wasn't," The Devil exclaimed.

She tilted her head at him. Sensing he was maybe being a little loud, he toned back his exuberance.

"I was only asking her if she knew what she was doing, that's all. There's a difference between running on automatic and free will. You know this."

"She still let that Demon commit judgement on her father," She said. "That's unacceptable."

"Her father was a rapist!" The Devil cried.

The words seemed to carry out across the gold course. They seemed crass, rude, out of place in this environment. They were out of place. Upstairs had a strict entry policy and talking about those sorts of things was prohibited. The Devil half expected club security to reign down on him.

"Yes, he was," She said.

"You knew that too," said The Devil. "And yet you still let her wind up there, you still made her confront all of that. Why would you do that to her?"

"What makes her so different to anybody else?" She asked. "Why should Jill Gideon be spared all the heartache and pain while somebody else, anybody else has to endure it? That wouldn't be fair."

"It wasn't fair shocking her like that. Especially when it was you who shoved her into my path in the first place," said The Devil. "That's right, I remember, the flowers in the hospital, the mysterious card she got. White roses, a dead giveaway."

"Some things need to be done," She said firmly. "That's just the way of things. You know that, you know that more than most."

"Yeah, I do," said The Devil. "But I also know that good people deserve to be treated well. And they deserve the benefit of the doubt instead of being shoved through the system."

"Is that why you took the blame for taking her to meet her father?"

The Devil felt empty. It was like somebody had reached into his stomach, pulled everything out and left a gaping hole. He could almost feel the gentle breeze passing through it.

"Why did you do that?" She asked.

He had no answer. He didn't even know where to start thinking of one. The situation had spiralled so quickly out of control he hadn't really thought about it all. When Jill was holding on to him, she needed to hear the truth. But he couldn't ever tell her that. It would have destroyed her.

Instead, he had told her what she wanted to hear. He was The Devil, the master of the black arts. She had followed him around faithfully, knowing exactly what he was. And yet somehow, she had been able to see something different in him, something else.

The smoke and mirrors were gone but so was his protection from her. Jill Gideon was the Human who made The Devil Human. In doing so, she had brought out a side in him that he never thought existed. It was compassion, it was faith, it was hope. All of those things, rolled into one.

In turn, it meant that she could trust him. That was why she had asked him for the truth, if he had been instrumental in bringing her face-to-face with her real father. She knew what the answer was before he answered it. But he still had to confess. Confession, The Devil had learned, was only as true as the person telling it.

That was why he had lied to her. If he hadn't, he would have undone all the good work they had achieved together. Only now, in the bucolic splendour of Upstairs, did he realise this.

"What can I say," he mused. "I'm a liar, a cheat, a gambler and a sinner. I just couldn't help myself."

It hurt him to say that, especially to Her. He felt like he was owed something better, something nobler. But that was the way of things, as She so often said. Everybody had their place in creation. The Devil's was to play the bad guy.

"It's been a difficult time," She said, starting off across the fairway again. "But a rewarding one all the same I think."

"If you say so," said The Devil glumly.

"Why don't you come back with me to the Club House and we'll have a little drink to celebrate."

"Celebrate what?" he asked.

"Oh, I don't know, anything really? Making it through another day, seeing another sunrise. Does it have to be anything in particular?"

The Devil stared ahead across the rolling fields. In the distance, he could see the sloped roofs of the Club House, shimmering in the heat. He knew he didn't have any choice but he wanted to pretend, just for a moment, like he did.

When that moment passed, he nodded. She put her arm around him and they walked off into the distance together.

THIRTY

The bar of the Club House overlooked the main entranceway. A large, open balcony was peppered with tables, chairs and giant umbrellas. Guests sat around chatting politely, their conversations light and pleasant.

Jill had absolutely no idea where she was. Other than the fact she was perched on a stool, sipping what looked like a tropical cocktail and wearing a club polo shirt and slacks, she was totally confused.

The last thing she remembered was being in Rafferty's dingy living room. There was a terrible sense of urgency about the place and she could picture a large man dressed entirely in black. The Devil had held her, taken her out onto the veranda. And then there was nothing. The darkness had come and swallowed her whole.

The next thing she knew, she was at this bar. A friendly man with a thick, grey beard had served her without speaking. She hadn't thought to question his motives, or the drink he had placed in front of her. She didn't think she had to. The whole place had a familiar, comfortable feel to it.

Two old women came up to the bar beside her. They were old, both on their seventies, dressed in colourful blouses and beige trousers. One said something to the other and they both laughed. When they saw Jill staring at them, they smiled.

"Hello dear," said the one closest to her. "How are you getting on?"

"Eh… fine, I guess," said Jill.

"Have you just arrived?" said the other old woman in a broad New England accent.

"Yeah, I think so, although, to be perfectly honest, I'm not quite sure where here is and how I came to be here."

The old women giggled. They were each served similar looking cocktails and clinked each other's glasses. When they were done, they offered the same courtesy to Jill.

"Don't worry," said one of them. "They'll be along in a minute to sort you out. I'm sure you'll be fine. And if you ever want a quick round of nine, just let me or Betty know. Take care of yourself my darling."

"But, wait, hold on," said Jill.

The two women walked off further into the bar, lost amongst the others. Jill wanted to follow them but she didn't. Something was telling her to stay where she was. Like there was a voice in her head, advising her, controlling her, she knew she couldn't go after them.

She shook her head. This couldn't be happening, surely this wasn't what she thought it was. She was a doctor, a woman of science, not superstition. Every medic alive knew that once you were dead, that was it, nothing else, game over.

So why didn't she believe it now? Why was she standing in the middle of a golf club bar, wearing a uniform and sipping an exotic cocktail. She had fallen from Rafferty's balcony; she had felt the wind race past her, whistling in her ears. She had felt everything break when she hit the ground. Why wasn't she dead?

"This is an urgent call for Doctor Jillian Gideon," came a voice over the public address system. "Would Doctor Jillian Gideon please report to the front reception please. Once again, a call for Doctor Jillian Gideon."

Jill left her drink and moved towards the exit of the bar. She raced down a flight of stairs and slid her way through the people who were milling around the reception area. Spying the front desk, she waved her hands frantically.

"I'm here!" she said, slamming into the tall, mahogany counter. "I'm here, it's me, Jill Gideon, Doctor Gideon, Jillian Gideon, that's me, I'm her."

A slender, balding man with a thick, bushy grey beard similar to the barman's appeared behind the desk. The nametag on his polo shirt read Peter and Jill looked suspiciously at him.

"Doctor Gideon?" he said, looking at some files in his hands. "Jillian Gideon?"

"Yes, that's me," she said, catching her breath.

"Ah, lovely, welcome Doctor Gideon, always nice to have another member of the medical community amongst us."

"Really?" she asked. "I wouldn't have thought there was much use for it Up here."

"Oh you would be surprised," said Peter. "You wouldn't believe what happens around this place. Anyway, I'm rambling. I'm just looking for a signature and then you can go right up."

"Right up? Right up where?"

"Upstairs," he smiled.

"You mean..." she pointed to the ceiling.

"Oh yes, you have an appointment. But you'll have to be quick, there isn't a lot of time. Lots of people to see and get put through the process. Then again, I'm sure you're used to that, being a doctor of course."

He laughed but it sounded more like a snort. Jill took her paper and signed the bottom of it without reading the print. She figured that if she couldn't trust this receptionist, who could she trust.

"That's lovely, thank you Doctor Gideon. Gideon, that's a good name you know, got lots of history."

"Yeah," said Jill. "I know. Especially around these parts."

Peter nodded and looked a little put out. He pointed towards a corridor that was lined with doors.

"Just down there, sixty-sixth door on the right," he said.

"Sixty-sixth?" she repeated. "You sure?"

"Yes, of course I'm sure," said Peter, looking a little put out.

"You're the boss. Thank you."

She left him at the reception and started down the hallway. There was a pleasant smell here, like a morning in the countryside. A gentle breeze was wafting up the corridor, the far end obscured by sunlight. Jill felt very relaxed, almost sleepy.

When she reached the sixty-sixth door, she stopped. She wasn't sure what to expect on the other side. Doors hadn't exactly been her best friends recently. Deciding she had already come this far and that there was little use in dallying, she knocked hard on the wood.

The door opened smoothly, like it was automatic. She stepped through the threshold and found she was in a large, open space. The roof had vanished, in its place an endless, spiralling column of clouds. Ahead of her was a desk and behind it an athletic looking woman writing with a quill.

"Eh... hello?" she said.

"Ah, hello, hello, come on in," said the woman. She stood up and welcomed Jill with a friendly handshake. "Can I get you anything? Tea, coffee, biscuits, a bun perhaps?"

"No, I'm fine, thank you," said the doctor.

"Please, take a seat."

From nowhere, a chair had appeared behind her. She sat down

and crossed her hands across her lap. She felt like she was at a job interview, wondering how much was too much to say. Should she make conversation or just remain politely quiet?

"Don't worry," She said. "It's not an interview, nothing like that."

Jill tried to conceal her surprise but she couldn't. She let out a gasp and quickly wished she hadn't.

"You're… Him, aren't you?" she asked.

"Well, I used to be," She said. "Although I'm test driving this new body so I suppose, to avoid confusion, I guess you could say I'm Her."

"Right," said Jill, totally confused.

"How are you finding the place? Is it to your satisfaction?" She asked.

"Yeah, yeah it's lovely. I've already been challenged to a round of golf by two old dears, which is nice. Although I can't say this was what I was expecting."

"No?" She asked. "And what were you expecting?"

Jill puffed out her cheeks. She didn't know what to expect. She hadn't really given it any thought.

"Do you know something," she smiled. "I have no idea, whatsoever."

She laughed. There was something familiar about Her but strange at the same time. Jill felt like she knew this woman in front of her all of her life but they had nothing in common, no history. Every moment was like meeting for the first time and being reunited with an old friend. She had never experienced anything like it before.

"We get that a lot," She said. "It's only natural I suppose."

"I'll bet," agreed Jill.

"Look, I'm not going to lie to you Jill, I couldn't anyway, even if I tried. So I'll cut right to the chase," She said, leaning forward on the desk and tenting her fingers. "You shouldn't be here."

"I shouldn't?" asked Jill, suddenly concerned.

"No, you shouldn't, not here, not now anyway."

"What does that mean?" she asked. "Should I be, you know, Down There instead then?"

She laughed again, flashing brilliantly white teeth. She adjusted her golf visor and fixed her dirty blonde ponytail.

"No, what I mean is, you shouldn't be here, in this realm, on this plane, right now. It's not your time."

"It isn't?" asked Jill.

"No," She said. "You see, you've found yourself embroiled in a bit of a tiff, a challenge match if you will between Myself and, well, you know who else."

"Yes," said Jill. "Only too well."

"Quite."

"Is he here?"

"We'll get to that," She added hastily. "But what I'm trying to say is, your case has been one that I've struggled with. It's not been easy, not by a long shot and I'm frightened that if I carry on, it'll be a big mistake."

Jill wasn't concerned as much as she was confused. She too leaned forward, trying to grasp what was being asked of her.

"What do you mean, a mistake?" she asked.

"Put it this way. The only reason you've come to the Club House is because you were taken, saved if you will, by our mutual friend."

"Saved?" Jill blurted. "You call being thrown off a balcony twelve storeys high saved?"

"Oh yes, I don't doubt it," She said. "If that Demon had touched you, there wouldn't have been anything I could have done. It was well within its right to do what it did to Thomas Rafferty and because you urged it on, you would have gone the same way. But, as I said before, you're here, now, in the wrong place at the wrong time."

"Now *that* does sound familiar," said Jill.

"Yes. Well, the situation being what it is, you'll have to forgive me if I seem a little reluctant to go jumping in with a decision."

Jill could sense she was standing at a crossroads. She might not understand all of the cosmic rules and regulations that went on over her head but that didn't seem to matter anymore. Her hatred for The Devil was slowly ebbing away. He had saved her, by all accounts, of his own accord. And if She hadn't seen it coming, then what did that mean?

"Do you remember the bouquet of flowers you were sent a few days ago?" She asked.

"Yes, the white roses."

"Do you still have the card?"

Jill patted the pockets of her slacks. To her surprise, she felt the hard edge of the card. She pulled it out and handed it over to Her.

"No, no," She said. "Please, read it aloud for me."

Jill unfolded the card and looked down at the words. They were still there, like they had been when she had first opened it. That time felt so far in the past now, it was almost ancient history. All that had gone on since then came flooding back into her head.

She started crying again, her chin puckering and nose running. She waved her hand in front of her face, apologising.

"Sorry," she said.

"That's alright," She answered. "Just read the card aloud for me, that's all you have to do."

Jill caught her breath. She wiped her eyes and cleared her throat. She read through the words once more in her head before announcing them to Her.

"Find out who you are," she said.

She smiled. Jill smiled too, laughing a little as she wiped her nose. She reclined in her chair and looked up to the endless sky above.

"And do you think you achieved that?" She asked. "Do you think through your journey you found out who you are Jillian Gideon?"

Jill nodded. She held onto the card tightly and kept nodding. When her tears retreated, she spoke softly.

"Yes, I do," she said. "Yes, I do."

"Then it's settled," She said, getting up from Her chair and rounding the desk. "It seems that we don't have a place for you just yet Up Here. And I don't think he'll be wanting you Downstairs any time soon either, especially judging by all the bickering you two do."

She placed an arm around Jill's shoulders, hugging her in close. The doctor wiped her cheeks and smiled. She couldn't stop smiling, even if she wanted to. She wanted to fall to the ground and cry some more. But she didn't.

"I don't know what to say," she whispered softly. "I wish you could help me put into words just how thankful I am. Thankful for all of your help, your guidance, your…"

"Interfering," She smiled. "No, I don't think I'll be helping you on that one Jillian. But I must warn you, this isn't the end of it I'm afraid. It's only the beginning. I'll be watching you carefully, making sure that my decision hasn't been a wasted one. Where you end up is still very much in the air Jillian, I can't stress that enough. Your involvement in all of this has been surprising to say the least. And while I'm satisfied that you're not ready to come to this plane just yet, you may still be punished for what you've done."

Jill found that she was outside the office. She nodded solemnly, understanding everything she had been told. It was fair and just and there wasn't a great deal she could do to argue or protest.

She had willed the Demon to take Rafferty away and in doing so had acted above her station. The hate and lust for vengeance she had displayed were unforgivable but she knew that. She was a responsible Human Being, or at least, she liked to think so. It would therefore fall at her door to take any and all punishments that She saw fit.

"I understand," she said. "I completely understand."

"Good," She said. "Then you should be heading home. Head back to the front desk and Peter will arrange everything."

Jill went to speak again but the door was closing. She vanished behind the polished mahogany as it clicked shut. Looking down at her hands, she noticed that the card had vanished.

She took a long sigh of the clean, fresh air and started back up the corridor. She was going home.

THIRTY-ONE

The Devil whistled a jaunty tune as he walked down the corridor towards his office. He didn't know what the tune was but it was strangely familiar. It was going to drive him mad all day. But that was alright. After the few weeks he had endured on Earth, anything would be a relief.

As he strutted confidently, the interns and other members of staff all cowered and smiled. He could tell they were happy to see him, he could see their teeth.

It was nice to know that in his unexpected absence, the place hadn't gone totally to, well, Hell. The building was still intact, in Hell's nerve centre, and it looked like most were still bothering to turn up for work. Two major ticks, he thought, considering he employed some of the worst people known to have ever existed.

He reached the door to his office and straightened his tartan tie. Unless he was mistaken, he actually felt a little nervous. He checked his watch, but he didn't have to. Alice would be in, behind her desk, typing, filing, answering the phones. It would be like he had never left. So why was he so worried?

"Good morning sir," said an intern, pushing a trolley full of papers. "Good to see you back in action."

"Yes, good morning," he replied, to the lad still in his teens.

A motor scooter accident, pretty bad by all accounts. The Devil didn't know his name but he remembered his arrival. Had he not been high as a kite on drink and drugs, he probably would have made it Upstairs. As it happened, he had an eternity of damnation to look forward to. That and an endlessly full e-mail inbox.

"Drugs are for mugs," shouted The Devil.

"Drugs are for mugs," nodded the boy.

The intern was a welcome distraction. He took The Devil's mind off his impending reunion with his secretary.

Realising he had been loitering in the corridor for long enough, he took a deep breath. The nagging feeling that his trip to Earth had left more than just a rash on his backside and some broken bones was beginning to gain strength.

He pushed the door open and strode into the office, his arrival announced in a billow of wind. Alice was there, behind her desk, typing, as he predicted. She had to grab a stack of papers before they blew away.

"Ah, good morning," she said, smiling. "So you're back in the pink then."

"Red, actually Alice, I prefer red," he leered. "Just check out the tie."

He pointed at the tartan. She slowly took off her glasses and began chewing on one leg. The action was simple enough but he knew she was doing it deliberately. It made him tingle.

"I take it you've been debriefed on what happened?" he asked, trying to distract himself again.

"Yes, we received a full dossier from Upstairs, full of clauses, waivers and all the other nonsense they like to pad it out with. Honestly, you think they would learn to use contemporary English, it was all doths and thous and beheaths."

She leaned down and pulled a massive stack of paper out from beneath her desk. Thumping it down hard, she peeled the top page off and handed it to him.

"They're like lawyers Alice," he said. "They're full of their own sense of self importance. And you know me so well. Do you honestly think I'm going to bother reading this drivel?"

"I didn't think so," she said firmly. "So I've prepared a reduced, edited version for you and it's sitting on your desk."

"Lovely," he said.

He was about to vanish into his office but stopped. He turned back to his receptionist and loosened his collar.

"Alice, could I trouble you for a second?" he asked.

"If you must," she smiled, placing her chin in her hands. "You do it all the time, what makes you think I'm going to refuse you now?"

"Oh and don't I know it," he whimpered. "But it's a rather delicate matter, one that I'd rather you didn't share with anybody. Is that still okay?"

"Go on," she replied.

The Devil licked his lips. It was good to feel his own mouth again instead of a stranger's. For the duration of his escapade, he had felt like he was French kissing somebody he didn't know. Not that he was totally against that. He just liked it to be on his terms.

"Am I good person?" he asked.

"Pardon me?" she choked.

"A good person, me? Do you think I'm a good person?"

"I'm… I'm not quite sure what you want me to say to that," she replied. "I mean, you're The Devil, after all. I somehow don't think it's in your nature really. Otherwise, what's all of this about then?"

She waved her hands about the office. He nodded and scratched his chin.

"Is that what you wanted me to say?" she apologised. "You sort of caught me off guard a little."

"No, no, blimey, not at all Alice," he apologised too. "It's just, well, as you know, that little adventure I had, on Earth, it got me thinking."

"About if you're a good person?"

"Sort of, yes. I don't know. You spend a lot of time around Humans and Him, who is now sporting a She outfit I should add. It sort of drives you mad. I just thought well, you know, I'd check. Always nice to hear it from a friend."

Alice eased herself out from behind her desk. She was wearing a particularly tight pencil skirt and blouse that accentuated all of her ample curves. He knew she had chosen that outfit deliberately. It was one of his favourites.

She rounded the desk and strutted up to him so that she was close enough he could feel her breath on his cheeks. She reached up, fastened his collar again and straightened his tie.

"You are the worst creature imaginable," she said, softly and deliberately. "And there's absolutely nothing anybody can do about that."

She leaned in closer and whispered in his ear. The Devil felt every hair and vessel of his form stand on end, charged with alluring electricity.

"That's why you're my favourite," she kissed his cheek. "Welcome home."

She pushed herself away and replaced her glasses on her nose. Flattening her skirt, she returned to her seat and immediately began typing again, as if nothing had happened.

The Devil was speechless. He had missed Alice, he had missed Hell, he had missed everything. Only when his mind clicked back into action did he realise he was standing, idle, staring at his secretary.

"Yes," he said, clearing his throat. "Yes, yes, I agree, yes."

He stumbled around a little before finding his way back to the door of his private office. He turned the handle the wrong way and bashed himself against the hard wood. Rectifying this mistake, he eventually navigated it successfully.

"Thank you Alice," he said.

"I know," she said with a knowing, sly grin.

He closed the door and stood for a moment, letting himself cool down. The dank, emptiness of his office was just what he needed.

He turned around and stared at his desk, his Inbox pile almost reaching to the roof. That didn't matter though, it could have stretched all the way Upstairs. He was getting back into his groove. And he knew he had the staff to take care of business while he was away.

But more importantly, he shook off any lingering doubts. The Humans could have their emotions, The Devil didn't need them. At least, he didn't need them in as large doses.

He clicked his fingers and skipped across the floor. He was smiling again and it felt good.

"Still got it," he cackled. "You never lose it."

He launched himself into his chair and spun around, legs kicking out. When he stopped, he clicked away his dizziness and focussed on his desk. There, sitting in front of him was a large, white box.

He slid forward. Cautiously, he read the name written on the card. Without knowing it, he let out a long, protracted groan.

"You've got to be kidding me," he said. "Really? Already? I thought You took your time over this sort of thing? Bloody hell."

The Devil was back in Hell alright. But it looked like he was heading to Earth a lot sooner than he had hoped.

THIRTY-TWO

Cathedrals were dismal places, The Devil had always thought. Built for the sole purpose of worshipping Him Upstairs, gloomy and dreary seemed to be the order of the day. Perhaps it was the candles, or the stained glass windows. Humanity had never really been able to grasp illumination very well when it came to their places of worship.

He lurked at the back of the chapel, watching. Ahead of him, down the central aisle, a gaudy alter stood silently. The place was quiet and peaceful, he would give it that. There were only a few faithful worshipers in at this time of the day.

A large bust of a man he didn't know stood beside him. Leaning on it casually, he drew the disapproving tuts of two old women who were handing out hymn sheets.

"Relax," he said. "He won't mind."

They scurried off, talking unmentionables between themselves. Do-gooders, he thought, never got a good word to say about anybody. He wondered if they ever had time off.

His moment of dreaming was interrupted by the sight of a familiar face. Jill Gideon stepped through the huge stone archway of the door and proceeded towards the row of pews near the far wall. She bowed and crossed herself as she passed by the central alter, slipping into an empty row and dropping to her knees.

"About time," he said, starting off towards her.

His heels clicked off of the cracked and broken stone of the floor. As churches went, this one was in a particularly bad state of disrepair. He wondered where the money went every collection.

"Oi, oi," he said, taking a seat beside her. "Bet you didn't expect to see me here did you?"

She looked at him once and then returned to her prayers, hands clasped over the back of the wooden bench in front. He wasn't sure what that ignorance meant. Was he guilty of something? He was always guilty of something. That was part of his job description. But he wasn't sure if there was a particular crime he had committed this time.

Suddenly, the organ wheezed into life. A short scale was played on it, the powerful sound blowing away any cobwebs that the tiny congregation may have had. Even Jill, trying her best to ignore him, jolted a little on her knees.

"That's a bit much isn't it?" he said with a subdued laugh. "Here we are, trying to get some airtime with Him and Elton John over there decides to take the keyboard for a walk."

Jill laughed but tried to stop herself. She feigned a cough but The Devil had seen her. That was all he needed.

"Blimey, I reckon it's woken everybody up though," he looked about the place. "And by the looks of it, they needed some excitement. Look at that one over there," he pointed at an old man, hunched over on his side, dozing. "They should start charging him rent if he stays any longer."

"You finished?" she said, climbing back onto the pew.

"So you're talking to me now then," he said.

"I'm not talking to you, I'm not talking to you ever again," she tried to keep her voice down. "And I'm especially not talking to you here."

"Why not?"

"Because," she spat. "It's a chapel for god sake. And you're well… you know what you are."

"Get over yourself Gideon, I'm Human now, it doesn't matter," he cracked his fingers. "And as it happens, when I'm not being crammed into one of your sweaty, itchy, endlessly clumsy bodies, consecrated ground is about as far as I'm allowed to go."

"What?" she asked. "That doesn't make any sense? Why would you only be allowed on blessed land? You're the last person that should be allowed here."

"On the contrary, it makes perfect sense. Ethereal, remember, we're all the same. We can only tread where Human kind has said we can. It's a sort of gentleman's agreement on His part. Also keeps us all in check."

She stared at him for a long moment. He was still the same but she wasn't. Having your eyes opened to a whole other world just simmering away out of sight could have that effect on a Human.

The Devil had been surprised how well she had taken the whole ordeal. The only real side effect had been her renewed faith. He could scratch that one up to experience and be done with it all.

"How's the side? And the jaw? And the eternal pain in the arse?" she asked.

"Good as new, thank you. It seems as though the only thing yet to heal is my ego. Do try to keep up Gideon."

"Alright, bloody hell."

They both looked at each other and started to laugh. Their hilarity drew some odd looks and disapproving murmurs but neither of them cared. Despite all that had gone on, The Devil had grown strangely accustomed to having his human companion around him. For Jill, being able to speak to somebody honestly had been a refreshing change.

"What are you doing back here?" she said. "I thought you would be on holiday by now. I see that Hellcorp is rocketing up the stock markets."

"Of course it is," The Devil said smugly. "I knew it would. Creighton Tull is an excellent puppet and front man. Crafted from the finest minds that Hell has to offer."

"Yes, yes, I've heard the sales pitch, I don't need to go through that whole rigmarole again, thank you very much. Especially after what we've just been through. And *especially* not at Mass."

"Fine, suit yourself." The Devil crossed his legs awkwardly, bashing them off the hard wood of the pew in front.

"You never answered me," she said, not looking at him.

"No, I didn't," he replied.

"Well?"

"Well, Doctor Gideon, as it happens, our little jaunt has raised some eyebrows in certain corners of the universe."

"What do you mean?" she asked, a little more anxious.

"It seems that your intervention and overall usefulness have bought you some favour in circles that most men and women fear to tread."

She turned to face him, her eyes wide with a strange, panicky madness. She instinctively grabbed his sleeve, tightening her grip until he made a small yelp.

"Steady on," he said. "This is a Hugo Boss."

"What are you saying," she said. "You mean, I'm going… you know, Down There. What has She said to you? Did She talk about, you know, our meeting?"

The Devil smiled wryly. He took great enjoyment in watching Humans squirm. When it was all said and done, there were no atheists in foxholes. And there certainly weren't any when death was staring them in their clammy, greasy faces.

"Oh god," she said, holding her forehead. "Oh god, what have I done? What have I done? I should have been more polite, I should have… I should have, well… I should have done something."

She wrapped her knuckles against the hard wooden seat. This drew some looks of confusion from the nearest worshipers. The Devil threw them a scowl and they went back to their silent contemplation.

"Oh god," she began to cry.

"Oh bloody hell," he said with a sigh. "Would you give over. Honestly Gideon, I thought you would have learned better by now. Crying doesn't cut any mustard with me love."

He handed her a silk handkerchief and she blew her nose loudly. Handing the sodden cloth back, he threw it onto the floor and kicked it under the pew in front.

"I'm sorry you know, I really am," she said. "I thought I was doing the right thing, I thought I was making up for being a lapsed Catholic, for all those years I turned my back on, you know, Him, Her, Them. But it's not worked has it? I'm damned, totally and utterly damned. Destined to spend the rest of my miserable life unhappy and then die, only to be even more desperately unhappy with you in my earhole all day and all night."

"Thanks for that," said The Devil, polishing his nails.

Watching Jill cry made him think. Their little escapade, his task, had given him a new outlook on Humanity. Especially in the grand scale of things.

The way he saw it, they were the conscience of existence. Totally driven by a sense of justice and greater good, they were the ultimate barrier and difference between him and Her. They always had been and it appeared they always would be.

No matter how they were dressed or what technology they possessed, Humans were, inherently, Human. There was nobody else like them in the Multiverse. And for The Devil's thoughts, that was probably a good thing.

"Are you finished yet or should I nip out and buy a box of sweeties?" he said sardonically. "And seeing as you've just polished off what was once a very nice, very expensive silk handkerchief, I should maybe buy another one of those too."

Jill looked up at him, her eyes red raw. Two great bubbles of snot hung from her nostrils, the skin around her nose blotchy. She was the epitome of misery, a picture of the blues. The Devil's chest burned a little but he acted quickly and caught it early.

"Here," he said, reaching into his inside pocket.

He produced a perfectly crisp, white rose. Its stem was a brilliant green, with fine leaves dotted around the head. In the gloominess of the chapel, the white petals were brilliant and bright. Jill looked at it curiously.

"What's this?" she asked.

"It's the motherboard from a crashed alien spaceship."

"Really?"

"No, of course it isn't, give me strength," he sighed loudly.

She sniffed and took the rose, spinning it slowly in her trembling hands. She caressed the petals and smelled its sweet aroma, a relief washing through her as she did so.

"It's beautiful," she said.

"It should be, especially where it came from."

"Wait," she said, suddenly suspicious. "You mean this isn't just an ordinary rose?"

"When has anything ever been ordinary when it comes to me and the people I work for?"

Jill didn't answer him. She couldn't take her eyes from the rose in her hands, the sweet aroma intoxicating. She took another long sniff, the scent making her aching joints relax.

"That," said The Devil, seizing his chance. "Is your passport."

"My passport?" she asked. "Passport for what."

"What do you think," he rolled his eyes upward towards the draughty cloisters.

"What do you mean?" a pulse of excitement and trepidation made Jill's skin tingle.

"What I mean is that this little flower here is a gesture, a symbol, a gold star from Her."

"What?" she said, words catching in her throat. "Her, Her?"

"Yes, Her, Her. The definitive Her, the genuine article, so to speak. The one who's been driving me nuts for so long I can't remember the last decent conversation I had with Her."

Without thinking, Jill threw her arms forward and hugged The Devil tightly. More tears rolled down her cheeks but this time, they were for joy. She had never felt so happy, so relieved, so glad to be alive.

"Wait, hold on," she said, trying to compose herself. "Does this mean She's not pissed off with me?"

"Not at all," said The Devil, sluggishly. "In fact, you might say She's been so moved by your eagerness to help and, I'm quoting here, putting others in front of yourself, has scored some major Brownie points with the bigwigs Upstairs."

"What does it mean though?" she said, still looking at the rose.

"It means Doctor Gideon, that you've got a get out of jail free card. A selfless act, on a pretty grand scale, has bought you a ticket to the promised land when you die."

Jill could hear what he was saying but she couldn't comprehend what it meant. She knew he wasn't joking, she had learned to trust him. And while that idea had proven folly for so many throughout history, she knew then, in the chapel, that The Devil wasn't lying to her.

"I don't know what to say," she whispered. "I mean, I thought He, She, said that I would have to wait and see."

"Yes, I'm hardly surprised by that," he said lethargically. "She's always a bit ambiguous when it comes to detail. But it would seem that She's had a change of heart and, more importantly, is now using me as Her bloody delivery boy."

"I'm speechless."

"Oh please," he said, getting to his feet. "Don't get all sentimental on me, not now. I've got better things to be doing than listen to you whinge on about how eternally grateful you are for His boundless forgiveness and compassion."

He straightened his suit jacket and adjusted his cuffs. Slickening back his curly hair behind his ears, he wagged a finger at her.

"That's the end of it, do you hear me."

She smiled warmly. Rubbing more tears away from her cheeks, she nodded happily.

"Thank you," she said.

"For what?" he fastened the buttons of his jacket.

"For -"

A blast of sound from the organ drowned her out as the opening notes of *How Great Thou Art* sounded out around the dingy cathedral. The Devil puckered his lips and shrugged his shoulders.

"That's my cue," he said.

Jill moved to get up. As she did so, The Devil was shoved violently out of the way. He collapsed onto her and she helped him back to his feet.

"What the fu... fu... fudge?" he said over the din.

A man wearing a thick, black coat had pushed him out of the way. He walked quickly and with purpose down the aisle beside the pews before coming to a halt at a statue of Mary in a shrine.

Beneath the idol was a row of votive candles that flickered as the man neared them. The Devil and Jill looked on, both silent and shocked.

"He's in a bit of a rush, don't you think?" he said as the music grew louder.

"I don't understand," she said.

The man bent down to the candles and, with deliberate breath, blew out each and every one of them. The lights were snuffed out one by one until the whole rack was little more than a smouldering collection of burned down wax.

"What the hell!" shouted Jill. "He can't... he wouldn't..."

She forced her way past The Devil but he stopped her. He could feel her trembling with anger, her fists clenched into tight balls, the stem of the rose bending at an awkward angle.

The Devil knew how angry she was, he could feel it. He thrived on that anger, it made him strong, more powerful. Or at least, it normally did.

The rage that was pouring from Jill wasn't the usual hatred or malice he was used to. It was something altogether purer, more just. He didn't know who this man was but he wasn't anything to do with him.

At the shrine, the man in the dark coat spun on his heels, an arrogant smirk on his face. Jill made another attempt to get away from The Devil.

"That bastard!" she shouted over the music. "Doesn't he know what those candles mean to people? The disrespect, that utter ignorance I mean."

"Easy," said The Devil as the man approached them.

He walked past the pair, Jill staring him down. When he breezed close to her, he made a kissing motion with his lips before throwing his head back and laughing.

"Bastard!" she shouted but the organ was drowning her out. "I can't let him do that! I can't! Why is nobody else helping?"

She tried to break free of The Devil but he was too strong for her. The man reached the end of the pews, none of the gathered congregation daring to look at him. He was headed for the door when something in The Devil's mind snapped.

"You know," he said. "I don't think I'm going to let him get away with that."

He let go of Jill and sprang quickly into a bolt. He raced down to the end of the pews and hurled himself across the back of the church. The man was reaching the stone doorway into the lobby when he caught him, bundling him into a wall.

"Oi!" he shouted. "Get your fucking hands off me!"

The Devil spun him around. There was a bright flash as a sliver of light danced across the sharpened blade of a flick knife. The man plunged the blade into The Devil's chest with enough force to break his collarbone.

But nothing happened. The Devil tightened his grip on the man and drove him harder into the wall. Thinking it was just unlucky, he sank his knife two more times before panic began to set in.

"Not nice, is it?" said The Devil, smiling with razor sharp teeth. "Not nice when something you don't expect happens to you, is it?"

"What the fuck!" said the man, stabbing more and more out of sheer panic.

"Let me tell you something friend, a little bit of friendly advice from somebody you can't even begin to comprehend. This type of behaviour isn't cool. It's not clever, it's not big and it most certainly doesn't make a difference. You can blow out as many candles as you like but make sure they're on your birthday cake, do you understand me?"

"Eh?"

The Devil gave him a firm slap across the face. The hit was so hard, a tooth dropped from the man's slack mouth, rattling on the marble floor beside his knife.

"Now I'm going to let you off with a warning this time compadre. And believe me, there won't be a second. You're lucky it was me you pissed off and not somebody else. Somebody much, much worse. You hear me?"

He grabbed the man's face and forced him to look into his eyes. His pupils dilated as fright greater than any human had ever known took a firm grasp on him. Through The Devil's eyes, the darkest corners of Hell were shown in all of their dreadful glory, the future of sinners old and new exposed to a mind that could barely count to ten.

Intelligence hardly mattered; the point was always the same. The hypnotic trance was broken only by Jill's footsteps.

"You got him," she said, out of breath.

The Devil let the man go and he almost fell over himself running through the door. He raced off into the rainy night, vanishing amongst the grey smudge of the storm.

Jill watched him go. She held the door open and then turned back to The Devil.

"What did you say to him?"

"Oh nothing," he replied. "Just a little friendly advice. It goes a long way you know, especially from the right person."

"I agree," she caught her breath and looked at the rose in her hand.

"You better go back in," he said, fixing his tartan tie. "You'll miss all the best bits. I'm told they're very good, full of drama, all that game."

"They are," she said with a sad smile. "Why don't you join me, learn something new?"

The Devil let out a cackle and rubbed his hands together. When his hilarity died down, he winked at her.

"Too busy Gideon, too much to do, too little time. You know how it goes."

He went to step out into the rain but she stopped him.

"Wait!" she shouted. "You can't, I thought, you know, when you're like that, you can't set foot in the mortal world?"

The Devil widened his eyes. He nodded, scratching his head as if he had forgotten. Then he stepped out into the rain and she gasped.

"There, see," he said, the shower darkening his suit with huge blobs. "Nothing to it."

"You bastard," she gave him a wry smile. "Do you ever tell the truth?"

"Only when I lie," he answered. "See you around Gideon."

He turned on his heels and walked off into the night storm. Jill watched him until he was little more than a blurry silhouette. She peered through the rain and thought she saw a cloud of dust kick up from where The Devil had once been.

The rose was still in her hand and she looked at it again. Touching each of the beautiful petals in turn, she felt a great sense of contentment deep within her soul. After a few moments of listening to the rain beat against the ancient chapel, she headed back indoors and joined the congregation.

THIRTY-THREE

The soft, opal water lapped against the golden sand at its own, relaxed pace. Washing over the coral far beneath it, the hiss of the tide joined with the chirping birds and gentle whisper of the palm trees.

The Devil stretched out his arms and legs and wriggled his toes. There was sand everywhere, even in places he was still discovering. Bizarrely, he didn't mind the irritation, knowing he had a very long time to contemplate why.

He squirted out a blob of sun cream and applied it to his exposed skin. He was wearing a sun hat, sunglasses and a decorative Hawaiian shirt. Trying to blend in had become something of a bad habit.

The balmy atmosphere of Jamaica was almost perfect. If it hadn't been for the blasted sun, he would have sworn he was in paradise. The temperature reminded him of home but it was so much quieter. Screaming and roaring infernos could become wearing.

No, he was happy. This was why he wanted a holiday. Some peace and quiet with only himself for company. He deserved it, he had earned it. Nothing was going to ruin it now.

To celebrate, he took a large gulp of the blue cocktail he had ordered. The ornate monstrosity tasted terrible but it looked the part. Even if he had almost poked his eye out with the decorative umbrellas and straws. He was there to be a tourist, not a critic.

He replaced the half coconut shaped beaker on the table beside his lounger and let out a satisfied sigh. Listening to the water, he could feel himself falling asleep.

"Excuse me sir," came a voice from behind him.

In an instant, three days of relaxation were lost. His jaw clenched shut, tendons stretching to their limit and his blood pressure rising. He thought about ignoring whomever it was that was talking to him. Sometimes ignorance was bliss.

Then he remembered he was the only one on the beach. Everyone else had been banished to a three-mile radius.

"Excuse me sir," came the voice again.

The Devil clenched his fists tightly and sat up. Whipping off his sunglasses, he took in the resort attendant standing over him.

"Yes!" he snapped.

"Sorry to disturb you sir," said the young man, forehead sweaty and glistening in the sun.

"No you're not," said The Devil. "If you were so sorry, you wouldn't have bothered me in the first place."

The attendant looked confused. Humans, they were always so quick to please without thinking through the consequences. They were also massive cowards, ready to pass the buck at any and every opportunity.

"What is it?" said The Devil, pinching the bridge of his nose.

"A phone call for you sir," replied the attendant.

A shiver went down The Devil's spine. The temperature was a comfortable thirty-six degrees but he had been chilled to his mortal marrow.

"A telephone call?" he asked suspiciously. "From who?"

"They didn't give a name," was the response. "All they said was you were to be spoken to immediately sir."

"But… nobody knows I'm here."

"This man certainly seemed to think you were staying at the resort. In fact, he seemed to know that you were on the private beach sir."

That tore it. The Devil shook with rage. Only He could wind him up so badly.

"Thank you," he said, seething. "But if you would tell the gentleman on the phone that I'm not to be disturbed, that would be wonderful."

"No offense sir, but you could tell him yourself."

The attendant produced a mobile phone from the pocket of his Bermuda shorts. The Devil rolled around some bile and venom in his mouth before snatching the phone from his hand.

"Thank you," he said. "Thank you so very much. Remind me, did I tip you this morning at breakfast?"

"No sir, you didn't," said the attendant, his shoulders perking up at the prospect of money.

"Good!" The Devil cackled.

The young man turned away, muttering to himself obscenities that would have made even The Devil blush. And obscenities were on The Devil's mind as he pressed the answer button on the waiting call.

"Not like you to let your guard down," came Her dulcet tones.

"Really?" asked The Devil. "You couldn't let me have a few days rest?"

"I'm not here to disturb your holiday old boy. It's just a friendly, how are you type phone call."

"Oh please. Don't give me that old rope. Since when have you ever just called to say you love me. I smell a rat, a big rat, the *biggest* rat."

"On the contrary," She said calmly. "I'm merely making sure that you're happy with your decision."

The Devil went to answer back flippantly but stopped himself. He had learned not to trust a word She said. The last time he did that, it had proven costly.

"Yes," he answered eventually. "I am as it happens. Why?"

"No reason at all old boy. I just like to check up on you from time to time."

"Oh don't I know it."

She laughed softly. There was a rustling of papers from the other end of the phone and the hairs on the back of The Devil's arms and neck stood on end. Something was wrong, She was up to her old tricks.

"Well, if that's all you wanted me for," he said, "I'll let you get back to work. Overseeing creation must be a dreadful press on your time. Lovely speaking with you, bye."

"Before you go," She said, "there is just one other thing I'd like to discuss with you."

The Devil ground his teeth, mashing them together and hoping they would disintegrate. He had a migraine coming, a fully blown, ten on the Richter scale level headache that would make his skull feel like it was an imploded neutron star.

"Yes?" he said, feeling the anger rise from the ends of his toes.

"I've got another case for you."

The Devil was never in control, not really. He was a slave to his emotions, no matter how much he tried to deny them. That was why he threw the phone in the ocean and marched straight back to the hotel, cursing, swearing, stomping his way across the rich, white sands of the Caribbean.

He knew he was in for it, but he didn't care anymore. The holiday was ruined; he might as well pack now. She would be on

Her way down shortly and that meant it was back to business.

"Three hours I got," he said, throwing his hands up into the air and shouting at the heavens. "Three measly hours!"

Jonathan Whitelaw is an author, journalist and broadcaster. After working on the frontline of Scottish politics, he moved into journalism. Subjects he has covered have varied from breaking news, the arts, culture and sport to fashion, music and even radioactive waste – with everything in between. He's also a regular reviewer and talking head on shows for the BBC and STV.

HellCorp is his second novel following his debut, *Morbid Relations.*

You can follow Jonathan on Twitter @JDWhitelaw13 and on Facebook **https://www.facebook.com/JonathanWhitelawAuthor/**

HELLCORP

ACKNOWLEDGEMENTS

I'm always amazed and humbled by the help, patience and support that all of my close friends, family and loved ones have shown me with this book and my writing.

While I could spend an eternity listing them it would probably take up a whole other novel. In short I'd like to thank my parents and parents-in-law for their backing and encouragement. I'd also like to thank the Urbane team, especially Matthew Smith for his tireless efforts, support and constant answering of all my e-mails.

I'd be remiss if I didn't thank all my school religious education teachers who put all these ideas in my head in the first place.

And of course the music of AC/DC, without which I'd never have found that Highway to Hell.